# We

## RAE LLOYD

*For the ones who live in the spaces between the rules*

# CONTENT WARNINGS

Trigger Warnings

This book contains themes and scenes that may be distressing for some readers, including:

- Hospital scenes
- Gun violence
- Stillbirth and pregnancy loss (secondary characters, primarily off page)
- Childbirth (graphic, on page)
- Homophobia
- Sexual content, including mmf intimacy (on page)
- Strong language

While We is ultimately a story of love, forgiveness, and found family, it also explores the raw and sometimes painful realities that shape these bonds. Reader discretion is advised.

*If I know what love is, it is because of you.*
*Hermann Hesse*

Babe,

Listen to these songs. They remind me of us.

xoxo,

Jax

way after forever by vaultboy

MAD by Martin by Garrix, Lauv

Waves of Blue by Majid Jordan

WALKING AWAY by Justin Bieber

THINGS YOU DO by Justin Bieber

Be Your Friend by Cheat Codes, Edward Maya, Enisa

Don't Let Me Drown by Burna Boy, F1 The Album

Eyes Off You by PRETTYMUCH

Body Talk by Kane Brown, Katelyn Brown

Sexy Love by Ne-Yo

Love U Like That by Lauv

Call It by Soleroy

I Wanna Dance with Somebody by Hard Lights, Behmer, The High

Loved By You by Justin Bieber, Burna Boy

I n a rush of amniotic fluid and blood, I delivered my fifth baby of the night, and gently laid him on the blanket covering his mother's chest, still slick with vernix. One of the nurses suctioned the newborn's mouth with a blue bulb syringe, and a beautiful, piercing cry filled the room, a sound we heard often, but were always grateful for. It never got old. That first cry always hit me in the gut, reminding me why I chose this. I guided the proud father through cutting the cord, then watched as he leaned over to kiss his wife on the forehead.

"Good job, Mom," I said, congratulating her as I applied pressure to her abdomen and gently tugged on the umbilical cord to encourage the placenta's delivery. My hands moved on autopilot, stitching up a few small tears from the birth, cleaning my patient up, and running through the checklists of tasks that I'd done hundreds of times before. The end of my shift was almost in sight. My limbs were getting heavy, my brain was buzzing with exhaustion. Twenty-four hours on shift. If I hadn't been running on coffee and adrenaline, I would've been sleepwalking by now.

After finishing the stitches, we took the baby for his Apgar

scores. He squealed in protest as we checked his reflexes, skin already a healthy pink. When I brought him back, I helped my patient latch her baby onto her breast. Over the sounds of suckling, I let her know that another doctor would check in once she was transferred to the Mother and Baby Unit.

"Thank you." She sounded grateful—and exhausted. I held back a yawn until I stepped out of the room, then finally let my own fatigue wash over me.

"Long night, Dr. Hennessy?" One of my favorite labor and delivery nurses, Charlee, took the iPad I handed her, flashing me a smile, making something shift in my chest. Something I really didn't have the energy to name. God, she was pretty. I looked away, reminding myself, she was married. She was married, my co-worker, and my friend.

"Five babies, so not too bad. But I've been here since Friday morning."

"Aw." She pouted, making my heart pound beneath my scrubs. I needed to get laid, badly. But honestly, I didn't have time. As a fourth-year resident, I was *so* close to finally being done with school and training. This year, as Chief Resident, I'd taken on a mountain of new responsibilities, and sleep was already a rare luxury.

Making things worse, when I moved from Boston to New York for my residency, the only apartment I could find was miles from the hospital—and traffic made the commute a daily nightmare. I was burning the candle at both ends, and barely managing daily life, let alone finding the time, or energy, to meet someone.

You had to be awake to have sex. Or did you?

I chuckled to myself, said goodbye to the nurses, and headed to my locker to change into the scrubs I wore home, grab my things, and begin the long ride back.

I fell asleep in the Uber, and my driver had to shake me awake.

"Sorry, man," I mumbled, bleary-eyed and barely conscious as I stumbled out of the car. It took me three tries to get the combination on my door lock right. Once inside, I collapsed onto my bed, fully clothed, shoes still on. I didn't even have time to make it under the blanket. Just hit the mattress and let the world fall away.

Six hours later, it was nearly noon on my first day off in what felt like forever. I stretched, finally removed my shoes, and pulled off my scrubs in preparation for a long-overdue shower.

Growing up with a father who was a surgeon, I thought I'd been prepared for life as a doctor. But somehow, the grueling hours and the near-unconscious exhaustion I now felt on a daily basis had still managed to surprise me. Either my dad had figured out some kind of work-life balance that I hadn't, or choosing OBGYN over general surgery had been one of the dumber decisions I'd made in a life full of questionable choices.

I sighed. That was the burnout talking. I truly loved my field, and I was just a few months away from finishing residency at the ripe old age of thirty. After that, the plan was to move closer to home and join a smaller practice, where I could finally have office hours, fewer nights on call, and zero twenty-four-hour shifts.

I was already in talks with a few practices, and honestly, I couldn't remember the last time I'd been this excited about something. Who would've guessed that Liam-from-twelve-years-ago, F-boy, weed-loving, sex-obsessed Liam, would end up in a specialty that brought babies into the world?

I laughed, running a hand through my hair.

Gross. I really needed that shower.

I kept the water slightly tepid, which helped me wake up fully. I needed to be bright-eyed and bushy-tailed, my mom was throwing Shaen's baby shower today, and I had to drive an hour north to get there. Everyone was excited for the party because this baby had been a long time coming.

I could still remember the day my best friend Shaen and my other best friend, and cousin, Remi got engaged at twenty. I'd joked that Shaen must be knocked up. But she wasn't. Then they waited four years to get married, mostly so Remi could finish school and get a better job. They wanted to save up and pay for their own wedding, even though my parents had all but begged to foot the bill.

The timing worked out. By then, all our friends were home from college and able to attend.

In typical Shaen fashion, she planned everything down to the year. She decided they'd wait one more year after the wedding to start trying, because if she got pregnant at twenty-five, she'd have the baby just before turning twenty-six, and that sounded like the perfect age to become a mom.

I had just started med school at the time, drowning in classes and late-night study sessions, so I clapped for her plan and assumed, like everything else in her life, it would go exactly how she envisioned.

But it didn't.

Shaen and Remi tried to get pregnant for four years. Now Remi and I were both thirty, and Shaen was twenty-nine. After a chemical pregnancy, two miscarriages, and countless negative tests, she was finally close to nine months pregnant.

I cried the first time I heard the baby's heartbeat. Being in the field made me emotionally invested already, but this? This was personal. She was my best friend, and by marriage, my cousin and now, she was finally going to be a mom.

Which was ironic, considering she'd spent the first half of her life actively avoiding and fearing getting pregnant.

As if she could hear my thoughts, my phone rang.

**'Shaen bff I'm pregnant answer the phone immediately'** scrolled across my screen. She'd changed her contact name, and I hadn't had the heart to change it back.

"Hey, babes." I put her on speaker as I applied deodorant.

"Did you leave yet?" she asked, a little breathless.

"Just about. I'm getting dressed." I zipped up my fly and walked into my closet to pick out a shirt. I mostly lived in scrubs, but today I finally got to wear real clothes.

"Okay, drive safe."

"Okay, Mom."

I heard her inhale sharply, and then she squealed, soft and high-pitched. "I'm gonna be a mom, Liam!"

"You're already a mom, Shay Shay, the baby's just not out yet," I said gently.

She sniffed. Pregnancy had turned my little ice queen into a soft, emotional mess.

"Stop it." I laughed. "I'll see you soon."

"Bye." *Click.*

The phone went quiet. I grabbed the presents from the kitchen counter, scooped my keys off the table, and shut off the lights in my apartment, the one I barely lived in but paid an astronomical amount of rent for.

"Hi, Mom." I hugged her, inhaling her familiar scent. I instantly felt calmer in her arms.

"Hello, my love." She stood on her tiptoes to kiss my cheek. "Did you sleep?"

I nodded.

"You look tired."

"I *am* tired."

"How many babies?"

She took the gift bag from me and placed it under the balloon arch, pink and blue balloons twisted into a social media-worthy display, where the other gifts were stacked.

"Last night? Five. This month so far? Fifteen."

"I'm so proud of you. And soon you'll be done with residency and can settle down. You'll need to find a nice girl and have some babies of your own."

She squeezed my hand.

Charlee's face flashed in my mind, and I shoved it away, irritated that my brain kept going there. And then, uninvited, something else, something much worse, tried to worm its way to the surface.

I squashed it before it could even become a thought.

"Sure, Mom. Let me just graduate first, and then we'll talk."

I heard Shaen's voice and followed it down the hall to my old bedroom, now converted into a guest room.

Three years ago, Shaen and Remi had bought a house not far from my parents'. It sat on a big plot of land, perfect for the dog rescue she'd always dreamed of running. Now it was a full-blown, highly successful business. Her social media had hundreds of thousands of followers. She'd even been interviewed on the news several times after her rescue helped shelter dogs from states hit by natural disasters. It had been her passion for so long, and I was proud of her for making it happen.

I pushed open the door and found my best friend lying on the cream-colored duvet of the king-sized bed, shirt pulled up, Doppler out, crying. Lia, her other best friend, and my high school girlfriend, was beside her, trying to calm her down.

"What's wrong?"

"I just wanted to find the heartbeat before the party, and I can't find it, and I just—I…"

I held out my hand, and Lia silently passed me the Doppler. I'd bought Shaen a high-grade one because she'd always struggled with anxiety. Layer that with all her losses, plus pregnancy hormones, and she had been a full-blown wreck at the start. I'd taught her how to find the heartbeat, and it had helped ease her mind, most of the time.

I added a little more aloe vera gel to her stomach and placed the Doppler on her firm, round belly.

Less than two seconds later, the beautiful flutter of her baby's heartbeat filled the room.

Right on cue, she started crying again.

"Shaen, get it together, girl. You gotta go out there, entertain your guests, and open presents." I laughed and leaned in to hug her. She pressed her tear-streaked face into my shirt and took a deep, shuddering breath.

Once she calmed down, I sat back, grabbed a wipe from the farmhouse-inspired nightstand, and cleaned off the gel. Then I gently tugged her white maternity shirt down over her stretched skin.

"Fuck, Liam. I'm a mess." She sniffled, but thankfully, the tears had stopped.

I rubbed her back, brushing her long blonde hair to the side so I wouldn't mess it up.

"Hi, Liam," Lia said softly, giving me a quick hug.

"Hey."

It wasn't weird between us, too much time had passed for that, but there was always this odd energy. Like, *I knew what your vagina felt like before your husband did,* but obviously, neither of us ever brought it up.

Lia had married one of her college professors after graduation. At first, it stirred up a bit of drama in our friend group, he was twelve years older than her, but at one gathering before the wedding, my mom clapped her hands to shut everyone up and gave a little speech about acceptance.

She'd said, *We don't get to judge how different someone's love may be. We just have to accept it. Because if someone we love is happy, then we don't question how they found that happiness.*

Something had stirred inside me that day, but I ignored it.

Just like I'd been doing since college.

And just like I was still doing now.

I helped Shaen off the bed, she couldn't pull herself up at this point. She was only five-foot-three and growing my six-foot-four cousin's baby. At nearly nine months she was carrying big. Though you'd never hear me say that out loud, Remi would murder me.

"Hey, turn around," I said, guiding her to stand in front of me. I reached my hands around her and gently lifted her belly, taking some of the pressure off her back.

"Oh my god that's so good," she all but moaned.

Of course Remi chose that precise moment to walk in.

"I'm not even gonna ask." He pretended to walk back out.

"Come here." Shaen motioned for him to return.

Remi listened immediately. He adored her.

I wouldn't admit it out loud but ever since breaking up with Lia at the start of my freshman year of college I'd notoriously been a fuck-them-don't-date-them kind of guy. Lately I'd secretly begun to want what Shaen and Remi had. I wanted unconditional love and a person to be my safe space. I wanted cuddles and an opinionated five- foot-three wife who told me what to do.

*Boss me around baby, I can take it, please and thank you.*

Shaking free from the thought spiral I showed Remi how to gently support Shaen's swollen stomach. Then I kissed her forehead before stepping back to give them room. Seeing a man care for his pregnant wife was inevitably part of my job—but somehow, this felt too intimate. Too personal to intrude on.

"I'm gonna go get food and see if any of the guests want to give me a quick blowie before the party starts." I said it to take my mind off the intense thoughts going on inside my head and to make Shaen laugh. Which she did and Remi said, "Wouldn't expect anything less from you, Liam."

I grinned but it was overshadowed by the ache that crept in every time I acknowledged how long I had been hiding behind this character. The sex-obsessed playboy who forgot her name before she even came.

Because now I wanted more.

But what I wanted felt completely unattainable.

Plus I wasn't sure what would hurt worse. People not taking me seriously and laughing about my latest escapades if I ever spoke my deepest desires out loud or the possibility of wanting something I'd never get at all.

The first time I laid eyes on my husband, he was kissing another man.

It had been six years ago while I was in an accelerated nursing program, and I was stretched thin between school and life responsibilities. I'd taken a rare night off from studying to celebrate Halloween. I predictably dressed up as a sexy nurse, and went out with my friends. The club was packed, energetic, and everything I needed to let go and enjoy myself for a night.

I was several drinks in when the world around me seemed to slow and I caught a glimpse of the hottest man I had ever laid eyes on. My stomach flipped. A couple dancing in front of me blocked my view for the most part but every time they moved, I saw a little bit more of his profile. Flashing strobe lights cast a colorful glow across his strong arms. I caught a quick flash of his bristly cheek and defined jawline before the couple shifted again, blocking my sight.

I squeezed past them, jostling my drink in the process, and finally, there he was in all his tall, brown-haired, broad-shouldered glory.

I watched as he laughed, then placed his hands on the cheeks

of the man in front of him, bent his head and kissed the ever-loving shit out of him. I'd never seen something so hot in my life—and I didn't know what it meant for me, but I couldn't look away.

"Well fuck," I muttered out loud. "The hottest ones are always gay."

A girl standing in front of me heard and turned to see who I was looking at, then laughed.

"Jax? He's bi—maybe you still have a chance."

I doubted it based on how much he obviously liked what he was currently doing, and I said as much out loud.

The girl laughed again and took my hand. "Come on, I'll introduce you to my brother—you're exactly his type." She winked and I wondered if I was just a little too drunk and making this entire scenario up in my head.

Yet, what felt like moments later, I found myself dancing, sandwiched between hottie number one, Jax, and hottie number two, whose name I didn't catch over the deafening music. I found that I *loved* the feeling of both of them around me. Two pairs of strong hands on my waist and hips. Two voices encouraged me to keep moving exactly like that. For the first time in ages, I felt wanted—and not by one person, but both. Like I belonged exactly there.

I was crowded on all sides, and the chaotic security it lent me was something I had never experienced before.

Two more drinks, and an hour later, I found out what Jax tasted like when he kissed me, while the other guy practically licked his way down my neck. I let go of every thought, every worry. Then they kissed each other while still holding onto me, and I died and went to *bi heaven*, because I had *literally* never been this turned on in my life.

Unfortunately, moments later, it all came crashing down when Jax looked at his watch and announced he had a flight to catch. The fantasy shattered like glass. He was leaving? We traded numbers and a few more soul-scorching kisses before he left.

Two days later, he texted me, apologizing for his forward behavior. He assured me that he was usually much more reserved than that, and he had drunk way too much that night.

I texted back saying I had too much to drink as well and asked what it was like flying hungover. He told me he didn't know, since he had still been inebriated when he got on the plane and ended up barfing in the tiny airplane bathroom, and at six feet tall, that was no easy feat.

We kept texting for weeks after that until he finally asked me out over Christmas break.

We casually dated from December until March, when I broke up with him for a brief month. I told him I didn't want to hold him back from the rest of his sexual needs. We'd talked about him being bi, and although he'd never done anything to make me feel this way, the worry that I wasn't the right person for him ate away at me until I finally called it quits. I was scared to be someone's compromise.

I was absolutely miserable for the entire four weeks we were apart, and I felt intensely relieved when we got back together in April. He called me drunk one night and told me how mad he was—that I'd assume I wasn't exactly what he wanted and needed, and that he couldn't believe he might be falling in love with someone who would break up with him over something so insignificant.

We'd been together ever since.

He proposed a year later and loved to tell people how his sister had found the love of his life in a packed New York City club. He conveniently left out the other guy in that scenario. Not only did we not talk about that part of our meet-cute but I never told him how much I had loved it.

Fast forward to now. We lived in a rent-controlled, two bedroom apartment in NYC that I had inherited from my grandmother. I was an L&D nurse at NYU and Jax worked for his uncle in construction. We had our routine down pat. We worked a lot, and sometimes, when we had time, we hung out with friends or went on a rare date night. But for the most part, our lives were spent working to pay the bills and pay down my student loans. Our life together felt exactly how I had imagined it would be once I reached my upper twenties, yet it also felt like the days had flown by, turning into years. Suddenly, we'd been married for so long, and I wasn't quite sure how it had happened.

I lay awake in our bed, horns blaring outside our window, Jax snoring next to me. His scruff had grown in, and his brown hair was a mess. I scooted over and laid my head on his defined chest, right over his tattoo. He let out a huff of a breath, and in his sleep, he wrapped his arm around me, keeping me close to him.

I loved him so much—yet I worried.

Despite his assurance so many years ago, I still worried that I wasn't enough. How could I be? All I had was a vagina.

My sweet husband, who was on the quieter side and tended to be more shy, said a lot when I got alcohol into him. Unlike his usual more reserved self, those were the moments when he shared stories with me, things he'd experienced with his former male partners. He never got too graphic, but I knew there were things he'd done that I could never provide.

Last year on his birthday I'd brought up the idea of pegging. He'd blushed, and told me to stop, said he loved me and he didn't need anything else. He had proceeded to eat me out with so much gusto, trying to prove how much he "loved that pussy."

The thing was I was confident in how much he loved it. And me. But I couldn't help but wonder if he was trying to convince *himself* that it was *all* he loved.

Once I tried to explain to him that it was like me loving dessert. I could be happy with cake, but what if I also loved ice cream? What if I found out I could never have ice cream ever again? How would I feel?

Jax had proceeded to get mad at me.

"Well, what do you want me to do, Charlee? Cheat on you?"

He left in a huff and came back a few hours later with one of those individual slices of cake from 7-Eleven. I didn't bring it up again.

I sighed and got out of bed, my feet hitting the cold floor of our bedroom, sending a shiver up my spine. I had a shorter-than-usual shift this morning. Then I had the hospital's yearly holiday party tonight.

I showered quickly, washing my hair and shaving all the important parts before drying off. Then I put on the scrubs that I wore to work, even though I'd have to change into hospital-issued ones once I got there. I blew out my long, dark hair and applied a quick face of makeup, just a bit of mascara to my lashes, some blush to brighten up my face, and a swipe of lip stain to bring out the natural hue of my lips.

After putting everything away in our tiny cabinet beneath the sink, I stepped out of the bathroom and saw that Jax had woken up and was sitting in bed, looking at his phone.

"Morning." I leaned down to give him a kiss.

"Mmm, don't leave. Let's play hooky."

He grinned up at me, wrapped his arms around my waist, his knees caging me in on either side.

"We've got bills to pay." I softly bopped him on the nose.

"Ew boring." He pretended to sulk.

"Don't forget, you're leaving work early today. We've got the holiday party tonight."

I eased his arms open and scooted away to grab my badge and stethoscope.

"I'll be ready… Remind me again why I can't just wear jeans?"

He stood and stretched, and I watched appreciatively as his ab muscles rippled with the motion.

"You're not wearing jeans to a fancy party, Jax." My husband was a blue-collar man through and through. He lived in Levi's, boots, caps, T-shirts, and plaid-button downs. Since I had gotten my job at NYU three years ago, I'd forced him into a suit once a year for the party, and he despised every second of it, but he did it anyway.

"Be a good boy and clean up your neck too. I'll see you soon. Love you."

I gave him another kiss, and he swatted my ass as I walked out.

I WAVED hello to the security guard at the front desk, as well as the receptionist near the elevators, then pressed my finger to the electronic screen to clock in and start my shift.

In the locker room, I changed into my pink scrubs, wrapped my stethoscope around my neck, pulled my hair back, and clipped my badge to my pocket. I texted Jax to let him know that I was at work and would talk to him soon, then stuffed my phone into my pocket and headed to the main desk to see how many laboring moms we had with us this morning.

That's where I found Dr. Hennessy, leaning against the desk with his phone out, showing photos to two of my co-workers. He looked up as I approached and grinned.

"Morning, Charlee." He shifted over to make room for me and turned his phone around so I could see the screen.

It was a photo of his best friend Shaen. She had that gorgeous pregnant glow and was sitting on the couch, surrounded by baby gifts, ripped wrapping paper at her feet. She was holding up a newborn onesie that looked like a doctor's white lab coat, complete with a printed stethoscope around the neck and the words *Dr. Lewis* on the fake pocket.

"Is this not the cutest fucking thing you've ever seen?" He looked so excited as he waited for me to answer.

"That is adorable."

He leaned in to show me a closer shot.

"Did you have that custom-made?"

"Of course I did."

He swiped to the next photo and showed us the Owlet Dream Sock monitor that he'd gifted her as well.

"You're the best cousin ever," Reina, one of my co-workers said, clearly impressed.

"Godfather," he corrected her. He was very proud of his role in this baby's life.

"How was the party?"

I took an iPad off the charging dock to log into the electronic medical records system.

"So good. She only cried three times and she loved all the presents."

He looked so genuinely happy and it was sweet to see how much he loved his friend.

"Did their parents show up?"

I'd been kept up to date on all the family drama and had found myself fully invested.

Dr. Hennessy—or *Liam*, as he kept telling me to call him, and I kept refusing—had started his residency here right before I had started as a nurse. Much of his residency had been spent rotating through different departments, so he wasn't always on L&D with me, but we'd still become fast work friends.

During the time he *had* rotated in my department, he'd become my favorite doctor to work with. Not only was he funny and kind, but he was also an incredible provider, I had seen him do some amazing things in the delivery room. The patients always loved him, partly because his bedside manner was impeccable, and if we were being honest, because he looked like he had just walked off a runway to be here.

His light brown hair had natural blond highlights through it and was longer and styled in the front, kept shorter, and tapered on the sides and back. His eyes were a deep, gorgeous blue. He had full lips, a strong jawline with just the right amount of facial hair, and a smattering of freckles across his nose.

In other words all the nurses on the floor called him *Dr. McHottie* behind his back.

I was convinced that more than one of the midwives had a massive crush on him.

Although I'd heard whispers of his supposed playboy reputation, I didn't pay them any mind. Not only was it irrelevant to me, I was happily married, but I'd also spent so many long hours working alongside him and had never seen any sign of that alleged side of him.

Instead, I just knew him.

I knew what he was like as a friend, he was always excited to tell me all about his best friend. I knew that he loved his family, and of his plans for after residency. I knew his favorite movie as he was always quoting it. I knew how he took his coffee and even had it saved on my Starbucks app for when we ran out of anything good in the break room and decided to have some delivered. I knew he always wore a specific design on his socks when delivering babies because he claimed it brought him good luck.

I had never seen him speak to anyone in the hospital without being completely professional, let alone flirt with them. If he *had* slept with someone in the hospital I would have found out about it because he was my friend, though ironically, we didn't talk outside of work.

"Remi's dad, Dermont, came. He bought the baby the fanciest stroller you've ever seen." Liam rolled his eyes because Dermont was always buying them outrageously expensive things.

"His mom 'couldn't' make it as usual but she did send some nice gifts and Shaen's mom actually showed up."

"Aww, that's nice. I'm so happy for them."

"One of these days, you have to meet her. You'll love her," Liam said just as his pager beeped.

"We've got a blood pressure dropping in room four. Let's go."

Instantly, the chatting, easygoing version of Liam was gone, replaced by the focused doctor I'd seen countless times. We ran to room four—and just like that, our day officially began.

APPARENTLY, our shifts ended at the same time today, so we headed to the elevator together as my phone rang. Jax's smiling contact photo filled my screen.

"Hey, babe."

Liam pressed the button to the lobby.

*Thanks,* I mouthed.

I could barely hear Jax over the sound of jackhammers and trucks in the background.

"You cut *what?*"

"My arm. I think I need stitches." I finally heard him say.

"Crap. Are you okay?" The hospital's holiday party was starting soon, but I figured we'd make a detour to get him stitched up, and assuming he felt up to it, we'd just show up late.

"Are you coming home now? We'll stop at urgent care on the way out. How bad is it bleeding?"

Liam kept the elevator door open for me as I distractedly stepped out. I held my phone to my ear with my shoulder while digging in my bag for my car keys.

"I can do it." I heard Liam offer.

"Do what?" I finally got my keys and pulled them out of my bag, only to send a tampon and tube of lip gloss clattering to the floor. "Shit."

I tried to bend down but Liam beat me to it.

"I got it." He scooped them up and dropped them back into my bag.

"Gosh, thank you." I didn't even have the energy to be embarrassed. The man looked at vaginas for a living, and we were both adults.

"No problem. Assuming it's a simple cut and he doesn't need further care, I can stitch him up," he explained as he followed me out to the parking lot.

"I wouldn't want to put you out of your way like that."

"I'm not going home. It's way too far. I was gonna hang around here and then head to the party," he told me. "I really don't mind, and it'll save you a trip to urgent care. As long as you don't mind me using your bathroom to change into my suit."

I nodded in understanding.

"Babe, one of the doctors that I work with says he can come over and stitch it up for you. We're coming home now. How far are you?" We headed to my car as Jax told me he was around ten minutes away. I relayed the information to Liam, who gave me a thumbs-up.

"Perfect. See you at home. Love you." I hung up and slipped my phone into my bag.

"Thank you so much. I hope this isn't too much of an inconvenience."

"Not at all. My apartment is so far away. I needed a place to hang out anyway. If anything, *I'll* be inconveniencing *you*." He laughed.

I backed out of the spot and merged into busy NYC traffic.

"Why do you live so far from work?"

"It was the only thing I could find at the time. My lease is actually already up. I was going to find something else, but I'll be moving again in six months, so I figured, why bother? But the drive every shift is really starting to wear me down."

"I can't imagine. I'm always exhausted after a shift and I'm only fifteen minutes away."

As if to prove my point, we pulled up at my building and, with a rare moment of luck on my side, I found a parking spot right in front.

"*Damn.*" He looked positively jealous. "I didn't know you lived so close to work. How does it feel to be God's favorite?"

I laughed and turned off the car.

Jax was already upstairs when we got inside.

"Jax, you remember Dr. Hennessy, Dr. Hennessy, this is my husband, Jax." Although they met briefly each year at the holiday party, I reintroduced them as I hung up my bag and coat.

"I've been telling her to call me Liam, but she won't listen." There was suddenly an edge to his voice I hadn't detected earlier, and I glanced between the two of them curiously as Liam stepped forward.

"Hey. I'm Jaxon. Jax. Her husband. Yeah," Jax said in the slightly shy tone he always used around new people.

"Let's see the damage." Liam stood with his hands on his hips in front of Jax, who got up from his chair and began to unbutton his long-sleeve shirt. I noticed that Liam was about an inch taller, but despite his obvious muscles, Jax was still much broader.

I winced when I saw the bloody paper towel wrapped around Jax's arm.

"No bandages at work?" Liam joked lightly.

Jax shrugged. "I grabbed the closest thing I could find," he grunted.

I came over holding a warm washcloth, a tube of antibacterial ointment, and a bottle of painkillers. The paper towel had stuck to areas of the wound, and when Liam gently peeled it off, fresh blood welled up.

"This doesn't look like it hit any tendons. I'm not an orthopedic surgeon, but I feel comfortable closing the fascia."

Jax nodded as Liam examined the cut, then turned to his bag and laid out his supplies.

"I'm gonna numb you and then I'll close it."

"You can just skip the numbing if you want," Jax hissed as I dabbed at the area with some rubbing alcohol wipes.

"Oh so you're a tough guy huh?" Liam winked as he prepped the needle.

I caught it then—just a flicker—the way Jax's eyes tracked Liam's movements.

*He likes what he sees,* I realized with a start, *interesting.*

The awareness landed soft and strange, low beneath my sternum. Not jealousy. No, it was a curious ache, a flicker of heat. Something I wasn't ready to name.

"I'm numbing you anyway. Hold his hand, Charlee." Liam took the cap off the needle.

"Yeah hold my hand, Charlee," Jax echoed, grinning.

"You boys are stupid." I laughed, grabbing hold of his big, calloused hand.

It took seven stitches to close the gash. I watched as Liam used a simple interrupted suture stitch, his lip held between his teeth as he focused.

"Looks good." He nodded as he examined his work and I began to clean up the counter. Liam placed a bandage over the wound, his voice calm and instructive as he went over aftercare with Jax telling him how to keep it clean, what to watch for, and when to follow up with another provider to make sure it was healing properly.

Jax nodded, although he was already well-versed in keeping cuts clean, it was something that happened at least a few times a year on different job sites. As he stood he asked, "Wanna watch the game until we have to get ready?"

"Hell ya." Liam tucked his supplies back into his bag and the two of them disappeared into the living room.

I shook my head, laughing to myself. Men made friends so easily. I wished it was as simple for women. I kept my friend group small, partly because I didn't have a lot of time to be social, but mostly because women could be catty and I had zero time for drama. Jax had three sisters whom I loved, I still stayed in touch with two girls from nursing school, and one girl from back home. Other than that, I had my work friends and Jax. I didn't need more than that.

"Babe," Jax called over the sound of the sports announcer. "Can you bring us a beer?"

"Sure." I popped the cap off two bottles and brought them into the other room.

"Thanks." Jax ran a hand down my arm as I handed them their drinks. Liam lifted his bottle toward me in a silent thank you.

"How long do we have?" Jax looked at his watch.

"We should probably leave within the hour."

"I'm gonna go start getting ready now, 'cause I need all the time I have to make myself pretty."

"You're always gorgeous," Jax said, though his eyes were already drifting back to the flat screen.

Liam's eyes flickered—just for a moment—from the TV to me, and then back again. So quickly that I almost thought I'd imagined it.

D r. Freaking Hennessy was hot. Like capital-H hot. I remember thinking that every time we met briefly at the hospital's holiday party. Just minutes ago, he had literally stood between my legs while stitching me up, one lip pulled between his teeth as he concentrated. It had made me feel all hot and bothered, which, in turn, annoyed me. *I'm married,* I reminded myself. *I love my wife, adore her.* She was everything I want and need, and most importantly, I am loyal and respect our marriage vows. I would never touch another person in a sexual way. I had never wanted to, nor would I ever even consider it. But sometimes my thoughts would run amok, and that inner turmoil was a tremendous source of shame. It wasn't even about him—it was about me. About something waking up inside of me I didn't know still lived there.

I was still wrestling with the chaos in my mind when Liam stood and took the empty beer bottle from my hand.

"Where's your recycling?" he asked.

"You don't have to do that," I protested. Liam made a tsking sound with his tongue and watched me as if insisting that I let him discard the bottles.

"Under the sink in the kitchen," I acquiesced, watching him walk away. I couldn't help but notice how his scrubs clung to his taut ass cheeks and how his chest filled out his top perfectly. He was, without a doubt, exactly my type. With his tousled hair, bright eyes, strong jaw, and a personality that balanced intensity, intelligence, humor, and carefree charm.

*He's straight and you're married*, I reminded myself again as I stood almost feeling the need to physically shake my traitorous musings that made my stomach clench. I shouldn't have been watching him like that. But I had. And it scared me more than it turned me on.

"We should get ready or Charlee will have our asses," I told him.

"Charlee? She's so sweet at work," Liam said, sounding surprised as he grabbed his bag and the suit he had draped over the back of the couch.

"Oh she's sweet," I confirmed. "She's also obsessed with being on time." Liam nodded.

"Got it. Where should I change?"

*Right here*, I thought, and mentally slapped myself.

"Take the other bedroom. It's empty." I showed him the door to the second bedroom that we had yet to furnish. "There are towels in the cabinet if you want to shower."

"Thank you." He smiled at me and then shut the door behind him.

I'd realized I was bisexual in high school. The same feelings of interest that I had developed for girls bubbled up inside of me for boys too. When I jacked off, I thought of boobs and rounded hips and broad chests—and the shape of a dick behind the quarterback's football uniform. At first, I felt confused. Why did all my friends only talk about pussy and boobs and which cheerleader they wanted to fuck, while here I was, equally excited by the idea of getting a blow job from a girl as from a guy? It made me feel alone, like I'd missed a memo everyone else got. Once I understood that I liked both men and women, I simply embraced who I was. I didn't publicize it, but I didn't hide it either. If people found out, so be it.

I hadn't explored much in high school, and although I was naturally an introvert, in college I managed to push outside my comfort zone and I slept around a decent amount—sometimes just with a man, sometimes just a woman, and sometimes with both at the same time. If I was being honest with myself, those encounters had been my favorite because it was the best of both worlds in one bed.

Then I met Charlee, and I fell in love almost immediately. I had never been in love before—lust, sure, but love had never been on my radar. Not until my black-haired, tan bombshell showed up at a club, ironically led by my sister. She'd been wearing a sheer white bodysuit with red nipple covers, emblazoned with a medical cross insignia, and a tiny, red, latex skirt. When she had maneuvered herself between me and the guy I'd been kissing earlier, it turned out to be the highlight of my night. My heart had kicked up a notch at the feeling of her lips beneath mine and my date's hands running down my arm. In that charged moment, it didn't take much for me to drum up a vision of him above me and her below me—ripe for the taking.

Even though the night had been cut short by my flight, I had dreamt of her and him entangled next to me as I slept on the plane. Which was why I was pretty shocked, as the more I got to know her, the less I thought of me—and her—with anyone else. Once we started dating, I quickly discovered that I wanted monogamy. My nights with other men became a distant memory and I wanted nothing else but her. Body, mind, and soul. She offered something steadier—a certainty built on real connection—and it made all my past, fleeting encounters pale in comparison. The thrill of meeting someone new and giving into the impulse of desire became a fading memory, echoes of something

I no longer craved. She may not have a dick but she had my heart, and that was what mattered most.

As I entered our bedroom, I found Charlee standing by the long white dresser, brushing her hair. She wore a black, gauzy dress that appeared sheer in all the right places. Her lips were red, her amber eyes heavily lined, and her hair floated around her.

"Damn, baby." I ran a hand appreciatively down her ass.

"You like?" She grinned, her tone teasing.

"I love." I peeled off my already unbuttoned shirt, watching her step into a pair of heels before giving me a twirl.

"You win." I tossed the shirt toward the laundry basket. It hit the rim and fell to the floor.

"What do I win?" She picked up the shirt, and this time, it made it into the pile.

"Everything. You win it all." I unzipped my pants and watched her eyes drift downward as I pushed them down my thighs. She came over and gently cupped me through my boxers. I immediately stiffened.

"Oh I've won alright." She winked. I held back a moan.

"That's rude, Charlee," I chided as I pulled on the crisp white button-down shirt she had prepared for me last night. "You can't start something when you can't finish."

"I'll finish later," she promised, and I looked forward to it.

We had an active sex life. I loved our connection—how much I still desired her all these years later—but sometimes a nagging voice in the back of my head wondered if she was overcompensating. I knew she worried I wasn't fully satisfied, that being dedicated to one woman for the rest of my life left me somehow bereft of dick. I snickered to myself at how ridiculous it sounded. In all seriousness I was profoundly happy with her. She was my best friend, my partner in life—the person I would happily grow old with.

Sure, I occasionally missed the feeling of strong arms holding me down, a stubbled cheek pressed against mine or a deep voice panting in my ear. But I also knew what I had given up when I had chosen to dedicate my life to one woman and I didn't regret it. Not ever. Because she was worth it and I loved her.

I found Liam and Charlee talking in the living room. Liam looked devastatingly handsome in his black suit paired with a black shirt—a few buttons left open and no tie. His dirty blond hair was a startling contrast to my wife's dark hair as they stood close to each other, leaning over his phone screen.

"Ready?" I asked while I grabbed my jacket.

Liam looked up, stuffed his phone in his pocket, and walked over to join me in the front hallway.

"Right on time." Charlee sounded pleased.

"I've already ordered an Uber," Liam announced.

"Oh you didn't have to do that," Charlee replied.

"It's the least I could do—after all you let me hang and get changed here." Liam held the front door open for the both of us, then shut it behind him, carefully turning the lock.

"You mean we let you use our completely bare spare bedroom? That's so nice of us." Charlee laughed.

Liam shrugged. "I'm not picky."

I liked him. He was personable and funny, and weirdly enough I found myself appreciating how thoughtful he was to my wife—holding the elevator door for her, pointing out a bump in the sidewalk so she wouldn't trip, even asking the Uber driver to pull up right in front of the venue so she wouldn't have to walk too far in her heels.

Once we made it inside and through security Liam thanked us again, and promised, "See you in there." He even hugged Charlee briefly before disappearing into the crowd.

"How's your arm?" Charlee asked as we handed our coats over to the woman manning the coat check.

"Throbs a bit," I admitted. "But I'll be fine."

"Let's drink the pain away," she declared, leading us to the open bar. After waiting ten minutes in line, she ordered a boozy hot cocoa, two shots of whiskey, and two marshmallow mules. "Nurse's orders," she said as she handed me my drinks.

"That is such solid health advice. Thank you," I joked, sucking down both shots before sipping on the mule.

"Let's get some food, and I'll re-introduce you to everyone." Charlee was not only beautiful and friendly but also very likable so we were stopped to say hi at least three times before we got to the buffet. We took our plates and joined the line for dinner. As we moved toward the chafing dishes, I noticed Liam and another man join the line behind us, deep in conversation.

"Dr. Shaw, Dr. Hennessy." Charlee bobbed her head in greeting, balancing her plate in her manicured hands.

"Charlee. Jax. Hey!" Liam had clearly gotten into the alcohol already as he appeared even friendlier than before, if that were possible.

"Jason, this is my favorite nurse, Charlee and her husband, Jaxon." Liam slung an arm over my shoulder as he introduced me to his colleague—oddly choosing to use my full name. Jason grunted a hello.

"Jason's an anesthesiologist. So he's very smart—but very lacking in social skills." Liam laughed.

"Hey," Jason protested. "All of my patients are asleep. What do you want from me?"

We walked the length of the buffet, chatting with the two of them. Liam suggested that we load up our plate with one or two things and share family-style at the table instead of making multiple trips back and forth. We all agreed, and I found myself scooping up an array of meatballs, pigs in a blanket, and sliced venison.

Then Jason decided that we needed more alcohol, so we grabbed a couple more drinks each before finding a table near the dance floor with enough space for the four of us.

"You know, I'd be fine without a holiday party every year if they would just pay us more instead," Liam said, digging into a slice of steak.

"Seriously," another co-worker chimed in from across the table.

"Do they pay residents?" I asked.

Liam nodded. "Oh yeah. I work around eighty hours a week for a whopping $110,000 a year which has barely made a dent in the nearly $300,000 that I've racked up in student loans."

"Bro, that's just about what Charlee makes," I blurted, holding back a snort. I meant it as a joke, alcohol always loosened me up —made things funnier and made me say dumb shit apparently— because the second it left my mouth I regretted it.

"Jax," Charlee, hissed, horrified. While Liam wasn't her boss, he was a doctor and she was a nurse, and I knew that dynamic could get complicated.

I swung my eyes from her face to Liam's, ready to apologize, but I found him laughing.

"It's true." Liam pretended to cry. "Be my sugar mama, Charlee, I'm broke and my living situation sucks."

I shrugged at my wife in silent question, and she proceeded to fill me in on his awful commute and how he had six months left to his residency. Liam leaned in and added that he planned to get a job closer to his parents once he graduated—he was looking forward to finding an apartment there and for his commute from hell to be over.

"Why don't you move into our second bedroom?" I heard myself say. The words came out before I was able to think them through.

Charlee froze, her fork halfway to her mouth. Liam blinked, surprised.

"Come again?"

"That's what she said." Jason snickered as if he weren't a full grown adult and a doctor on top of that.

"I mean, I'll talk to Charlee about it first," I added quickly. "But you saw the bedroom and if it's only temporary…"

I downed the rest of my drink and looked away. Liam's eyes looked even bluer under the warm lights, and between the alcohol that had entered my bloodstream and the way he distracted me, I felt heat creep up my neck. Maybe the offer was stupid. Having that beautiful man in our apartment every day suddenly did not sound like such a good idea. Not because I didn't trust myself—I did—implicitly. But because if he didn't move in, I would likely never see him again and that was for the best.

"I—I don't even know what to say." Liam looked like he had plenty to say but he was interrupted by a man in a suit coming over to introduce him to a woman with a severe blonde bob and a pair of pink glasses that dominated her face. He stood and they walked a few steps away. I watched him shake her hand.

When I turned back I found Charlee watching me with an unreadable expression.

"All jokes aside, Liam is the best," Jason said around a mouthful of food. "I've known him for years. He's respectful, generous, and trustworthy. If you're serious you'd change his life —I have never seen him this exhausted."

I winced imagining commuting that far on top of such long and intense shifts.

"Oh and charge him rent," Jason added as he stood up. "Don't feel bad, his daddy is loaded." Jason winked as he meandered off toward the bar.

"I'm sorry," I murmured to Charlee. "I don't know why I said that. I just felt sorry for him…"

She nodded slowly. "It's actually not a bad idea. If we charge him rent, I can throw all of it at my student loans and get them paid off faster."

That didn't sound terrible to me either.

"And it's only six months," I added.

"Let's be crazy and do it," she whispered loudly.

I grinned and nodded, but before I could say anything else, Liam returned with shots for the table and another cocktail for Charlee.

After that next drink, I was left feeling warm and happy. My gorgeous wife was by my side, my belly was full, and I felt like I'd made a new friend. What else could a guy ask for?

Dancing was not really my thing when I was sober, but drunk? I was all about it. After the usual speeches and announcements from the executive hospital staff and medical director, the music picked up and the dance floor filled.

Charlee ground against me, and I kept my hands low on her hips as I moved with her. She and her group of friends were laughing, spinning, and basically taking over the dance floor.

Suddenly, Liam appeared in front of us, moving to the music, a huge smile on his face. For a moment, I was flung back in time —a flash of a memory with Charlee and the man dancing behind her clouded my vision. I could taste the vodka on her breath and I could feel his hand on mine as we kept her solidly between us.

I hardened in my pants.

Slowing my steps, I gently pulled away. That heat was creeping up my neck again. I handed Charlee off to her co-worker.

"I gotta pee," I mumbled. "Watch her for me."

"I got her," Liam assured me and I knew he did.

I playfully spun Charlee while we waited for her husband to get back from the bathroom. Her hands were small and warm in mine.

*Focus,* I told my brain. Why did my palms sweat when she laughed like that?

Fuck, I liked her. I liked her chill personality and her sarcastic banter. I appreciated her meticulous professionalism at work and her ability to calm down even the most anxious patient. I liked her beautiful face and her ass.

*Nope,* I quickly redirected my thoughts.

*She's married.*

Oh yes she was. And I liked her hunk of a husband and his tight ass too.

*Jesus.*

When I drank it was harder for me to lie to myself, and self-deception was a skill I'd been perfecting since college.

It had never been a secret that I liked sex. Before Lia, I'd hooked up with plenty of girls. Then we'd dated through the end of high school. But once I started college and we broke up, I sampled the options and really upped my body count.

At first, when I found myself noticing a guy's body or imagined myself touching him, I told myself it was just appreciation. I was a sexual guy who could admire beauty no matter the gender. But one night in my freshman year things changed.

I had gone out with my friends and stayed behind when they left to finish up a game of darts I had been playing with a good-looking guy from Switzerland, who'd been hitting on me all night. When I finally won, he stepped in close, caging me in against the dark wood-paneled wall behind me, and kissed me.

I kissed him back. My heart thundered. My stomach twisted. What the hell was I doing?

And suddenly everything I thought I knew about myself imploded.

He ended up giving me a blow job in the alley behind the bar but I couldn't bring myself to reciprocate and I had gone home feeling dirty and confused.

I didn't tell anyone what happened, not even Shaen. It sat inside of me like a secret brick.

And it kept happening.

Some nights I'd hook up with girls. Some nights I'd let a guy pull me into a dark corner to kiss and end up with his mouth on me in his car or in the bathroom of the club. I never reciprocated but I got much better at navigating it with smoother excuses. This went on for years and still I never told anyone.

It wasn't that I thought my family or my friends would be upset if I came out as bisexual. I knew they would accept me and love me no matter what.

It was more that I didn't want anyone rolling their eyes and saying, "Liam loves sex so much he'll do it with anyone."

Because it wasn't that.

It was something bigger and deeper than that. Something that felt like it lived in my chest, in the ache behind my ribs.

Yeah I loved sex but I also loved the feeling of being with a woman and knowing I could protect her and take care of her.

Giving pleasure to a woman was something I enjoyed doing, often. Slowly. Thoroughly.

But with men, everything felt different. Even. Balanced.

We could protect each other so to speak. My strength was matched with strength. I could feel it pressing against each other, fighting for control, neither of us submitting. It's what made the kiss all that much better. That tension lit me up.

I loved the feeling of broad shoulders beneath my hands and muscles surrounding me. I found I could be rougher when getting head. They weren't as delicate and while sometimes I needed delicate, gentle, soft. A warm heat to sink into, sometimes I craved the ability to take. I wanted to give into something harder. Rougher. I wanted to make them gag while they gripped my thighs with their big hands.

I liked cuddling with girls and listening to them go on about their day with their warmth pressed up against me and I also liked the idea of laying next to a guy talking about sports after I'd just fucked the shit out of him, although I had yet to actually act on that.

I wanted both.

I wanted all of it.

I wanted Charlee.

And I wanted Jax.

And I couldn't have either.

I knew I should say no to their offer of living in their second bedroom while I finished out my residency. It was the smarter, safer choice.

Which is why I knew—without a shadow of a doubt—that if the offer still stood I would accept.

I WAS SO DRUNK. Sitting in the back of an Uber with Jax's big thigh pressed against mine, I thought I might actually combust.

Charlee was next to him, near the window, rambling about how much fun she had and how every day should be like this.

Jax was listening to her intently. His love for her was so obvious it almost made me feel like an intruder just being in the car with them.

Earlier, Charlee had declared that I absolutely couldn't make it all the way back to my apartment in my current state. Instead, I was going home with them. I'd sleep on their couch in borrowed pajamas from Jax.

I didn't have the heart to tell her that I slept naked.

I'd just nodded. Because I was finding that life felt a hell of a lot better when Charlee was in charge.

Despite it being two o'clock in the morning, my phone rang and I saw an incoming FaceTime from Shaen. It took me several tries to press the button, but I eventually managed to answer.

"Hi, Shay Shay."

"Did I wake you?"

I snorted. She obviously wasn't *that* worried about it if she was calling.

"Nope." I panned the phone to show her Jax, Charlee, and then the Uber driver.

"Are you drunk?" she asked suspiciously.

"Very," I admitted.

She sighed. "Well at least one of us is having fun."

Jax must've relaxed his leg, because now his thigh was pressed even closer against mine—and I was actively fighting an erection.

"What's wrong, baby?" Her face was a little blurry, but I could hear the anxiety in her voice. She sighed again.

"Nothing in particular. I just can't sleep, and I'm getting so anxious about pushing this baby out." She sniffed.

Charlee reached out her hand. "Give me that."

I blinked but dutifully handed her the phone with no hesitation.

"Girlfriend?" Jax asked, his stubbly face close to mine.

I shook my head. "Best friend. She's married to my cousin."

"Ah," he replied.

Charlee was smiling into my phone.

"Hi Shaen, I'm Charlee. I work with Liam."

The sound of her voice finally saying my name zinged through my veins. I liked it way more than I should have.

"I'm an L&D nurse, and I just wanted to tell you—you can do it. I know it's scary, especially because you haven't done it before, but I promise your body knows what to do. You're gonna do amazing."

Shaen responded, and before I knew it, they were chatting like old friends. Charlee finally handed the phone back when we pulled up outside her building.

"I like her," Shaen told me.

"I like her too," I heard the alcohol say.

"And you promise you'll make it to my delivery?"

"I promise," I assured her. "I'll even do the delivery."

"You're not delivering my baby," I heard Remi grumble in the background.

"I'll have you know I'm very good at it," I retorted.

"He *is* very good at it," Charlee chimed in, leaning over—practically climbing into Jax's lap—to put her face back in front of the screen again.

"Liam is good at a lot of things," Remi shot back. "Doesn't mean I want him doing it to my wife."

Charlee cracked up, and when I looked up, I met Jax's eyes from over the phone screen. He was watching me, and when he caught me, our gazes locked, and he looked away.

Just like that the moment was over.

Once upstairs, Charlee made us all drink a big glass of water. It was such a simple thing, so Charlee, and it grounded me more than I expected. We stood in the kitchen and downed them under her watchful gaze. Then she brought over a white sheet, a large grey blanket, and two thick pillows to turn her soft, plush couch into a makeshift bed.

After I changed into a pair of blue sweatpants that she gave me, I handed over my laundry. She insisted that I let her wash it so it would be ready for me to wear tomorrow. Jax decided he was hungry and placed an Uber Eats order from Domino's. So once again, I found myself sitting next to him—this time on the smaller couch—waiting for the food to arrive. We flipped through the sports channels until Charlee came out wearing a pair of loose shorts and a big T-shirt that looked like they both belonged to Jax.

"Is everyone sobered up enough to talk about what Jax said earlier?" she asked, folding her legs beneath her as she lowered herself onto the oversized green velvet chair with a floral print across the back.

I instantly felt more alert and nodded.

"Sorry if that caught you both off guard. When I drink sometimes I just say my inside thoughts," Jax explained to me.

"I understand and I don't expect you to follow through." For a moment there, I'd imagined how much better my life would be if I lived just a short fifteen minutes from the hospital. But I understood that it wasn't something that would actually happen. They hadn't even discussed it—it was just a thought Jax had accidentally blurted out. Plus, while I knew Charlee really well, having worked with her on and off for almost four years, I realized that to Jax I was practically a stranger.

"So, we did talk it over briefly, and being that in six months you'll be graduating and moving back closer to home, we think it can work. If it makes things easier for you to be closer to the hospital, then we'd be happy to help you."

My heart squeezed in my chest, and hope flared up inside me.

"We would charge you some rent, if you don't mind, and all I ask otherwise is that you bring your furniture—'cause as you saw, we have none," Charlee added with a giggle and a shrug.

Her dark hair cascaded over her shoulder with the movement, and I was momentarily distracted by it.

"No shit," I recovered and spoke, sounding as flabbergasted as I felt, turning to Jax. "But you barely know me."

Jax shrugged. "If Charlee says you're good people, then you're good people."

I was instantly jealous of how trusting he was of her. I wanted that. I wanted a relationship that was about more than sex. I wouldn't have been caught dead saying that four years ago, but between turning thirty, finally being close to graduating, and being surrounded by so many happy couples in my friend group, my aversion to a long-term relationship had waned. I found myself craving the intimacy that a relationship—like the one Charlee and Jax had—offered.

"Are you sure I wouldn't be in your way?"

"You're usually at work," Charlee pointed out.

"True." She wasn't wrong.

"If you have a lady friend over, just put a sock on the door handle," Jax joked.

"I-I wouldn't..." I stumbled over my words, realizing that our bedrooms would be right across the hall from each other. *These are my friends*, I reminded myself, *my married friends*. I wouldn't say I had a lot of rules for myself when it came to sleeping around, but if someone was married, that was an immediate no. That—and always wearing a condom—were definitely two of my holy grails.

However, it wasn't often that I found myself so attracted to two people whom I couldn't pursue for multiple reasons. *I have to get laid*, I told myself again. *I just had to fuck this itch right out of me and then it would all be fine.*

My brain tried to remind me that this wasn't a new fixation— no, in fact, I had been thinking of Jax and how gorgeous I found him to be since the first time Charlee had introduced us at a holiday party three years ago.

"Hey. Dr. Hennessy—sorry I mean, I'm Liam. Nice to meet you."

I had stumbled over my words as I took in his dark hair, bits curling over his forehead and falling into his deep brown eyes. His face was covered in a layer of scruff that made it look like he had purposefully gone for a grungy-chic look but in reality, I assumed it was probably there because he couldn't have been bothered to shave before coming to the party. His lips were full, his nose straight, and his jawline defined.

We made some small talk, until he said, "Well look out for Charlee at work for me" and instead of saying, *Sure* or *Definitely* or *You got it*, I'd said, "You too," then shuffled away in embarrassment, barely looking at Charlee, who had laughed at me.

Charlee—who now sat in front of me in her oversized pajamas with her pert little nose, pink rosebud lips, and long, thick, dark hair.

My brain tried to force me to acknowledge it. That I was actually attracted to more than just her face and body. I respected her work ethic and how calm she remained in chaotic medical situations. I looked forward to talking to her at work. I felt safe and seen around her.

*Too much!* I halted the chaos in my mind. *Sometimes friends think their friends are hot, and still respect everyone's boundaries*, I rebuked my subconscious. *It's not a big deal.*

The song lyric, *friends don't look at friends that way*, suddenly played on the TV.

*Touché*, I told the universe.

After I finally agreed to this crazy idea of uprooting myself from the apartment I had lived in for the last four years and moving in with my co-worker slash friend and her hot husband, we decided it was finally time for some sleep.

I lay on the couch, listening to Charlee and Jax getting ready for bed. Water flowed through the pipes, the toilet flushed, their footsteps creaked on the wooden floor—then Charlee's giggle drifted through the quiet, light and familiar.

I was so used to living alone, existing in silence, me being the only one making any noise in my apartment, that nostalgia from my childhood—growing up with so many siblings—washed over me, and I suddenly felt at home.

I pressed deeper into the soft pillows beneath my head and curled up under the thick blanket.

I had another rare day off the next day, and then I was back on shift again for the foreseeable future, so the only logical thing to do was to be spontaneous and move all of my belongings in tomorrow.

I had already emailed my landlord to let him know. My lease had ended back in June, and I'd been paying month to month ever since, so it was just a matter of telling him I was leaving.

I rented a truck on a car rental app and texted my guy friends group chat, asking if anyone could drive down to the city and help me move. It was an ungodly hour, so I didn't expect to hear back from anyone until the morning.

*Worst comes to worst I would do it myself.* But I would have to be careful. My hands were my money makers: all $110,000 worth.

Days off were usually spent with a round of morning sex, after which I would go back to sleep and Jax would leave for work. A few hours later, I'd warm up the breakfast Jax had left for me in the fridge, run some errands, fold some laundry, and then catch up on my shows until Jax got home.

Today, however, was the complete opposite.

We were up way earlier than my hangover wanted to be. Liam had ordered greasy breakfast sandwiches, and I forced one down praying that it would make my pounding headache and nausea disappear. Then Jax took Liam to pick up the moving truck. The two of them met up with Liam's cousin Remi and a few friends at his apartment before Jax headed off to work. Four hours later, Liam was officially moved into our spare bedroom, the extra furniture still in the truck. I was told the plan was their friend Carter would be driving it back to Liam's parents' place to store it until he moved back in six months.

"I can make my own bed, Charlee," Liam protested as I stuffed his pillows into silky pillowcases. His bed was massive, with what looked like a high-end mattress and a thick down blanket.

"Yeah but so can I." I shooed him away.

"Why do you have so many fucking clothes when all you wear is scrubs?" Remi shouted from inside the walk-in-closet.

We'd gotten really lucky with this apartment—spacious, good-sized kitchen, two full bathrooms, decent sized closets, and even a washer and dryer, which was practically unheard of in our building.

"Your mom buys them for me," Liam didn't miss a beat, a smirk tugging at his mouth.

"Yeah fuck you." Remi walked out holding an armful of hangers. He was really tall, broad, and definitely attractive. He and Liam had been bickering like teenage boys all morning, which gave me a glimpse of a more unfiltered version of Liam. It also made me feel like I was suddenly part of this chaotic, close-knit circle of his.

"Hello?" A knock sounded on the front door—which we had left slightly ajar—followed by a voice calling down the hall.

"Is that Shaen?" Liam sounded surprised.

Sure enough Liam's best friend stood in the hallway—heavily pregnant and holding a tray of coffees.

"Babe." Remi rushed to her side. "How did you get up all those stairs?"

"I'm pregnant, not paralyzed," she deadpanned, handing out the drinks. She had even brought one for me—somehow knowing that I liked extra cold foam. I suppressed a laugh and it came out as a snort. Liam caught the sound and grinned.

"Shaen, this is Charlee. Charlee, Shaen." He stepped aside as she waddled over to me and pulled me into a hug.

I wasn't tall—five four and a half (don't steal my half)—but even with her big belly she still felt tiny next to me.

"It is so nice of you to let Liam stay here. He's the worst so brace yourself." She said it with such a straight face that I almost couldn't tell if she was joking.

"That's how she says she loves me," Liam said, ruffling her hair. She smacked his arm.

"I tolerate you," she corrected.

"You love me," he crooned, smacking a loud kiss on her cheek.

I glanced at Remi, who rolled his eyes like, *"Whadya gonna do?"*

"Julia had an appointment in the city, so I tagged along," Shaen explained her appearance as we moved back toward Liam's room. Remi ducked into the closet again, this time hauling in multiple pairs of shoes.

I finished making the bed and started gathering up empty boxes—the room was now basically unpacked. I figured we should store them under the bed as Liam would be packing back up in six months anyway.

"It's nice to finally meet you in person," I told Shaen, who was perched on the edge of the bed, her belly taking up most of the space in front of her.

"Oh my gosh, same," Shaen exclaimed. "I've been wanting to meet Liam's *work wife* for forever." She grinned at me and sipped her coffee.

*Work wife.*

The word stunned me for a moment. I nearly dropped the stack of flattened boxes I was holding. No one noticed. The conversation flowed around me, warm and familiar. The bond between the three of them was undeniable, their ease with one another, effortless.

When the boxes were all put away, I excused myself to the quiet of my bedroom and closed the door behind me. It was strange—this feeling like I was intruding in my own home. A home that had never been this loud, this full. Suddenly I was awkward in my own space, almost clumsy with it.

I slid down to the floor, my back against the door, took a steadying breath and pulled out my phone to text Jax.

CHARLEE:

Hey babe

My text went through, but I didn't expect a reply. Jax rarely had his phone out while he was working—it was too easy to lose it in a pile of tools or accidentally drop it into a bucket of cement.

Still, sending the text grounded me. Knowing he was out there on the other side of my little screen breathed calm into me. He was my anchor. Always had been. When I had a rough delivery at work or a stressful day back at school, just messaging him—or scrolling through old photos of us—was enough to help me focus and remind me of all the good I had, even when the world felt a little off its axis.

I was generally low-maintenance and it really didn't take much to make me happy. But life had a way of throwing you off-balance, and when it did, I held onto Jax. Jax with his endless calm and steady loyalty. And if all else failed, his ridiculous collection of memes that always made me laugh.

I smiled as I got to my feet, already feeling more centered. *Sudden change would rattle anyone*, I reminded myself.

Dr. Hennessy—Liam—and I had gone from strangers to co-workers to favorite co-workers to actual friends over the past few years. And then, in what felt like a blink, to roommates.

I was genuinely happy to help him. I was even more than thrilled to use the rent money to knock down my student loans. Plus it was only six months.

*By the time he moves out, this place would probably feel empty and lonely without him.*

"Charlee!" I heard a knock on the door behind me as Liam called my name. I stood to open it and nearly stumbled into him, where he stood in the doorway, one shoulder pressed lazily against the frame.

"Come on, we're getting lunch." He tugged me out of the room and herded me down the hall.

"Where are we going?" I laughed as he held out my coat and then handed me my purse.

"Shaen is craving fajitas," Remi announced matter-of-factly which I took to mean we were now all getting fajitas. As if on cue, Shaen waddled out of the bathroom.

"Sorry if you've been waiting I had to pee—again." She rolled her eyes in exasperation, and Remi helped her into her coat, zipping it up carefully over her belly.

"They're so cute it's disgusting," Liam said, catching me watching them.

"I could absolutely vomit," I deadpanned. He grinned.

The waiter led us to a table with four chairs. Remi and Shaen naturally sat on one side, which left Liam and me to sit across from them. He pulled out my chair before his own.

"Thanks," I murmured but he was already scanning the menu.

We got guacamole, chips, nachos, and picadillo to start. Shaen chose a fajita combo plate and practically cried when it arrived, taking a bite of the steak fajita as if it were the best thing she'd ever tasted. I went with a beef burrito and fries, which Liam kept stealing off my plate.

"I told you he's annoying," Shaen said, laughing as I swatted Liam's hand away.

"So obnoxious," I agreed, speaking around a mouthful of my burrito and washing it down with a sip of margarita.

I really liked her. I didn't regret keeping my friend circle small —it had always served me well—but sometimes it was nice to make a new female friend. Shaen didn't seem like the type to do drama. She was straightforward, honest, sarcastic in a refreshing way and by the time the waiter came back with the dessert menus, I felt like I'd known her for years instead of just hours.

Remi and Shaen ordered a Mexican sponge cake. Liam asked for churros with a chocolate dipping sauce.

"And for your wife?" The waiter turned to me.

"Oh I'm not—I'm, I'll have…" I tripped over my words and if not for my tan skin tone, I knew I'd be red as a beet.

"The wife will have the pineapple cream crepe," Liam said smoothly, leaning over to see which one I was pointing to and ordered for me without skipping a beat.

"Excellent choice, Senora." The waiter seemed pleased and then walked away toward the kitchen. Shaen and Remi were both laughing again.

"It wasn't that funny," I muttered, flipping my phone over to check if Jax had responded. He still hadn't seen my message.

"The idea of Liam settling down and getting married is always funny." Remi chuckled.

"Yeah whatever." Liam was still smiling, but something else had flickered beneath it. An emotion I couldn't quite place, but one that belied his lighthearted grin.

"Why's that?" I asked.

"Well, he's Mister Playboy. He's a 'fuck-'em-and-leave-'em' kind of guy. Commitment doesn't really mix well with his preferences," Remi explained.

"We love you exactly as you are—body count and all," Shaen added, reaching across the table to pat her best friend's hand.

I felt a sudden urge to defend him.

"Obviously you know him way better than I do, but from what I've seen at work, Liam would make a great husband." The margarita had the words falling out my mouth before I could even comprehend what I was saying. All eyes turned to me, and I quickly gulped down another swallow of alcohol.

"Do tell," Shaen encouraged, clearly intrigued.

"Well, he's always respectful to all the nurses. He has a ton of patience with the moms. He remembers almost everyone's birthdays and he's the first one to chip in when we buy a gift for one of the staff. I mean—" I shrugged. "As someone with an awesome husband myself, I'd say I'm a decent judge of good husband material. And if he's been around the block a few times, that probably just means he's good at what he does."

I blinked as the words left my mouth. I wasn't shy by any means and I didn't usually censor myself—but blurting out that Liam was probably good in bed. That was new.

The table was silent for a second before Remi and Shaen burst out laughing again.

"I love her. We are keeping her," Shaen declared as she stood up, presumably to go pee again. Remi followed, saying he was going to find our waiter and ask for the check.

When it was just the two of us left, I busied myself with brushing crumbs into a little pile on the white tablecloth, avoiding looking at Liam. When I heard him clear his throat, I looked up—only to find his gaze unexpectedly bright, almost like he was trying not to cry.

"That was really nice, Charlee. Thank you."

He said it so quietly that I almost didn't hear him over the music, and it was in that moment that I realized that there was a lot more to Liam Hennessy than met the eye.

The next morning, I heard Liam's footsteps in the hallway at 5:45 a.m., and a few minutes later, the smell of coffee drifted down the hall into our room. He'd brought some fancy coffee maker with him from his old apartment, and Charlee had stuffed our much less fancy coffee pot into the top of a closet to make room for his on the counter. Last night, when Liam gave us a tutorial—how to steam the milk, what grinds to use, what button and knob did what—I already knew Charlee would be asking for one of her own when he moved out.

She murmured in her sleep and shifted slightly from where she lay, her head on my chest. Emotion rippled through me. Everyone had warned us that things fade over time—that we'd fall out of the puppy-love phase and into the routine of married life, where we'd have to prioritize keeping the spark alive. But at the risk of sounding cliche, I fell in love with her all over again every morning. She was the yin to my yang. Where I was more reserved, she was outgoing and lively. Where she could some-times let herself get lost in a spiral of overanalyzing, I was logical and unbothered. She liked the middle slice of a loaf of bread; I

preferred the crusty ends. We just worked. We made sense. Loving her was the easiest thing I'd ever done.

I felt the deep, steady love I had for her ache in my chest. The emotion skipped a beat behind my ribs—and I resisted the urge to kiss her so she could catch what little sleep she had left. I knew she had a long day ahead.

The soft click of the front door closing and the lock turning back into place shook me from my thoughts. Liam had left—6:05 a.m. sharp. Charlee had ten more minutes left before her alarm went off. She snuggled closer to me, hooking her leg over mine. Even half-asleep she found me. I stiffened in my boxers at the feel of her warm body pressed against me. I closed my eyes and willed it away. We didn't have time for shenanigans this morning.

I must have drifted off again because the alarm startled me awake. Charlee rolled away to grab her phone and shut it off.

"Morning," she mumbled, still half-asleep. She looked adorable with her hair wrapped up in a weird contraption that I had yet to figure out, but loved watching her pull free. Somehow, it magically left her long hair in perfect curls overnight. She pushed her glasses on, stumbled out of bed, and shuffled toward the small en-suite. She didn't bother closing the door, and I could hear her peeing.

Maybe it was weird, but the first time she'd peed in front of me, I'd felt infinitely closer to her. It was its own level of *I feel safe with you*. I'd never say it out loud, but I cherished how much she trusted me.

The toilet flushed, the rip of her opening a pack of lenses and then the sound of her electric toothbrush filled the air. That was my cue. I got out of bed, shivering as my feet hit the cold floor. I pulled on sweatpants and slid my feet into a pair of slippers, then headed to the kitchen to make her lunch. It was our thing. When she worked days, I made her lunch. Nights, I dropped off dinner. On her days off, I left breakfast for her in the fridge.

My sisters had once joked that I hadn't married her for her cooking skills. Charlee raised an eyebrow and said, "Don't worry. I make up for it." I grinned at the memory as I spotted half of a burrito in a Styrofoam container in the fridge, leftovers from her dinner with Liam and his friends.

I scooped out the meat and veggies, tossed them in a pan with some chopped onions, shredded cheese, and six scrambled eggs. Once everything was cooked, I toasted two baguettes, spread the mixture on, topped with a generous squeeze of spicy mayo and sriracha. I wrapped the sandwiches in parchment paper and sliced them in half before packing them into two lunch bags.

Charlee's bag got a container of cut-up fruit, a bag of chocolate drizzled popcorn, string cheese, a bottle of iced tea, and a chocolate bar. Liam's bag had similar options, but between remembering his muscles—which I tried very hard not to notice—and the mention of his workout routine, I swapped the iced tea for water and the chocolate for dried edamame. I liked taking care of her. It made me feel useful and needed.

I grabbed my notebook and wrote Charlee her usual note before zipping her bag closed. I had been leaving notes in her bag since the first time I made her lunch and I hadn't missed a day since.

As I recapped the pen, Charlee walked in wearing her gray scrubs with little pink bows printed all over them. I handed her a thermos filled with Liam's fancy coffee, and she moaned appreciatively.

"I love you way more than I love this coffee, and today I love this coffee *so much*." She took a long sip. "Fuck, that's good." She set the thermos down, then grabbed her coat, badge, and keys.

"Two?" she asked, noticing the lunch bags. I pointed my chin toward the bedrooms.

"For Liam?"

I nodded and gave a quick shrug—*Why not?*

"That is so nice of you, babe." She leaned up to kiss me, and for a moment I got lost in it, my body reacting instantly as she pressed against me.

"Tonight," she promised, clearly feeling how hard I was against her stomach.

"You'll have to stay quiet so our new roommate doesn't learn what you sound like when you come," I joked, giving her a wink.

"He should be so lucky," she shot back sarcastically—but something about the idea of him hearing her, hearing *that,* made my cock twitch even more. And I felt guilty the second it happened.

"I love you," she said, unaware, and kissed me again before heading out the door.

It was 6:35. I had forty minutes before I had to leave, and I *desperately* needed to rub one out in the shower—but I was afraid of where my mind might wander.

*Intrusive thoughts aren't cheating,* I told myself as I went back into our room. It's normal to find other people attractive. Par for the course of being alive and having eyes.

I was loyal. I loved my wife so much. My body's reaction to her offhanded comment didn't mean anything.

Nada. Zilch.

I ended up taking a cold shower.

When I got to the worksite, my uncle was on a call, so I waited in my truck until he finished up. I had a degree in civil engineering—an expensive piece of paper, honestly—because my uncle would have hired me without it. He wasn't just my boss, he was the person I turned to when I needed parental advice, since my relationship with my own parents had always been... strained. Some people got a dad. I got my uncle, and I was lucky for it.

My parents weren't bad people, they just weren't great parents. They didn't hurt us, and they provided what we needed. I think they wanted what was best for us—they just weren't really *there.* Emotionally unavailable, constantly preoccupied. They'd met later in life. My mom had been in her thirties, my dad in his forties when they had me, followed quickly by my three sisters. By the time the youngest was born, my mother was exhausted from having four kids in six years, so we learned to rely on each other.

We had each other's backs. I made sure my mom bought the girls' favorite snacks; they would help me with my homework so we could get in a quick video game before bed. When we were teens, they came to my games and I went to their dance recitals. Once I had my license, I drove them everywhere—even attempted to do their makeup for school dances. Mom was usually off with friends, doing errands or caring for her elderly parents. Dad was always working. It wasn't exactly a surprise that we weren't close.

When I quietly came out as bisexual in high school, suddenly I was *all* they could focus on. It wasn't even that they were morally against it—it was the inconvenience of it. It didn't fit the image. My dad was a respected lawyer. My mom played the part of his perfect wife. We lived in a small town in Indiana and having a son who liked boys and girls? That was just… weird to them. Off-brand. Problematic. Inconvenient.

My dad once asked me why I couldn't just pick one. "Why be greedy and like *both*?" he said. I'd mumbled a half-assed explanation of biology and how I was just born this way. He scoffed and walked off before I could even finish. After that I never brought anyone home, a boy or a girl.

My uncle and sisters met Charlee way before my parents did. Honestly, if I could've gotten away with never introducing her to them, I would've. I'd have happily skipped the part where I saw relief in my mother's eyes when she realized I'd be settling down with a woman. At our wedding, my dad had muttered something about me finally "making the right choice" and it had pissed Charlee off.

Sometimes I wondered if her obsession with me being able to

express all parts of myself— especially sexually—wasn't just about letting me be free. Maybe, in her own way, she wanted to give the proverbial middle finger to my parents once and for all. I didn't really know. I'd never asked. And if she brought it up, I usually shut down that conversation before it could go anywhere.

If we were watching a movie and she pointed out a hot guy, I kissed her instead of agreeing or disagreeing. If she suggested buying lube and experimenting with some "butt stuff" as she affectionately called it, I would change the subject or flat out say no. She once got invited to a party—rumored to be a sex party— by one of her college friends. She laughed, sounding flirty, and asked if I wanted to go "see what would happen." I shut it down immediately.

Because it confused me. Because I didn't know where her desire ended and mine began.

One: I'd made peace with not being with a man again. I didn't want a taste of something I'd already chosen to give up. I didn't need to remind myself of what I had left behind. I loved Charlee way too much to open any door that may lead to regret.

Two: I never really knew what *she* pictured when she brought it up. Me hooking up with a man on my own? Her watching? Or worse—her joining in? Did she *want* that? As hot as that idea could be—no matter how often those images crept into my dreams—as strong as I knew our relationship and our love was, the thought of possibly sullying the one thing in my life that felt perfect and steady, terrified me.

I was the kid whose parents didn't really love him, I'd be a fucking idiot to risk the love I *did* have for something as fleeting as lust.

With that, I shoved my thoughts down, grabbed my hard hat, and climbed out of the truck—Charlee's words from earlier flitted through my brain.

*"He should be so lucky."*

Images of Liam watching me make Charlee come clouded my

vision. Him running a hand over her curves, holding her down with my mouth on her. Her writhing breathless between us. His hand on mine, our arms touching. Her crying out, him moaning with her, me coming on both of them.

"Fuck." I rubbed a hand over my face like I could force the thoughts from my brain.

It was going to be a long day.

And an even longer six months if my imagination kept pulling this shit. It wasn't just lust—it was longing. And it scared the hell out of me.

It's crazy how every day
I love you a little bit
more.

Have a good day baby.

xoxo

Jax

My morning had been spent studying for my written board certification exam, which I'd be taking after graduation. I wasn't nervous about it—I knew I would ace it. Everything up until now had been preparing me for this moment. I was just sick of studying, sick of waiting, and sick of being *almost* a doctor with a crazy schedule, but not *fully* a doctor until I passed. I was ready to start living my life.

I knew my schedule as an OBGYN would still be long and hectic, but literally anything had to be better than being a resident. I checked the time, knowing I had to get upstairs soon to start my shift. My afternoon would be spent on L&D as I finished up my three-month rotation on the floor before moving to Chief Resident of Gynecology, where I'd be supervising junior residents and teaching medical students how to do surgical GYN procedures.

I was almost done. June 30th couldn't come soon enough.

I could almost—just barely—see the light at the end of the tunnel of complete exhaustion. However today, my eyes didn't burn with the same vengeance because it had only taken me

twenty minutes to get to the hospital instead of the usual hour, and I could've cried from the gratitude alone.

I stood, put away my books and shrugged on my lab coat before heading up in the elevator. I made a beeline for the break room to grab another coffee before starting my rounds, only to find Charlee by the fridge—and a smile broke across my face before I could stop it.

I *should* absolutely not be this happy to see her. *Down boy*, I chastised myself.

"Good morning." I tried to keep my tone even—just one roommate saying hi to the other. No big deal. Totally normal.

"Good morning." She turned at the sound of my voice, and her tone was anything but chill. Charlee was friendly and exuberant all the time, and there was nothing half-assed about anything she did. It was one of the things that I liked about her so much.

"Hey, I got something for you," she said, turning and pulling a black lunch bag out of the fridge.

"What's this?" I took it and unzipped it to peek inside. "Charlee Berman, did you make me lunch?"

"Nope." She grinned. "I don't cook."

"You don't cook," I repeated, already guessing who the lunch had come from. The image hit me fast—Jax, shirtless of course, his broad shoulders and thick chest on full display, deftly slicing up fruit. The thought hit me hard—so domestic, so normal—and something in my chest clenched before I reminded myself I was standing in front of his wife. *His wife.*

I coughed, shifting uncomfortably, at how naturally and quickly my mind had gone there.

"Jax made us lunch," Charlee explained, cutting through my mess of thoughts.

"Jax. That's… unexpected. And really nice." I zipped the bag shut again. "Thank you."

"He is unexpected and nice." Charlee smiled as she grabbed

her coffee and left the room to get back to work with an easy, "I'll see you out there."

I clumsily made myself a coffee as well and followed a few minutes later. Why did it mean so much that Jax had thought of me?

A FEW HOURS IN, I was finishing up charting when the ER called up to L&D letting us know that a pregnant patient had been in a car accident and was being sent to us. She was in labor and they couldn't find a heartbeat.

My heart sank.

This was part of the job. It was not all simple deliveries, crying babies, little toes, and happy endings. No my job also included cancer diagnoses, D&C's, infertility, and babies born sleeping.

The patient arrived bruised, her face had been stitched up, with an angry looking, mottled seatbelt mark across her chest. I had several nurses with me, including Charlee, a few medical students, and one of the attendings.

She told us she had been in labor and was on her way to her hospital when a car hit theirs and they flipped over the median.

"Is my baby okay?" she asked again.

I assured her that we'd do everything we could and that we would check on her baby again right away. Charlee dimmed the lights while the other nurse, Marissa, wheeled in the Doppler and ultrasound cart.

I searched for a heartbeat for five minutes. The room was so oppressively quiet, interrupted only by the patient's quiet, gasping sobs. My stomach churned, and the sandwich Jax had made threatened to come back up.

My professors and the doctors I shadowed told me I would

get used to it, that with time, the intensity of my feelings would dull. They didn't call it losing empathy, but they warned us that the more we did this, the more routine it would become, the less it would wreck us.

So far, it still wrecked me.

The attending tried next, but the result was the same. The impact had caused a fetal demise. We'd need to continue labor so she could deliver.

I explained it gently, trying to balance medical clarity while remaining cognizant and respectful of their unimaginable grief.

"I'm so sorry," I told her.

She nodded, face streaked with tears, quiet for now in her acceptance or perhaps her denial. I couldn't tell.

I ordered more fluids and a dose of misoprostol to keep labor moving. I held off on the Pitocin for now. She'd already been in labor before the accident. I wanted to see if her body would continue naturally with a little help before bringing on the more intense contractions that Pitocin offered.

As I left the room, I caught sight of Charlee fluffing the pillow behind the grieving mom's head, speaking to her in low, calming tones.

With a best friend like Shaen and a mom like mine, I'd always been a fan of women. But ever since I had chosen this specialty, I'd grown to be in awe of them.

Not just because they were so powerful when giving birth, literally digging into the depths of their pain tolerance to bring life into the world—but also because of how women showed up for each other in the delivery room. The crying sisters and the supportive doulas. The nurses who did everything from helping the patient stay medically informed, to acting as a labor coach, to being a needed best friend, cheerleader, a shoulder to lean on literally and figuratively, to physically holding them upright. The delivery room was always a beautiful scene of femininity.

The support these nurses offered went far beyond their

paychecks. My respect for these women had grown in ways that I struggled to explain.

I'd once tried to articulate it to Shaen—she teared up while Remi just asked where my balls were. I shut up after that. Later on, Remi slung an arm around me and admitted he agreed, but I didn't bring it up again.

When my shift ended, I gave sign-out on my patients for the incoming night shift and grabbed my stuff to go home.

*Was it home?* Or just a landing spot until the next destination?

It already weirdly *felt* like home—the Christmas tree in the corner, the small menorah in the window. Charlee's coat hanging next to mine and Jax's work boots lined up neatly in the entryway.

It took me two laps around the block to find parking. When I finally trudged up the three flights of stairs, I found Jax at the door, punching in the lock code.

"Hey, man. Thanks for the lunch," I greeted him with a gusto that belied my utter exhaustion.

"No problem. You'll have to tell me what you like and don't like so I can get the right groceries."

He opened the door and bent down to untie his boots. *Don't look at his ass, don't look at his ass,* I forced myself to keep my eyes up as I slipped past him into the apartment.

"I can also order groceries," I called from the kitchen where I rinsed out the lunch bag and left it to dry.

Jax shrugged in silent agreement and took a pack of steaks out of the fridge.

"Can I help?"

"How are your cutting skills?" He opened a bag of potatoes.

"Well, considering I cut people open on a consistent basis I'd say they're decent," I quipped.

"Well, it's not surgery but you can dice these while I get the steaks going."

He slid a knife and cutting board over to me.

"I can do that. Just gonna change first."

He nodded and I ducked into my room. I ended up jumping in the shower, where I let out a silent scream of frustration over how unfair the world could be sometimes.

I dried off and pulled on a pair of gray sweatpants and a soft blue T-shirt. I usually didn't wear a shirt at home, but it felt... distasteful to walk around half-naked in front of my landlords. Hosts. Friends...?

After the day I'd had, I felt compelled to text Shaen. She'd been my best friend since kindergarten, and we spoke every single day. But today, it didn't just feel like a want—it felt like a need.

LIAM:

Hey babe

SHAEN:

Hey yourself

LIAM:

How u feeling? Baby kicking?

SHAEN:

Kicking up a storm. Bad day?

LIAM:

That's good. Tell baby Uncle Liam says hi. Ya shitty day

SHAEN:

I'm sorry. Wanna talk about it?

LIAM:

Nope. I just can't wait till I graduate. All I do is study and work and I'm fucking tired Shay Shay.

SHAEN:

Being an adult can suck some days. For example
my vagina hurts all the time now

LIAM:

Spare me the details (grimacing emoji)

SHAEN:

And here I thought you loved that topic (laughing
emoji)

LIAM:

Firstly not urs. Never urs. Secondly u'd think but
the only vagina I've seen lately is one with a baby
coming out of it or one I'm doing a pap
smear on.

SHAEN:

Sounds like Uncle Liam needs to get laid

LIAM:

He really does

SHAEN:

Any possible prospects?

LIAM:

Nah. I may have a crush on someone but it's not
gonna happen. I wish though

This was the perfect chance for me to tell her. To admit that
I'm bisexual. To apologize for keeping it from her all these years,
hoping that if I didn't say it aloud, it might just disappear. To
confess that I might be developing feelings for a married couple I
have no business crushing on. That I'm tired of meaningless
conversations on boring dates with girls who just want to get
some. That I yearn for what she and Remi have—a genuine
connection, someone to come home to. That I want people to see

that silly, spontaneous Liam is still here, but I've grown, evolved, and desire more to life than just a good lay. But instead, when she pressed me about my crush, I deflected, saying Jax needed my help with dinner. I felt a pang of guilt as I shoved my phone into my pocket. It didn't feel right keeping this from her, but after having this epiphany so long ago, it almost seemed too late to share.

Charlee had returned home sometime during my shower. I could hear the soft murmur of her and Jax talking in their room. The weight of today was sitting solidly on my shoulders, so I distracted myself by peeling six potatoes then cutting them into precise little squares. I dropped a generous slab of butter into a pan, and once it began to sizzle, I put the potatoes in, seasoning them as they cooked.

"You cook?" Jax's voice startled me. I turned to find him right behind me. The scent of his cologne mixed with the subtle aroma of a day spent working outdoors. I quickly turned back to the stove and busied myself with moving the potatoes around to prevent them from sticking.

"I wouldn't call myself a gourmet cook, but I get by."

"Noted," Jax grunted, sliding behind me to grab plates. I stood perfectly still, careful not to accidentally touch him, because even a brush of his skin on mine would be too much. This was getting ridiculous. I couldn't remember the last time I'd been this awkwardly worked up about someone, let alone two people.

As if on cue, Charlee padded into the kitchen wearing another oversized T-shirt and striped pajama pants.

"You okay?" she asked, popping the tab on a can of seltzer. I watched as she filled three glasses with ice, poured in the seltzer, then topped each generously with vodka from the freezer. I raised an eyebrow at her.

"When a case like that comes in, I need a little something to help me fall asleep."

"They told me it gets better," I admitted.

"What? Having hard days?" She took a sip, then handed me a glass. I nodded.

"I mean I guess—it's not as bad as when I first started, but it's still sad enough to want to take the edge off."

I took a large gulp of my drink, followed by another, nearly finishing the glass.

"Is it hard for you?" Jax's question caught me off guard. I wasn't used to decompressing the day with people who understood what I was going through. My classmates and I would dissect these days clinically, trying to keep emotion out of it. My mom always encouraged me to call her after tough days, but I didn't want to overwhelm her; hard cases occurred more often than I wanted her to know. I would never share these stories with Shaen, as she was anxious enough about her own pregnancy. So, I usually processed everything alone, leaving the day behind me with an intense workout at the gym, then filing it away under things I didn't want to talk about anymore.

"I... it's not my favorite part of the job," I stumbled over my response. Jax nodded. His face was unreadable, and his eyes gave nothing away.

"That's what makes you a good doctor." He had served steak, a salad, and the potatoes I had made on three plates, balancing them as he carried them to the table.

"What does?" I took the vodka, and another can of seltzer with me as I followed him into the other room.

"Your heart."

Charlee nodded and held out her glass for me to pour more alcohol into.

"Thanks for saying that," I told my new friend and interim landlord. He smiled, and we all dug in. I discovered that alcohol, laughter, and a home-cooked meal were a pretty effective antidote to a hard day.

I was pleasantly full from Jax's delicious cooking and feeling the vodka's warmth as I opened a package that had been delivered earlier today.

"Oh, it's that couples game I bought," I said, holding it up and waving it around.

"Couples game?" Liam asked with a mischievous grin. "Do tell."

"Not like that." I laughed. "It's a stack of questions to help couples get to know each other better. I was planning to bring it to Jax's sister's place for Christmas, but now we're not going since I have to work the day before Christmas Eve."

"Let's play it now," Jax suggested.

"You don't have Christmas plans?" Liam interjected.

I shook my head. "Our families don't live nearby, and with me working the day before, we can't catch a flight in time. But it's fine—we'll celebrate here."

I began unwrapping the game and poured more vodka into our glasses.

"Come with me to my parents. Everyone will be there." Liam began to clear the table.

I glanced at Jax, who shrugged, indicating that he was okay with it. Though introverted by nature, he didn't mind meeting new people.

"Your mom won't mind?"

Liam pulled out his phone and pressed a button.

"Mom?" he said after two rings. "Yes, everything's fine."

He grinned, clearly amused by her response.

"Hey, I was wondering if Charlee and Jax could come with me for Christmas Eve?"

He laughed again and covered the speaker.

"She said Shaen and Remi love you, so she has to meet you now."

"Yes, I know, Mom. Of course, Mom. Yes, I'll see you on Tuesday then. Okay, love you."

He hung up.

"Well that's settled then. All my brothers will be there—there are a lot of them—plus Remi and Shaen. Lia and her husband. Carter, my dad's sister and her family, a few neighbors, and my mom always cooks way too much food. You're in for a treat."

"Thank you, that's very generous of you," Jax said, ever the gentleman. If Liam's family was anything like him, I knew I'd enjoy meeting them—and, of course, spending more time with Shaen. I suddenly found myself really looking forward to next week.

We all moved to the couches. I sat next to Jax on the big couch, near the windows, and Liam took one of the oversized chairs across from us.

"Okay, the rules are, you either answer a question and keep the card, or if you get one you won't answer, you have to take a drink. The person with the most answered cards wins, the drunkest loses," I explained.

Liam rubbed his hands together in anticipation.

"I love winning and I love drinking, so I don't see how I can lose."

We all laughed. I pulled out a card and turned to Jax.

"What are two big sacrifices you have made for me?"

My heart thudded because I immediately thought of a significant one.

"Wow, right into the thick of it, huh?" Liam chuckled. Jax looked slightly perturbed, and I wondered how much he would share.

"I don't look at anything as a sacrifice because I love you, but for the sake of answering, we have nursing school loans to pay back, which we had to factor into our budget."

I nodded. "True."

"And living in New York City—as convenient as it is—is slowly chipping away at my mental health because driving here is the worst."

He grinned, skillfully answering without delving too deep, or appearing too vulnerable.

I handed him the card as Liam lamented the traffic.

"Okay, you ask the next one to Liam."

Jax turned it over and laughed. "This one won't work."

"What's it say?"

He showed us, and we all read aloud. "Explain how you felt when we had our first kiss."

I giggled and handed Jax another card.

"Whoops." I glanced at Liam, catching him watching me intently.

Jax read the next card, "Is your ex still in contact with you?"

We both looked over at Liam, who nodded. "That girl Lia, who I mentioned will be there on Christmas, she was my girlfriend through high school."

"Oh, is it weird that you still see her?" I asked, genuinely curious.

"Nah. She's Shaen's friend, and she's married. Plus, it's been so long, and our breakup was amicable. I was in Boston; she was in California. It wouldn't have worked."

"Liam and Lia," I pointed out the similarity in their names.

Liam shrugged. "Yeah, another reason why we were not destined to be together," he quipped, taking the card from Jax and drawing another.

"What's your biggest pet peeve?" he asked, turning to me.

"You'd think it would be something work-related because there are so many things that happen there, but actually, it's people who talk on speakerphone in public. Like, what the fuck are you doing? We don't all have to hear your conversation. It's so socially inept."

I realized I'd gotten a bit worked up when both Liam and Jax burst out laughing.

"Wow, Charlee is big mad about that one." Liam chuckled, handing me the card.

"Seriously, it's so annoying," I said, laughing at myself as I pulled out another question. "Describe how we first met. That's cute but not really something I don't know. I'll get another option." I fished around in the box, but Jax answered anyway.

"We met on Halloween. You were dressed as a sexy nurse, and I had come to the club with someone else."

He was looking at me, but I knew his words weren't meant for me. "I was kissing him, and when I looked up, my sister was walking toward me, followed by the most beautiful girl I had ever seen. We both danced with you that night, and then I got your number because I had to leave to catch a flight. But I texted you, and the rest is history."

I sucked in a deep breath. Had Jax meant to share that? Had Liam caught it? Jax leaned back on the couch, calm and unbothered as ever. His jeans rode low, his shirt stretched tight across his chest, cheeks slightly flushed, and his eyes clouded with a look I recognized. He was watching Liam, almost daring him to say something.

It dawned on me then, my husband found him attractive. It made sense—Liam was the kind of guy you usually only saw in magazines. I'd heard that people tried to recruit him to model. He had a face that made you do a double take because he was genuinely beautiful.

But my husband wasn't someone who was focused solely on the outside appearance. Though I knew he had a type, and Liam fit it to a T. Jax also had to like your soul before he'd look at you with eyes like that.

Surprisingly, I wasn't jealous—I was intrigued. Objectively, I knew Liam was a hot man. Realistically, I really liked him as a person. We had connected as friends. But could this be a moment? Could Jax finally give in and allow himself to enjoy another part of him? Could Liam be the answer to an uncomplicated experience with someone we both trusted? Could I possibly convince my husband that I would want to be involved too?

I had been craving something taboo like this since the moment Jax kissed me as he held me against his date's body. But it wasn't about me—it was about Jax. I wanted him for Jax.

The moment came crashing down when I remembered that Liam was straight. I blinked away the cobwebs of the elaborate storyline I had concocted in my mind and startled when Liam asked, "He?" His voice sounded hoarse and almost strained.

All three of us reached for our glasses at the same moment, the room silent as we drained them.

"I'm bi," Jax offered, refilling our glasses before getting up to grab more seltzer.

Liam watched him go, and remnants of my previous thoughts returned to my addled mind. Liam's hand tightened on his glass. I waited.

"Cool," Liam nodded. "I—" He took another drink and didn't say anything more.

I handed Jax another card because it was starting to feel awkward.

"How many partners have you had?"

Liam groaned when he heard the question, which intrigued me, and I said so out loud.

"I'll be honest I don't know, but it's been a lot," Liam admitted.

"Ooh, so the rumor is true—Dr. McHottie is actually a player?" The nickname popped out before I could stop it, the vodka loosening my tongue.

"Dr. Mc who?" Liam raised an eyebrow, clearly perplexed.

"Don't tell me you haven't heard the nurses call you that. Not me, of course," I added quickly, glancing at Jax, who was grinning.

"Why not you?" Liam pressed.

I ignored his question and repeated, "The nurses call you Dr. McHottie."

"I didn't know that." He gave a soft laugh, seeming oddly pleased with himself. "But for the record, I've never hooked up with anyone from work. I told Shaen back in college—I had no plans of shitting where I ate, so to speak."

"Smart move," Jax murmured. I looked at him, then back at Liam.

The room suddenly felt warmer. The air thicker. The lights brighter. I felt like I needed to crawl out of my skin because the unspoken tension was palpable, yet none of us dared to acknowledge it. It was eating me alive.

"So how many?" I urged, a bit too eagerly. I spilled some of my drink, a few drops trailing down my chin. I stuck out my tongue to catch them, noticing both Liam and Jax's eyes followed my movements. My heart pounded, catapulting in my chest.

Liam shrugged. "It's a lot. And... It's been both men and women. So I've lost count."

The confession hung in the air, heavy and unexpected. The words seemed to have left him in a chaotic rush. We all collectively took a deep breath, processing what he had just said.

"You're bi?" Jax's voice was deep and gruff, sending a shiver down my spine.

"No one knows," Liam admitted, his expression vulnerable.

"We won't tell a soul," I assured him, reaching out to touch his hand, but he pulled it away before I could.

"I don't know why I never told anyone." He sounded uncertain.

"Because people think we're weird," Jax offered. "It's exhausting to explain your sexuality, especially when people fetishize it. No one makes straight people justify who they're attracted to— why should we?"

"Maybe. But also... it's not really something I can have." Liam's voice was waning, his eyes were half-closed.

"Have what?" I asked gently.

"Both. I want both," he murmured, nearly asleep, even while sitting up. The words crawled behind my ribs and stayed there, heavy and lingering.

"Go to sleep, Liam," I urged.

His eyes fluttered open. "Did I win?"

"Yes." I smiled. It felt odd to call a grown man—especially a doctor—*cute*, but the term fit. His little "yay" that followed proved my point.

"Good night," he whispered, then stood, stumbled slightly, and made his way down the hall to his room.

I turned to find Jax towering over me, his gaze intense.

"I need to fuck you," he growled.

"We need to talk about it," I insisted. God, I hoped we were finally going to talk about this.

"We'll talk while we fuck." He took my hand and led me to our room where he immediately stripped me of my clothes.

There was no preamble, no foreplay—just a sudden, urgent need. With barely any warning I was on my back and he was fully thrust inside me.

"You're soaked," he said almost accusingly.

"And?" I challenged, breath hitching as he found that spot inside of me that made me let out a yelp.

"What got you going?" Jax demanded, his hips snapping against mine, the bed groaning in protest beneath us. I sighed, turning my head. We were so close in every way. He wasn't just my lover, my confidant, my husband, he was my best friend. We bickered over trivial things like him forgetting to bring the garbage down or my penchant for overpriced coffee. But never about the important things. On the things that really mattered, we were always united. We shared perspectives on politics, long-term goals, values, and morals. We gave one another unwavering support, whatever that looked like at that time.

Yet despite our seamless communication and deep trust, there remained a colossal, unspoken truth between us. A gargantuan elephant in the room that I had to summon immense courage to address—one he struggled to meet my gaze over.

"You're bi," I finally said, my words nearly drowned by the rhythm of our bodies, the sound of his skin slapping against mine.

"I know." Jax's eyes were watching me, weary, yet attentive.

"And you know that I feel guilty for holding you back from what you need…"

"I—"

"Shush." I pressed a finger to his lips as he tried to interject. He responded by circling my clit with his finger, eliciting a cry from me, my hips bucking against him. He smirked, and I felt the simultaneous urge to slap and kiss him.

"But there's more."

Now, he was fully present, listening intently as he moved within me.

"That night when we danced—you in front of me, him behind me—you kissed me while holding onto him, and then you kissed him while pressing me between you…" My words were cut off by

Jax's fervent kiss, his movements growing frantic, his arousal intensifying.

"You're so wet, Charlee," he whispered again, his eyes gleaming in the darkness.

"Baby, that night was so hot. I've always wanted more of that," I confessed, finally voicing my deepest secret.

"Why didn't you ever tell me?" he asked, his climax nearing—I could feel it.

"Because I love you so much. I never wanted you to think I desired someone else because you weren't enough. Because you are. It's not that. I just think it could be amazing to experience it together." He was strumming my clit now, focused solely on his determination to bring me to the edge before himself.

"I love you too," he panted, attuned to the sounds of his finger against my wet skin. It wasn't a rejection. It wasn't avoidance. It wasn't a subject change. It was a possibility. I clung to that, hoping that one day, he'd allow me to witness that side of him.

"Let him be *lucky*," Jax hissed into my ear.

"Huh?"

"Let him hear you come, Charlee."

I unraveled with a cry that Liam undoubtedly heard, followed by Jax's groan as he emptied himself inside of me.

Just as I thought he had drifted to sleep, Jax murmured, "Who would handle cleanup?"

I was instantly alert, picturing one of them cleaning up what the other left behind.

I was up before both of them the next morning. Charlee was sprawled across the bed, her hair wrapped up in its usual contraption, snoring softly. I prepared them steak salads with a side of hash browns from last night's leftover potatoes, added a doughnut for Charlee, a sugar-free muffin for Liam, some cut up veggies with a smaller container of ranch and a bundle of grapes for each. I scribbled a note for Charlee and tucked it in her lunch bag before zipping them both up and placing them in the fridge.

Now, I was on-site, wielding my nail gun and channeling my confusion and frustration on the wood before me. I learned early on that society didn't embrace 'different.' I learned it from my dad who would cringe when we kids were too loud in public. I learned it from my mom who invested so much time and money ensuring her clothes and bags were always in style. I learned it from the boys in gym class who hurled slurs at me, yet some of them sought me out for a blow job behind the bleachers at night.

Society claimed to celebrate diversity. They welcomed it. They offered parades and dedicated a whole month to pride. They assigned letters from the alphabet as tokens of inclusion. But in reality, different still made many uncomfortable. In fact

when I had kissed a man in public back in good old Indiana I was met with glares or outright hostility.

The idea of a polyamorous relationship seemed too radical, something that disrupted societal norms. In movies you never saw three people choosing to be together or getting married. You wouldn't find cake toppers featuring a trio instead of a couple. And certainly, there was a scant representation of a man married to a woman, loved her deeply, yet also found himself drawn to his roommate—the hottest man he'd ever seen.

I inhaled the crisp December air that seeped through the unfinished building. Society didn't have a place for love that didn't fit into their little box of tolerance. So much so that I had a hard time breaking free out of my own box of tolerance. I've always accepted my attraction to both men and women, never feeling ashamed or hiding it. However, my introverted nature meant avoiding calling attention to myself or disrupting the status quo. I didn't like breaking out of *normal*. I found comfort in my routine. Wake up. Shower. Prepare lunch. Work. Return home. Make dinner. Sleep. Some days I'd also fuck my wife, or go bowling with my friends when Charlee worked a night shift. But I just wasn't *that* guy. I wasn't one to attend a parade to validate my sexual preference or cause a scene. Honestly, if I hadn't been drinking the night I met Charlee, she might have never noticed me.

I just didn't know how it worked to stay *not different* after last night's revelations. Learning that Dr. Liam Hennessy was attracted to men just like I was and we were the first people he confided in, it was not just unexpected it disrupted my sense of normalcy. I had always perceived him as unequivocally straight —clearly I'd been off. Then discovering that Charlee had enjoyed being between two men, and watching me kiss him was equally as surprising. I was so thrown off by that. In an excited, exhilarated, nerve-wracking, am-I-nauseous-from-my-feelings-or-was-the- milk-in-my-coffee-bad kind of way. What did this mean for our relationship? Would this change everything? Or nothing at all? I would never jeopardize my marriage, yet the thought of being with her and another man had me stiffening up painfully in my pants. I sighed. As a kid I believed at thirty-four I would have my life figured out. For the most part I usually did but last night had things crumbling down around me and all I could think about was Liam's whispered words, "I want both."

"You're here early," my uncle called up to me.

"I'm taking time off for Christmas, so I thought I'd make up the hours now."

"You don't have to do that, Jaxon. You're a foreman; I don't even know why you're up there nailing."

He shook his head and walked away. When he promoted me to foreman, the role encompassed managing multiple sites and overseeing staffing decisions. Initially, I took the job to work and get my hands dirty. Nowadays, I mostly handled management tasks, contracts, and staff coordination. But on days like today, I needed to hold a tool and shut off my mind.

After completing my task, I headed to the trailer for a meeting with the project designer, engineer, and my uncle. Several hours and about thirty phone calls later, all to find the exact type of glass we needed for the windows, I finally checked my phone. I had been added to a group chat with Charlee and Liam. Charlee had created it, naming it "We at 3C". At first only "We" appeared in my message, but upon opening the chat the full name scrolled across my screen.

> **CHARLEE:**
>
> Figured all real roommates have a group chat. So here is ours.

> **LIAM:**
>
> I love a good group chat (naughty face emoji).
> Thanks for lunch, Jax

CHARLEE:

> Yeah thanks for lunch, babe. I saw your note (winking emoji)

LIAM:

> Hey I didn't get a note

CHARLEE:

> You're not special yet (sticking tongue out emoji)

LIAM:

> (Sad face emoji) what does a guy have to do to become special?

CHARLEE:

> I'll think of something

LIAM:

> Deal. I'm going into a C-section. Later

I groaned. Was it just me or was their banter adorable? I had only just begun to really get to know Liam, and already he felt like he would make a great permanent member of... the group chat.

I typed out a quick, rather boring but safe, response and then shoved my phone back into my pocket as I gathered my stuff and went back to my truck to drive home.

JAX:

> See you at dinner

I made lasagna and sauteed veggies, the savory aroma filling the kitchen. When Charlee came home, she mentioned that Liam might be on a twenty-four-hour shift and probably wouldn't be back tonight. Though he'd been stuck in a long case when she left, so she wasn't entirely sure. I wrapped up his meal and slid it in the fridge.

After dinner, I showered, then Charlee and I watched a movie together. By the end, she leaned in and whispered something about my note in my ear. I gathered her up in my arms and carried her to our room. I tried to kick the door shut, but it bounced off the frame and swung back open. I was too distracted to care.

Soon our clothes were off, and she was on her knees, sucking me. After a few minutes of watching her intently working on me, I groaned and pulled her off. I got between her legs to repay the favor. She came, gloriously loud. I wiped my mouth, crawled up the bed, and leaned against the headboard, pulling her into my lap. She lifted her hips, and I slid into her.

"Fuck," she whimpered.

I echoed her sentiment. I'd never get enough of this. It wasn't just physical, although physically it felt phenomenal, but the emotional closeness—it made my brain feel all fuzzy at the edges in the best way.

I held onto her hips as she lifted and lowered herself on me. Her breasts bounced in my face, and I caught one in my mouth, sucking until she gasped. Then I grabbed her hair and pulled her in for a kiss. She panted in my mouth, moving faster, chasing her second orgasm.

That's when I heard a noise. I looked up and saw Liam standing in the hallway, staring at us. My first instinct was to stop, to shut it down, to close the door, to make him go away. But I didn't. I stepped outside my box of tolerance and whispered to Charlee, "Is this okay?"

Sweat had her hair stuck to her temple, her lips were swollen, and her eyes were glazed over.

"Is what?" she asked, still trying to move her hips, but I was holding her still.

I gestured to the hallway. She turned, and I imagined what he could see of her. Her silhouette was slightly illuminated by the glow off my phone, her body curved and primed above me. Her body tensed, and a gasp escaped her lips. I could almost see her mind racing through her options. I had a blanket ready to toss over her the moment she said no, but instead, she looked back at me and nodded.

"Yes?" I needed her to say it—not just for consent, but to know we were stepping into this together.

"Yes," she said, sounding determined.

I hoped she wasn't just doing this for me. I wanted her to be doing this for herself—and, if I was being honest, for him too. I didn't have to be told twice. I took hold of her hips, lifted her off me, and slammed her back down. She let out a half-sigh, half-moan, arching her back, giving Liam a better view.

I was torn between watching her lean into another level of her sensuality and watching him watch her. Watch us. Watch me. I gave in, and looked back at him. He stood there in his scrubs, stethoscope still around his neck, holding the lunch bag I'd packed for him that morning. The intimacy of him watching my wife sliding down my cock, paired with the domesticity of that lunch bag, had me fighting not to come.

He shifted slightly, not moving closer, just adjusting his stance. His mouth went slack, eyes dilated as he took in the scene. He could have left. The minute he saw what was happening, he could have shut himself in his room. But he stayed. Even after realizing we both knew he was there, he stayed. What did that mean? Did he like what he saw? Was he silently judging me? Judging us?

My thoughts were short-circuiting from the intensity of the moment and the lack of blood flow to my brain—it was all in my cock. Charlee clenched around me, her body shuddering as she came. I followed soon after. When I looked back up, the hallway was empty. As I blinked, I wondered if I'd concocted the entire thing. If it was all a pleasure-addled fantasy.

I love the feeling of you clenched around me.

Have a good day baby.
xoxo

Jax

I was throbbing. Pulsing. Harder than I'd ever been in my whole life. I hadn't known it was possible to feel my heartbeat quivering through the length of my dick, but tonight proved otherwise. There was no blood left in my brain; it had all rushed south. The front of my scrubs tented obscenely, and I groaned as I peeled them off, freeing my cock from the prison of my boxers. It jutted out, angry and red, and when I palmed the length I shuddered—every touch way too sensitive. The ache between my legs was primal—but the longing in my chest was worse.

My shirt came off next, landing somewhere on the floor as I made my way to the bathroom and started the shower. It almost felt pointless to jerk off; I was so hard it seemed I'd stay that way all night. But of course, I did it anyway. It wouldn't take long. Even with my eyes closed, vivid images filled my mind: her body, lithe and muscular, yet full and rounded, moving up and down; his hands on her hips—huge hands—grabbing, holding. I bit down on my knuckle to stifle a shout of approval.

Flashes of him as she moved—wet and slick. Thick. Filling her. I wished I could join them. Be beside them. Feel them move with me. His arm next to mine as he held her body up, high

enough for me to lean in and get a taste. With that, I came all over my hand and the shower wall, standing there panting, eyes still closed, reluctant to open them and face the reality that the scene I'd just conjured was, and likely always would be, a fantasy.

I let the water spray all over me, cleansing my hand and my thoughts until it ran cold. Only then did I feel grounded enough to go to bed and fall into a dreamless sleep.

ON THURSDAY, I left early for a twenty-four-hour shift at the hospital. After I got off on Friday, Shaen asked me to come to their place for the weekend to help Remi build the nursery furniture. So it wasn't until Monday that I saw Charlee and Jax again in person.

The group chat had been active all weekend. Everyone acted like nothing had happened. Jax continued texting with his dry, short responses, and Charlee and I carried the responsibility of keeping the humor flowing for all of us. For every meme she shared, I had a funnier video, and for every quick one-liner I threw at her, she one-upped me.

I'd always liked her, but now I really liked her. I liked her wittiness and her casual way of putting us boys in our place while keeping it lighthearted. As the weekend crawled by, I almost wondered if maybe they hadn't actually seen me and everything had gone back to normal because they hadn't even known I was there. But every time I closed my eyes, I saw Jax's brown gaze staring right at me as he whispered in Charlee's ear and fucked her in front of me.

I wasn't used to this. Usually when I wanted someone, it was not complicated. I pursued them, we fucked, and that was it. Not only that, but other than Lia, my feelings were never involved. I wasn't hung up on how they made me laugh. I didn't think about the lunch they made me. I didn't feel huge relief that they now knew my secret. I wasn't wondering what they were doing while I screwed together a crib.

I knew I couldn't actually have them. They were a couple, had exchanged vows, and had promised their futures to one another. I was a co-worker, a friend, and despite how badly I wanted it, in all reality—lover was not going to make it to that description.

I heard Charlee and Jax in the kitchen while I stood by my bedroom door, debating how to act when I left the room. *"Hey, you guys fuck really well,"* was definitely not the right thing to say. I scoffed at myself. *You're a goddamn adult and a doctor*, I reminded myself. *Fucking act like it.*

With that, I opened the door and joined my roommates in the small kitchen.

"Morning," was all that came out of my mouth.

"Oh my gosh, hi! How was your weekend?" Charlee was all smiles, no trace of discomfort.

"I built a crib, a changing table, and a dresser." I took the coffee mug that she held out with a quick, "thanks."

"Wow, look at you. Next time, bring Jax. He's so good at building furniture." Charlee took my lunch bag out of the fridge and handed it to me. Our fingertips brushed, and a frisson of energy ran down my arm.

"How often do you think he's building baby furniture that he'll need my help again?" Jax laughed and ruffled her hair.

"I'm just saying, if he needs the help of someone big and strong, you're available." Charlee fake-pouted, but as she said it, Jax's eyes met mine, and the air around me stilled. He knew I had been standing there. He'd thought about it often since. I blinked, and he looked away. My heart started beating again, and I took a sip of coffee, scalding my tongue. They moved through the morning like nothing had happened. Meanwhile, I was barely breathing.

"I'm gonna drive up tomorrow morning if you want to join

me. Or I can text you the address if you want to come later." I began to leave the kitchen, planning to head to work early just to escape the sexual tension between us that was eating me alive. "My dad has the hot tub ready to go, and my mom always puts out an amazing breakfast spread."

"You don't have to ask us twice. We'll come with you." Charlee handed Jax his coffee and ushered us both to the front door. She still had her hair up in some elaborate situation that involved a pink rope-looking thing that I had no idea what it did, but I figured she wasn't leaving for work just yet.

"Sounds good. See you later." It sounded so domestic. So family unit. Jax opened the door and motioned for me to go in front of him. We walked down the steps together, chatting about the game last night, and then we went our separate ways—him to his truck, me to my Mercedes that my dad had bought me when I graduated Harvard.

It felt so easy and yet so complicated between us that I couldn't wait for a relaxed day with my family—full of alcohol, Shaen's Santa cookies, my mom's ravioli and roast, and all my family and friends piled into the house. If I was being honest with myself, I also couldn't wait for my parents to meet Jax and Charlee, because oddly, it felt like they had suddenly become important enough for them to know one another.

CHARLEE WAS either an amazing actress or she genuinely didn't care that I'd watched her orgasm all over her husband's dick the other night. We completed two deliveries together, and later, our schedules aligned for lunch at the same time in the break room.

"What did you get?" I peered over at her bag.

"Meatball sub. Fresh pineapple. Roasted veggies. Trail mix. Nutella cookie cup."

"And a note," I noticed. She blushed and slid it under the sandwich.

"And a note," she agreed. I desperately wanted to know what it said. Was it something sweet? Dirty? Both?

"What do you have?"

I opened my bag and pulled out everything that she had, except instead of the Nutella cup, he'd packed me a protein bar.

"He never gives me cookies," I observed.

"He knows you care about your muscles," she said around a mouthful of bread and meat, motioning to the six-pack she hadn't seen but seemed to know was there. Some sauce sat in the corner of her mouth, and I had to practically sit on my hands to stop myself from reaching over to wipe it off.

"Well. That's…" I was at a loss for words.

"Nice and unexpected?" She grinned. I nodded. She shrugged.

"Jax notices everything. He's just quieter about it than I am."

My mind stopped mid-thought. Did she mean something else by that? She was back to eating, hadn't skipped a beat or looked at me funny. *Fuck this girl was gonna be the death of me.* I quickly ate my lunch because I had a patient who'd been induced earlier, and I needed to go check on her progress.

"See you later." I gathered her garbage with mine and she smiled up at me. It was then I noticed that her gaze rested on my mouth briefly before flickering away. I held onto that for the rest of the day, even though I knew I shouldn't.

I WAS HOLED up in my room studying when I heard Jax come home—much later than usual. Charlee had gone to bed with a headache. I'd offered to go get her something, but she insisted she just needed to sleep it off.

The familiar clunk of his boots hitting the floor echoed

through the quiet apartment, followed by the soft hum of the microwave as he warmed something up. His footsteps approached down the hall, then paused. Moments later, a gentle rap of knuckles sounded on my door.

"What's up?" I called out.

"Did you eat?" His voice was muffled through the door, but clear enough. My heart leapt in my chest.

"Yes, thank you."

He seemed satisfied with my response, giving the door a light pat before footsteps retreated across the hall. I heard their bedroom door open and close.

I fell asleep surrounded by flashcards, my heart at peace. I may not have what I really wanted, but I'd definitely found something just as valuable—friends for life.

I ALMOST PREFERRED Christmas Eve over Christmas Day. The anticipation was the best part—the palpable excitement in the air, the flurry of preparations, the wrapped presents, and the gathering of people. It was more exciting for me than the actual unwrapping of gifts while nursing a hangover from the night before.

Up early, I ordered Uber Eats for all of us and packed an overnight bag. I had no idea where we'd sleep, with all my brothers home, every single bed in my parents' house was likely occupied. If I wasn't too drunk to drive, I figured I could crash at Shaen and Remi's.

"Happy Christmas Eve," I greeted Charlee and Jax as they came into the kitchen. "I got you breakfast, let's hit the road."

"Someone certainly loves Christmas," Charlee observed, her eyes still half-closed with sleep.

"I love family," I corrected her. "And if Christmas is a good excuse to spend time with family, then I'm all in."

"Not my family. I love my sisters but my parents… nah." Jax popped a bite of French toast in his mouth, chewing thoughtfully as he watched me.

"My family is okay. I only have one brother, and we're not super close, but they're not toxic like my in-laws." Charlee opened the bottle of electrolyte water I'd gotten her and took a sip.

"My family can be your family. There are enough of us to go around." I grinned. "Let's go."

The trip from the city to Rockland County should have taken an hour. With traffic, it took nearly two before we finally pulled up outside my parents' house. Jax took in the large home and its curved stone driveway nodding.

"I like it. Good architecture," he said in that slow, thoughtful way he had.

I grabbed all three of our bags from the trunk, and they followed me to the front door. As to be expected, my mom was right there to greet us.

"Darling." She hugged me, her perfume enveloping me in a tight, loving squeeze, just like she always did. "I'm so happy you're here. Are you hungry? I have food."

"I know you do, Mom." I laughed and kissed her on the cheek. "Mom this is Charlee and Jax. Guys, this is my mother, Julia."

She immediately hugged them both.

"I'm so glad you could come. You're so beautiful. Liam, you didn't tell me they were both so beautiful. Come meet everybody. Here, I'll take your bags."

She was her usual amazing tornado self, rushing around the kitchen and making us all a plate of brunch. Then she chatted with Charlee about her job as the owner of three med spas, as she was an aesthetics nurse injector. I heard her tell Charlee that she had Botox in the fridge if she wanted to try some. I loved my mother so much; she had the ability to make literally anyone and everyone immediately feel welcome, comfortable, and at ease.

I took Jax into the den, where my dad and three of my brothers sat watching the sports channel.

"Liam!" My dad stood and gave me a bear hug, then he shook Jax's hand. "Come sit." He motioned to the remaining loveseat, and we both sat down on it. I tried to hold my body to the side so that my leg wouldn't touch his, but of course, it did anyway, and I sucked in a breath when the outside of our thighs met. I was afraid any movement would make me sigh out loud.

"Thank you for having us, sir." The Midwesterner in Jax made him so polite.

"Call me Sam." My dad handed out beers. "Who are you going for tonight?" he asked, referring to the game, and he and Jax got into a conversation about football.

I heard Charlee laugh from the other room, and my body relaxed on its own accord. Jax's leg was solidly pressed to mine now; I felt his arm move next to me as he took a drink of his beer, and I felt my heart swell with happiness.

Everything was a confused mess, but it felt perfect somehow.

I can still taste you.
Enjoy your day.

xoxo

Jax

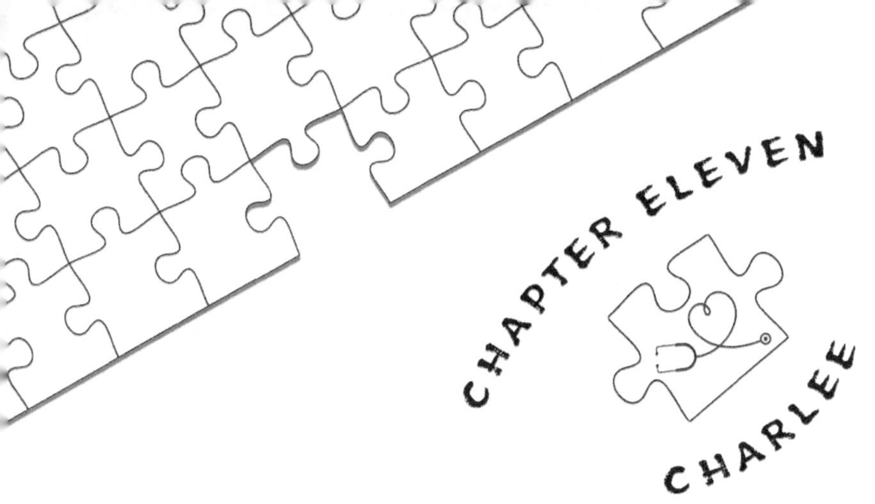


J ulia Hennessy might just be my new favorite person now. She was stunning, with an effortless grace that radiated warmth. The most maternal human I'd ever encountered. You could tell that every single person who stepped into her kitchen felt genuinely loved.

She introduced me to everyone as they came by to grab more food. I met Liam's older brothers—Landon and Ledger—and his younger brothers—Lance and Levi. Landon and Ledger were both married, so I was introduced to their wives and kids as well. It was a lot of L names and I quickly lost track as the kitchen filled up with young voices and laughter.

Lia and her husband, Jordan, showed up about an hour later. Lia was tall and willowy, and her husband looked significantly older than her. Several neighbors came by, as did Sam's sister with all of her kids and her husband.

Shaen and Remi arrived when it was time to start dinner, carrying several containers of desserts that Shaen had baked.

"Charlee. I'm so excited that you're here." Shaen gave me as big of a hug as her belly would allow. It seemed that everyone in Liam's life was open and giving with their love.

"How are you feeling?" I took the containers from her and carried them into the kitchen.

"Like I'm carrying a huge baby." She grimaced.

"You're almost done."

"I just hope Liam is off when I go into labor because I need him to be there." She followed me to the dining room, and we chose seats next to each other.

"He'll be there. The universe will make sure of it."

Shaen looked at me, teary-eyed. "I hope so. He's—" She was cut off as the guys entered the dining room and Liam announced, "Oh my god, Shay Shay are you crying again?"

"Fuck you." She sniffed. He came over, took her face in his hands, and kissed her forehead.

"You good?" I heard him murmur. She nodded. Their connection was so strong, I could almost feel it. Liam meant the world to her, I could see it in her eyes.

"I know it's hard to believe, but I used to call Shaen ice queen." Liam plopped down in the seat next to me, with Jax taking the chair next to him.

"It's not my fault. It's Remi's fault," Shaen interjected.

"What the fuck did I do?" Remi protested as he walked over to the table.

"You put a baby in me and messed up my hormones, and now I cry all the time."

"Ha, yeah I did do that." Remi sounded so proud of himself.

"I love how men act like they saved the universe when all they did was come," I said out loud. "Whoops, sorry." I forgot that these people were still getting to know me, but thankfully, everyone cracked up.

The rest of the group piled in, and we began to pass around the dishes. Liam wasn't exaggerating when he said his mother made too much food. There were five kinds of roasts alone and so many side dishes that I couldn't even fit them all on my plate.

"Okay, before we eat, let's just pause while Remi says grace,"

Sam announced. The whole table cracked up and Remi groaned. "Can you all fuck off?" I looked over at Liam for an explanation.

"The short version is, remember the guy I told you about who raised Remi? Well he is a pastor, and Remi isn't religious anymore, so we always ask him to say grace as a joke." I could feel Liam's breath against my neck, and my skin tingled in its wake.

No one would ever accuse Liam of being unhappy. He was the friendliest of the residents—always smiling, always in on a joke. But here, with his family, I could see how much more peaceful he was. Relaxed in a way I'd never seen before. His happiness was infectious, and I found myself deep in a philosophical conversation with Remi, and then chatting with Shaen about labor and what Liam was like in high school.

Julia joined us during dessert, settling into the seat beside me with curious eyes and a warm smile. She wanted to know everything—how Jax and I met, where we were from, and what made us choose our careers.

I told her I was born and raised in New York but my family had since moved to Arizona. That my golden skin tone and, as Julia had called it, my *gorgeous* hair, was most likely from my grandfather, who was part of the Tuscarora Nation—a local Native American tribe. I shared that my mother had been a doula, and that I'd wanted to be a labor and delivery nurse for as long as I could remember.

Jax explained how he had always liked putting things together, and with an uncle in construction, joining the family business just made sense. But he didn't say much about his own family—just glossed over the subject—as his parents weren't exactly a happy part of his story.

After the dessert plates were cleared, the alcohol came out. We'd sipped expensive wine during dinner, but now that the neighbors had trickled out, Liam's brothers started making cocktails that rivaled anything I'd gotten at a real bar.

Shaen leaned toward me.

"We're going to the hot tub, did you bring a bathing suit?"

I nodded, sucking down the creamy root beer rum drink Lance had handed me.

I changed in the hallway bathroom and tied a robe closed over my bikini. Jax was waiting for me and as soon as I stepped out, he snagged me another drink, and led me outside into the bitter cold. We ran quickly toward the massive hot tub, steam was rolling off the surface, the tub already close to full with Liam, Lia, Jordan, Remi, three of Liam's brothers, and his two sisters-in-law.

I stripped off my robe and made a mad dash up the stairs.

"Fuck, it's cold." My nipples were pebbling under my bikini top, and the contrast of the water on my cold legs was almost painful.

Liam drifted toward my side of the tub as Jax climbed in beside me. I took a generous gulp of the red drink in my hand.

"Holy shit that's good, what is this?"

"It's a blood orange ginger cranberry mojito," Lance informed me. Apparently, he owned several sports bars, which explained his expertise with alcohol. He and Jax launched into a conversation about the latest one he'd opened, their voices blending into the easy hum of the night.

Shaen joined us, bundled up in a huge coat, a knit hat pulled low over her ears, and a dramatic pout on her face.

"Liam won't let me go in the hot tub," she announced, crossing her arms.

"It's not like I'm just being an asshole," Liam argued. "The water is too hot for the baby."

"I know. Adult problems." She sighed. "It feels like it was just yesterday we were all hanging out in the hot tub in the Hamptons. Now here we are—you're a doctor, and I'm knocked up."

"You know, from what I hear, it actually makes sense that Liam became an OBGYN," Jordan suddenly piped up.

"And why's that?" Remi had his massive body folded so deep

in the water he looked like a floating head. With the amount of alcohol I'd consumed, watching him bob in place was dangerously close to sending me into a laughing fit.

"'Cause he gets to look at pussy all day," Jordan guffawed, way too pleased with himself.

The look on Liam's face had me sitting up straighter, contemplating hitting the man. He was so quiet, but I could see it—the way his shoulders tensed, the slight clench of his jaw. Jordan had gone on and on about being some important professor, but clearly he didn't have an actual working brain cell.

"Bro—" Remi started, but I interrupted.

"You're just saying idiotic shit because you can't handle the fact that Liam fucked your wife first," I blurted.

Jax stiffened beside me.

"For your information—" Jordan began, but Lia already cut him off.

"You drank too much, Jordan, let me take you home." She looked mortified, her face flushed with embarrassment.

"Liam is an amazing doctor." Shaen's tone was full of anger. "And it's honestly astonishing that someone of your supposed caliber would reduce everything he's worked for to something so ignorant."

"He literally brings life into the world," I added wholeheartedly, accidentally splashing Jordan with water as I waved my hand for emphasis.

"Okay..." Jax grabbed onto my waist and pulled me back against him, settling me closer to the curve of the hot tub wall.

"I'm so sorry." Lia was beside herself as she ushered Jordan toward the house, sliding the glass door behind them with a soft click.

"You know no one thinks that," Remi assured Liam once they were gone.

"Sure," Liam said with a hollow little laugh. But I could hear an edge of pain to his words. I reached out under the dark water and grabbed hold of his hand. He didn't look at me—didn't move —until he gave my hand a small, firm squeeze. I squeezed back, then let go.

Liam's friend Carter and his girlfriend showed up with more drinks and climbed into the hot tub with us. Liam's oldest brother yawned, claimed he was tired and headed inside.

"There's no way they're tired," Remi announced.

"Yeah, they're definitely fucking," Shaen added, still bundled up in her big coat. My fourth drink made that hilarious and I laughed so hard I got the hiccups.

Later, Julia came out to tell us she was heading to bed.

"I'm going to wake up early with the grandkids to unwrap presents," she said. "I am mortified that this happened, but I miscalculated, and I'm down to only one available bedroom—and you need two."

"Which room, Ma?" Liam asked. He was leaning against the edge of the tub, hair falling into his eyes, clearly feeling his drinks.

"Remi's old room."

"Is the pullout couch still in there?"

She nodded.

"That's fine, then, I'll take the couch, and Charlee and Jax— Jaxon—can take the bed. Do you mind?" He turned to me, his eyes impossibly blue in the moonlight.

I glanced at Jax, who answered in his usual polite way, "We just appreciate that you're allowing us to sleep over. Anywhere is fine. We can take the pullout couch."

"Nonsense. I wouldn't hear of it." Liam suddenly had a posh British accent that made Remi crack up before dunking him under the water, splashing Shaen.

Julia smiled fondly as she watched them. "I just love having my boys home. I do hope you'll sleep well, and I look forward to seeing you in the morning. Wear your pajamas—we always do hot cocoa by the fireplace on Christmas morning." She leaned over and kissed each of us on the cheek, then headed inside.

That's when I noticed she was still wearing her red-bottom heels this late at night.

"Is she a literal angel?" I wondered out loud.

"My mom?" Liam was back beside me, his hair plastered to his forehead.

I nodded, finishing my last drink and handed the glass to Jax.

"She must be. She's perfect." Liam leaned back, his eyes closed, as Shaen massaged his scalp. From what little I could see, his chest was perfectly sculpted, and I was pretty sure I saw a six-pack when he'd jumped to tackle Remi earlier.

*Don't look.* I peeled my gaze away before anyone noticed.

"So tell me about your dog rescue." I turned to Shaen.

She lit up, launching into stories about her work as I listened intently, trying hard to ignore the fact that Jax had his body pressed up behind me while Liam sat next to me—and every time the water shifted, his arm would float just enough to brush mine.

An hour later, the hot tub had cleared out. Shaen and Remi went home, promising to return in the morning. We followed Liam down the stairs to the basement, where the room we were sleeping in had a massive king-sized bed.

"It's extra long 'cause my cousin is a giant," Liam said, unzipping his bag and pulling out a toothbrush.

The pullout bed was more of a futon and I began to feel guilty at the idea of him sleeping on it.

"I'll sleep there. You guys take the bed," I told them as I pulled out my pajamas and made my way to the bathroom to change.

"I'm not letting you sleep there," Liam protested.

We each took turns showering and getting ready to go to sleep. Liam was last. Jax and I got into the bed and I pulled the blanket up to my chin.

"There is still a ton of space, babe. I feel bad letting him sleep on that," I whispered.

"So tell him to sleep in the bed," Jax mumbled, already half-asleep.

"With us in it?" I hissed.

"Isn't that what you've always wanted?" He smirked, eyes still closed.

My heart rate elevated at the thought of what I've always wanted and everything that had occurred the other night. Then I thought of my hair rolled up in my heatless curling rod and ran my tongue over the plastic of my retainers.

*Sexy.*

Before I had too much time to overthink it Liam came out of the bathroom as Jax let out a soft snore. The man was only wearing pajama pants and the six-pack I'd thought I'd seen earlier was definitely there. When did Dr. McHottie have time to work out with a schedule as crazy as his? But I was so glad he did.

I stared—blatantly—blaming the alcohol for my lack of subtlety. He was heading toward the futon when I whispered, "Jax said to sleep in the bed."

He halted. "I don't think—"

"There's a ton of room. You won't even know we're here." I lifted the blanket to show him.

"I'm too tired and too drunk to argue with you." He walked over and climbed in. I smelled his shampoo as he pulled the blanket over his body.

*I'm in bed with Jax and Liam.* My brain practically screamed: *Happy Christmas to me.*

"I know you're here." I heard Liam murmur as I drifted off to sleep.

I heard a whine, and in my sleep, I briefly wondered if I'd gotten a kitten. The kitten moved next to me, and I drifted back into dreamless sleep.

Then came a pant. A whisper. My eyes flew open.

I was in a bed—but not mine.

*I'm at my parents, it's Christmas.*

My brain scrambled to catch up. *Am I still drunk?*

I turned my head to the right. Charlee lay there, head thrown back, lips swollen, skin flushed. Jax was next to her, lying on his side, eyes on me. His hands were under the blanket.

Charlee let out a gasp. My brain finally caught up.

*He's touching her.*

*He's looking at me.*

Oh my god—what the fuck is happening right now?

*I must be so drunk.*

I closed my eyes, then opened them again.

Nope. Still awake.

He was *still* touching her.

Holy shit, I could *hear* how wet she was.

My cock sprang to attention, and I sat up slightly, heart

pounding. I should look away. Give them privacy. Leave the room. I kept looking. Eyes unblinking.

"Is this okay?" Jax asked, his voice low.

My mouth was as dry as cotton. I grabbed the water bottle next to the bed and took a big gulp. When I turned back, Charlee was watching me with hooded eyes. I lay back down, pulse thrumming.

"Is it okay *with you?*" My voice came out hoarse—thick with sleep, desire, and shock.

Charlee nodded.

"Do you want me to watch?" God, I would do anything they let me do. My libido was chomping at the bit, willing me to let it free.

Jax looked down at his wife. "Do you want him to *just* watch, sweetheart?"

She paused. My heart leapt into my throat when she shook her head.

Jax's eyes flicked back to mine. "Don't just watch."

Gone were the Midwestern manners. Gone was the quiet, polite man I'd come to know. This Jax was confident. Bossy. Commanding. I swallowed hard.

"I don't want to mess up anything between you. Or between us." I hated saying it. Every part of me just wanted to pull back the blanket and see exactly what Jax's fingers were doing to put that look on Charlee's face.

"We're just experiencing life, it doesn't need to mean more than that," Charlee whispered. "This won't change that I love Jax. And that you are our friend. During the day that is always true."

"And at night?" I asked, as Jax began to inch the blanket lower, exposing the top of her breasts.

"Let's see..." Jax said, eyes on mine.

"Yeah." I nodded. "Let's see."

The blanket dropped completely and I finally got a good look at what Jax was doing to her. His fingers were circling her clit—

wet and glistening. She let out that soft whine again, and her hips bucked off the bed.

"Taste her," Jax instructed. I took a deep breath. There'd be no going back after this. I knew what I'd agreed to—this just being an experience. Just tonight. But I'd had threesomes before, and I'd never been worried that I'd want more than just their bodies in the morning.

This time I already did. I'd already *been* wanting more. I wanted the impossible.

To hold Charlee's hand in public.

To call her *mine*.

To pick apart Jax's mind and figure out what made him tick.

To be *theirs*.

I thought of how Charlee had defended me in the hot tub. How she could see that Jordan's words hurt me, and had taken my hand under the water. Next time I wanted everyone to see, and the truth was, I wanted them both.

I looked over at Jax, his eyes steady, his full mouth pursed and focused, and then at Charlee's writhing body. I knew I would take whatever they would give me.

Even if it was just tonight.

Even if it was just their bodies. Because there was no way I could turn away now. I had to taste her. And I hoped he would let me get a taste of him too. I looked at Jax once more and he nodded as he smiled.

"Taste her," he mouthed at me. I leaned down and swiped my tongue across her, not just licking the sweet essence off her soft skin, but also Jax's finger that he had pressed against her clit. I heard him inhale sharply the second my tongue touched him, and I licked around it.

*Let's see what you got for me, Jaxon Berman*, I thought, *because I can take it.*

# *Jax*

As soon as his tongue swept over my finger, my brain short-circuited. I had spent years dodging Charlee's offers to have this experience, and to be honest, I didn't regret it. I valued her too much to let just anyone in our bed. In high school and in college, sex had just been sex—something two people did to offer physical release. But once I met Charlee and experienced sex paired with emotion, I'd realized it was sacred. Something to be shared only with someone you trusted and cared for.

That was why, when Charlee told me it was okay if I wanted to be with other guys, I couldn't fathom doing it. Because it would've just been physical and that would've made me feel used. Dirty. Aimless. I didn't want that.

But Liam—Liam was different. And if I was really being honest with myself, that scared the fuck out of me. Liam brought out a side of me that I didn't know if I had ever seen before and it made my stomach clench with fear and curiosity.

It had only been a week since he moved in, but I'd known him for years. With Charlee working so closely with him, I felt like I had a pretty good read on him. Still, I found myself wanting to know the simplest things—did he like his lunch, how his day went, was he sleeping well in his new room?

Watching his interactions with Charlee in our group text made me feel warm instead of jealous. On the drive up yesterday, they'd started singing along to the music—badly, but adorably—and it just felt *real*. Last night at dinner, I watched him around his family, saw how loved and relaxed he was, and I felt happy for him.

Then in the hot tub, when Charlee stuck up for him, I realized she might be feeling something similar to what I was. And surprisingly, it didn't bother me. In fact, it made sense.

Liam was my opposite in all the right ways. Where I was more reserved, he was vibrantly outgoing. Where I was careful and responsible, he was spontaneous. Where she lacked cooking skills, he and I could make sure she was fed—together.

It almost had me imagining nights where we all ate dinner, showered, and fell asleep in the same bed. I'd never considered anything like that before. But with him? My heart suddenly felt homesick for something I'd never even had.

I knew it could never really happen, not like that. But it would be a lie to pretend I hadn't wondered. I had never wanted to share Charlee with anyone. Until now. But with Liam, it didn't feel like sharing. It felt like something *more*.

His tongue circled around my finger, lapping at her with every pass. She was gasping, moaning, and pressing herself against his mouth. I moved my hand to cup his jaw, fingers slick and wet. He stilled and looked up at me. His lips were shiny.

I grew impossibly harder.

I imagined where his cock must be—trapped between his leg and the mattress—and felt precum leak from my tip.

"Would you like to come, baby?" I asked Charlee, not looking at her. My eyes were on Liam. My hand was still on his strong, scruffy jaw. I ran my thumb over his lips and he let out a small puff of a sigh.

"I need to," Charlee all but begged.

I hooked my other arm behind her back and under her hips, lifting her like a gift, offering her to Liam. Then I smoothed my hand along his jaw and around to the back of his head, threading my fingers into his thick, beautiful hair.

"Make her come," I ordered, breathless, holding onto control by the thinnest thread, vibrating, and about to snap.

I pushed his face toward her pussy, lifting her hips to meet his mouth. I held them there together. He didn't hesitate. He ate her like a man starved—lapping, licking, nibbling, sucking. I watched his tongue slide into her, then refocus on her clit, swiping his tongue around it—slowing down and speeding up in response to her sounds. He couldn't pull away even if he wanted to—not that he seemed to want to—because I was still holding him there, applying a steady pressure to the back of his head.

My arm ached from holding Charlee's hips up, but I flexed and kept her steady. She was almost there. I could feel it from the way her legs trembled, hear it in her breathy pants.

"Yes—right there. Right there."

I turned awkwardly and kissed her, swallowing up her cries just as he pushed her over the edge.

I looked back down at him. He was ravenous for her. Taking her right through her orgasm with strong, sure strokes of his tongue. She finally collapsed onto the bed, an arm flung over her eyes, half laughing and half crying at the intensity of it.

I tightened my grip in Liam's hair and pulled him up to his knees, closer to my face. His lips hovered just inches from mine. I could smell her on him. Feel his hot breath on my upper lip.

*Was I going to kiss him?* I hadn't kissed another man in years. Was it bad that I wanted to? Because I wanted to, *God* I wanted to. Would I be unloyal to Charlee if I gave in and took what I craved?

"Kiss him, Jax." Her voice came softly from below us.

We both looked down, chests heaving, his hand had ended up on the back of my neck too and he was gripping me hard. She smiled and nodded.

"Please." Her simple plea broke the last of my resistance. I crashed my mouth against his and felt the breath rush from my lungs. He tasted like her—and something uniquely male. The stubble on his chin scratched at my skin. It was nothing like Charlee's soft, loving kisses. He moved his mouth differently, his lips weren't like hers. And it made me crave more. Deeply. Desperately.

I pulled him closer, kissed him harder. He groaned against me, the sound vibrating in his chest and into mine.

"Fuck," I gasped, breaking the kiss. His lips were swollen, his eyes wild.

"Mmm," I moaned, pressing my forehead to his before diving in again. My kisses were sloppy now, eager, trailing down his chin, nipping at his neck, licking across his collarbone.

I felt Charlee's hand on my thigh, and I yanked my shorts down so she could take what she wanted. My dick was weeping, hard as steel and bobbing against my abs.

Liam's eyes dropped.

"Like what you see?" My voice was husky. Breathless. He nodded, frantically, and I laughed.

He looked back up at me. We were close. I could see the soft freckles across his nose, his long lashes. A flash of protectiveness rose up in me, sudden and fierce—like I wanted to hold him and tell him everything would be okay.

"I've never reciprocated," he whispered, lowering his gaze in shame.

"What do you mean?" Charlee sat up. We ended up in a loose tangle of limbs, her body between ours.

"I have been with men," Liam said quietly. "But only in the sense that they gave me head. I never gave it back. Never let them fuck me. It made me question myself. Like maybe I'm not really bi. Maybe I just... like sex." His voice was hollow, like he was reciting a story he'd told himself so many times, it had become true.

Charlee eyed me, a look that spoke of sympathy shone in her eyes. Then she grabbed her phone and typed something into Google.

"A man is bisexual if he experiences romantic, sexual, or emotional attraction to more than one gender," she read out loud, "or engages in a sexual relationship with more than one gender."

She glanced up. "It doesn't say you're only bi if you give another man a blow job."

"Are you attracted to me?" I asked, stroking his cheek.

He nodded, quickly. "Very much."

"You can be whatever you want to be. You don't need a label. And I'm happy to suck you off, no reciprocation necessary."

He smiled. "I want to though. I've just never felt safe enough to..."

Charlee slid closer and wrapped him in a hug before he could finish.

"I want you to tell little Liam in there," she said softly, "that it's okay to like sex. Most people do. There's nothing wrong with you. You're not 'acting bi' because you can't get enough with women. You do what you do because it's who you are—and it's okay. You're safe here."

Liam nodded. "Thank you, Charlee."

I was entranced watching them together. Her skin was so tan against his, he looked so muscular and strong next to her. He turned his head and their faces inched closer. I realized they were about to kiss and something inside me panicked.

"*Don't.*"

They froze, both looking over at me.

"I know—what the fuck." I tried to make light of it. "I just... I don't..."

"She's yours. I know." Liam eased back and gently unclenched my fist where I hadn't realized I'd been gripping the sheet.

"Jax..." Charlee sounded confused but she pulled away as well.

"I'd like to taste you," Liam said suddenly. "With her."

My cock pulsed at his words.

He motioned to Charlee. Images flooded my brain—Liam and Charlee on their knees, both sucking me.

I stuttered, "I-I'd be good with that."

Charlee giggled.

"She'll be a good teacher," I added, grinning as I saw that her hair had fallen out of its contraption.

The air shifted—away from the emotional tenderness we had all shared and back to the frenetic sexual tension. Charlee pushed gently on my chest until I reclined against the headboard. She pulled my shorts all the way off, then circled the root of my cock with her fist.

Liam watched intently.

"Did you like watching Jax fuck me the other night?" she asked, eyes on him.

Liam's eyes darted to her face. "I-I did."

I knew he had. But it felt damn good to hear him say it.

"Were you hard?" She was bold as she stroked her hand up and down my length. Liam's gaze dropped to where her hand moved on me. The front of his pants was visibly straining.

"I am. I was," he stammered.

"Good."

His breaths were coming out in short pants and my eyes closed on their own accord when Charlee leaned down and enveloped me in her mouth. Hot. Wet. Tight. My hips jerked and she gagged slightly as I hit the back of her throat.

My eyes snapped open when I felt the bed shift. Liam had bent down, his mix of light brown and dirty blond a striking contrast to her dark waves.

"Let me give you a taste before you take a bite," Charlee said with a teasing smile. I groaned when she swiped her finger across the head of my cock, now slick with precum, and held up her shiny finger to Liam.

Liam hesitated.

He looked at me. I nodded.

Then he leaned in and took my wife's finger in his mouth. I didn't even know where to look first. Charlee whose pupils had blown wide or Liam who was sucking precum off her finger.

# Charlee

My new love language was Liam Hennessy sucking my husband's cum off my finger. I must have been a really good girl this year because Santa had certainly shown up this Christmas Eve. Jax's fist in my hair tightened when I gripped his cock and held it out like a lollipop.

"Just lick the tip to start," I instructed.

I could not believe this was happening. I couldn't let my brain run away with the facts—that Jax and I were married, that Liam was my co-worker, that he paid us rent to live in the bedroom across the hall. No, I couldn't let reason and logic steal this moment from me. I was living out my hottest fantasy, and I wanted to keep it. I wanted this for Jax. I wanted this for Liam. I had called this a life experience, but I knew it was more. I knew it spoke volumes about the trust between us—not just Jax and me, but Liam as well.

I was very aware that it was the first time Jax had given in and initiated something like this since marrying me. Watching them kiss may have been the single hottest moment of my life. Emotion had tightened in my chest as I watched their strength, their need, their noises—if I hadn't just come, I would have combusted right then and there.

Liam leaned forward, his hair falling in his eyes, and stuck his tongue out to swipe it over the head of Jax's cock. Jax tugged my hair and groaned. I was wild with desire as I watched the scene unfold in front of me. I needed more. I rubbed my clit against the blanket, seeking some sort of relief.

Jax and Liam both turned to look at me. I stilled and encouraged Liam, "Now take some more in your mouth. Kind of pull your lips back to cover your teeth and..."

He did just that, taking in as much as he could into his mouth. Jax's hold on my hair was painful now, and I saw that he was fisting the blanket next to him as if to anchor himself. He let go of my hair and gently pushed my face closer to his crotch, closer to where Liam was sucking him with focus and need.

"Help him."

Jax's eyes were glazed over. The veins in his arms stood out, and his chest shone with sweat. I didn't have to be told twice.

Liam popped off. His lips were puffy, and he looked at me.

"You're doing so good," I encouraged. "Let me help you."

I leaned in and licked up the side, and Liam mimicked me on the other side. Our tongues danced dangerously close, then slid away. I kissed the head while he licked the crown. I took Jax deep in my throat, and when I pulled off, Liam took over. I left a line of saliva from top to root, and Liam followed me. At one point, our tongues moved in unison around the base, but I pulled away, remembering Jax saying, "Don't."

I wanted to kiss Liam, but I wanted to respect my husband's wishes more.

"He's close," I warned Liam. I could tell by Jax's deep breaths and clenched abs.

"I'll let him finish in my mouth. You jack him."

Liam nodded and waited while I took Jax in my mouth again, sucking and swallowing just the way I knew he liked it. Then Liam reached under and closed his fist around the exposed skin near my mouth, running his hand up and down like he was feeding Jax's cock to me. Every nerve ending in my body was on fire.

"Oh fuck, oh fuck."

Jax exploded in my mouth. I tried to swallow it all, but some dribbled out the side of my mouth and down my chin. Liam surprised me by catching it with his finger and licking it off. Jax ran his fingers through Liam's hair.

"You did so good," he murmured, then kissed him. Then he kissed me, keeping Liam's face right next to his so it almost felt like I was kissing both of them—although I was very aware that I wasn't. I wanted more, but I wouldn't push.

"You're next." I smiled.

"Maybe next time," Liam said, surprising me. "If there is a next time?" He sounded hopeful.

"Everything okay?" Jax had his worried face on.

"Yeah. I just need time to process." Liam was open and honest with his emotions, and I liked that. My tense shoulders relaxed with relief.

"Okay. So next time," Jax acceded.

My heart skipped with disbelief in my chest. *Next time*. Not just one time. I was already looking forward to it.

Jax fell asleep immediately, which made me laugh, because my brain was going a million miles a minute, and it would take me a while to shut it off.

Liam crawled back over us and lay down, this time closer to me than he had earlier. I could feel the heat of his body radiating near me, and without overthinking, I reached over and took his hand.

I fell asleep like that—Jax with his head on my chest, Liam on the pillow next to me, our hands clasped between us.

I t had been a week since I'd given a guy head for the first time. Since I'd gone down on Charlee. Since I'd kissed Jax. Since I'd questioned everything I thought I wanted with them, because I had felt closer to those two in that "life experience" than I had with anyone else I'd ever slept with—*and I hadn't even come*. I had chosen it to be that way but my body hadn't gotten the memo— I'd stayed hard for hours, and I'd held Charlee's hand while I lay there, unable to fall asleep.

The next day had been so much fun. We had hot cocoa and chocolate croissants in pajamas. All my nieces and nephews opened their presents under the tree. We stayed till dinner and then drove back so we'd be home early enough to get to bed on time since we all had work the next day. Charlee fell asleep in the back seat, so Jax and I had talked the whole way home. He seemed genuinely interested in getting to know me. He asked about my first time with a guy, why I hadn't told anyone in my life yet, and what I liked the most about my job. Halfway through the drive, his hand landed on my knee. Neither of us acknowledged it, but my breath caught and I felt it like a brand through my jeans.

We had all worked nonstop Wednesday, Thursday, and Friday. I spent Saturday studying, went home Sunday for my youngest brother's birthday, then we were back at work Monday and today. Everything felt fine. Normal. Great, even. Jax packed our lunches. I did dishes. Charlee washed my sheets. We chatted often in our group chat, but we didn't talk about that night or what had happened or if—or when—it would happen again. It was eating me up inside.

I didn't do weird very well. If I had it my way, everyone would come with a warning label and little subtitles so I knew what they were all about and what they were thinking. I wanted to know if Charlee's hugs in the morning meant something more than just a hug. Or if Jax saying good night through the door when he got home late, meant he wanted another *good* night or if he was just being polite. We had to talk about it, because I was horny and confused—neither of which I was enjoying very much.

Tonight was New Year's Eve, and on one hand, I was ready to go out, get fucked up, and recreate last week's events—except this time, I wanted to come too. On the other hand, I was so exhausted from non-stop studying and three back-to-back C-sections that I could very well just fall asleep on the couch without ringing in the New Year at all.

Both Jax and Charlee were in the kitchen when I got home. They greeted me as I walked in. I dropped my phone and keys onto the counter and announced, "I'm cool if you all want to just pretend that the other night didn't happen, but I need you to be straight with me because I don't do awkward very well, and I'll admit I'm kind of confused."

"I don't want to be straight with you," Jax replied cockily, and Charlee giggled.

"I'm serious." I could hear the exasperation in my voice. "I don't know what the fuck is going on. First you leave the door open so I can watch you fuck, and then no one says anything.

Then I wake up and you have me eat her out and suck you off, and still no one says anything about it. You have each other to talk things over. I don't. I'm alone in my room, confused as hell as to what is happening and why…"

"We are so sorry," Jax said sincerely. "You're right. We haven't handled this properly. In taking time to figure out our shit, we disregarded your feelings."

I nodded, feeling the anger seep out of me until only exhaustion remained.

"Let's sit and discuss it," Charlee suggested. Jax plated mashed potatoes and stuffed chicken breasts for each of us. Charlee brought over three cranberry cocktails garnished with lime.

"Happy New Year." She handed me one. I wanted to kiss that pink gloss right off her lips. Instead, I took a sip of the drink. We all dug in, and Jax began to explain.

"Obviously Tuesday night took you by surprise, and I apologize for that. I'm not sure if I read the cues wrong, but I kind of got the impression from you that you'd be down to…"

"Yeah I was definitely down. I'll admit I was a bit taken aback, but it ended up being great. Not planned or thought out, but I was definitely willing once I realized what was happening."

We all grinned, and they nodded in agreement with my words.

"We were wondering if maybe you'd want to keep doing it?" Charlee sounded tentative and almost shy.

"How would that work?" I wanted clarity—and fast.

Jax put his hands on the table, his expression serious.

"I figured we'd work that out. But being that we're married, you and I are bi, Charlee works with you, you're moving in six months, and you currently *live* with us… there are multiple dynamics at play here. If we explore this again, we'd want to keep it uncomplicated and enjoyable, so once you leave, our marriage and our friendship are still intact."

"What exactly do you mean by 'explore this'?" I asked. Did they want another quickie, or something more frequent?

"We want to put all the options out on the table," Charlee said.

"So what are the options?" I asked. Jax grinned, I loved the way his eyes scrunched at the sides.

"First we need to discuss boundaries and what we each want from this. Then we can lay out the options."

"Can I go first with boundaries?" I'd finished my drink and watched Charlee refill my glass.

"Go for it." Jax began eating as I shared.

"Whatever we end up doing, I don't want anyone at work or in my family to know. This is just between us."

They both nodded in agreement.

"This may be jumping ahead, but just so you know—I'm not ready to bottom. I don't know if I'll ever be. I'm not ruling it out, just not ready for now."

"Would you top me?" Jax asked so calmly, I choked on my own saliva and had to cough before answering.

"I think so."

He seemed pleased.

"Lastly, I need really clear communication. I am so swamped with work and studying that I literally don't have space in my brain to wonder what you really want or what you really meant. If you don't want me to do something—or sleep in your bed after or whatever—just say it. This is obviously casual, but I want to maintain our friendship above all else, and the only way that can happen is if you speak. Words. To. Me." I enunciated the end, which made Charlee laugh.

"All of that is exactly what we want too, and we'll respect your boundaries," Jax said. He turned to Charlee. "What are your boundaries, babe?"

"I would definitely want to explore whatever this could be, and honestly, I'm down for almost anything physical." She bit her lip, and all my blood rushed south. "I agree with everything Liam said about communication and keeping this private. I guess my only boundary would be that if you wanted to do something without me, you tell me before and after. I'd never want to ruin this with jealousy."

Jax's foot began tapping on the floor as he pondered through what she had just said.

"I don't know how I feel about you doing stuff without me, but I guess that's hypocritical, so I'd say let me know first before anything happens." He didn't sound so sure.

"We can have a rule that nothing happens unless all three of us are here," I proposed. "Obviously, you two can do whatever you want together and don't have to tell me—unless you want to." I winked at Charlee. She giggled again. Jax watched me flirt with her and took another drink, his foot inching closer to mine.

"Maybe we take it case by case," Charlee reasoned. "If something might happen and either Jax or I aren't here, we check in and see how the other one feels."

"Just to be clear—for me, I'm always a yes," I added. Both Jax and Charlee laughed.

"What are your boundaries, Jax?" We both turned to him.

"I don't want you to kiss Charlee." He almost seemed ashamed to say it, considering he had kissed me.

"Listen, I get it, and I'll respect it." I wanted to kiss her even more now that it was off the table.

"I don't like it, Jax," Charlee told him. "But like he said, I'll respect it."

She wanted to kiss me too. That knowledge made me feel hot. I pulled off my sweatshirt. I needed air. Or a distraction. Or maybe just to stop thinking about how much I wanted to kiss her.

"I know. I'm sorry I just can't wrap my head around it," Jax said, clearly conflicted.

"So he can eat me out, but he can't kiss me?"

"Right."

Charlee gave him a look.

"I'll keep your mouth so busy... you won't have time to kiss me," I quipped, trying to lighten the mood.

"I'll hold you to that." She grinned, and Jax looked relieved that I'd distracted her.

"So anal is off the table for Liam for now, and Charlee doesn't like it either. I'm okay if you want to have sex with me—and I definitely want to watch you fuck her." Jax's voice was low and gruff, and I found it hilarious that we were discussing this so casually over mashed potatoes and cranberry vodka.

"Sounds good to me," I agreed.

"I think I might be down to try DP," Charlee added, almost shy.

"DP?" Finally something I hadn't heard of.

"Double penetration," she explained.

*Fuck that's hot.* I kept my face calm and just nodded. No one said anything for a minute. The air thickened with possibility.

"If you fall asleep in our bed after, I'm fine with that," Jax said at last. "I just want to make sure we all agree that whatever we decide to do now, at the end of this, we remain friends—and don't let anything complicate that."

We all nodded. The only sound was Charlee's fork scraping her plate.

"So to be clear—I'm sorry for starting something last week without discussing it first," Jax said. "I'm not usually so spontaneous, I guess you're rubbing off on me."

"Or rubbing on him." Charlee wiggled her eyebrows.

"I'm serious, babe."

"I know. I'm sorry too."

"I appreciate that—but I'm not sorry it happened. It was hot," I admitted and Jax seemed pacified.

"So the options are, we don't do anything again and just stay friends. Or we go once more—since Liam didn't come last time and it's only fair. Or we agree to explore this as a more regular thing—a kind of sexual relationship—and see how it goes for the next six months, with the option to stop at any time if it doesn't feel right. But either way, the end of June is a hard stop."

"I vote the last option." Charlee had turned on the TV, and the sounds of Times Square filled the room.

"Liam?" Jax looked at me.

They made it sound like it would be so easy—to stop, to walk away, to say goodbye. I'd had just one taste, and I already knew my feelings were going to get involved. Which was ridiculous. I'd hopped in and out of beds for practically the last fourteen years and never felt this way. Not ever. Leave it to me to get emotional over a married couple who saw me as a friend and a conveniently available dick for their threesome fantasies.

I'd figure it out. I always did. But no matter what it did to me at the end, I wasn't turning this down.

"Option three." I was sure. Even if it broke me later. Right now, I wanted this.

"Yay." Charlee clapped her hands like we'd just picked a movie she liked.

"I like option three—as long as the communication stays on point." Jax started to clear the table.

I glanced at the clock. Ten thirty. The clubs would be open until four, and young Liam would've been smoking a blunt, throwing on something outrageous, and getting wrecked until last call. He'd have gone home with a stranger, and snuck out before sunrise.

Now? I just wanted to stay home, fuck my two friends and fall asleep between them. I wondered if they would be down to bring the New Year in with a *bang*.

P art of me was in shock that we'd just had such a matter-of-fact meeting about embarking on a sexual relationship, and the other part of me was excited to test the waters. Of the three of us, I definitely had the least experience. I had one boyfriend throughout high school, and we had only lost our virginity to each other in eleventh grade. Between his family always being home and me sharing a room with my brother, we didn't exactly have ample time for naked activities.

Once we broke up and I went to nursing school, I tried to make up for lost time. But I ended up in a few longer relationships, so by the time I met Jax, I had only slept with four other people. And I had definitely never had a threesome.

I planned to check out some romance books from the library to read about how this dynamic worked, not just to understand it better but also to do some research I could bring to bed with me. I held back a laugh so I didn't look insane, cracking up at my own thoughts and went to help Jax with the dishes. Liam followed behind, carrying our glasses.

"Are you both clean?"

"Well, it's only been the two of us for six years now, and yes, we're both clean," I told him. "You?"

"I literally haven't had time for sex since I started as Chief Resident, and I tested right after I started, so I'm definitely good."

"That's since… September?" I was shocked he'd gone so long. Liam laughed.

"Try July."

I pretended to faint in shock, and Jax rolled his eyes.

"You can't die if you don't have sex, Charlee."

"I challenge you to test that theory," Liam joked.

"With you both around? No thanks." Jax turned around to put away the plates I'd just dried. I looked over at Liam, who gave me a wink and disappeared down the hall.

A smile lingered on my lips and an inner sense of warmth settled in my chest. This was feeling so normal. Almost like we were a family of three cleaning up from dinner. I wondered what would happen next.

"Is it lame that I'm too tired to go out and celebrate New Year's?" Jax asked as we went into our room and he stripped down to his boxers in preparation for a shower.

"Not lame. Just proof that you're getting old." I loved to poke fun at him because he was eight years older than me.

"Well, if you're so young, then it's quite past your bedtime, young lady," he chastised. "Let's get you into PJ's."

I laughed as he chased me around the room, then tackled me onto the bed. His big body hovered over me, his arms caging me in, his weight pressing against mine just enough to thrill.

"We're solid enough for this, right?" He sounded wary all of a sudden.

"For sharing?"

He nodded.

"I think this will just prove how strong our love is." My grip on his arm was a little too tight and my smile wobbled. I'd be lying if I said I hadn't worried—just for a tiny, insane second—that maybe Jax would like being with Liam so much that he'd prefer him over me.

"You're it for me," Jax whispered against my lips. "This is just for fun."

I nodded in agreement as he kissed me greedily and then whispered, "Go get our fun."

"Now?" Jax peered down at me. I nodded.

"It's New Year's Eve. If you're too tired to go out, then let's have the party here."

He didn't have to be told twice and left the room in just his boxers.

I sprayed on a little perfume, brushed my teeth, freshened up every inch of myself with a warm washcloth, then slipped on a white corset with a matching thong that was sheer in all the right places. I placed a pack of condoms, lube, and a few bottles of water on the nightstand.

My pulse jumped nervously in my neck. Should I sit on the bed, legs spread, giving them a full view of what they'd be enjoying tonight? Or did I get under the covers so the lingerie was a surprise?

*What were they doing?*

I pressed my ear against the door but heard nothing. *Had they gotten started without me?*

My phone buzzed and the word **We** scrolled across my screen. I opened the group chat to find a photo that Jax had sent —of him kissing Liam.

My underwear dampened instantly at the words he had texted: *come here.*

I gathered the lube, condoms, and water in my arms, then doubled back to grab Jax and me a phone charger. I had a feeling we wouldn't be making it back to our room any time soon.

Liam's bedroom door was open, the lights off. Only the glow from the bathroom illuminated the room enough for me to see the two of them, locked in a struggle for dominance. Jax was on top of Liam, but Liam had a firm grip on the back of Jax's neck that made me wonder who had initiated.

I cleared my throat, and they both looked over at me.

"Fuck." Liam's eyes roved greedily over my body. Jax stood and took the water bottles from where they were slipping from my fingers. Liam took the opportunity to move his notebooks and loose papers off the bed.

"When do you sit for the boards?" I asked, as if I wasn't standing at the end of his bed with my nipples peaked under his gaze.

"It's complicated. There's a written exam that I'll take right after I graduate. I'm already studying for it. But there's also an oral exam that I'll take a year into practicing. I have to compile a case list where I log every surgery, delivery, office visit, and hospital admission I've done. Then, in November or December, I'll go to Chicago and get grilled on how l treated each case."

"I'll help you study for the written exam if you want," I offered.

"I'll take you up on that." His voice was muffled as he pulled off his shirt. My breath hitched in my throat as I got my first full look of his very toned and very chiseled body. His pecs were defined, with a dusting of chest hair, and that delectable V of muscle below his abs drew my eyes straight to the waistband of his pants. Liam winked when he caught me staring.

He had tattoos across his ribs. I climbed onto the bed to get a closer look. It was the words *I love you* over and over, each one unique. I reached out, running my fingers over the ink. Liam sucked in a surprised breath.

"What's this?" I asked.

He stood to remove his pants then climbed back onto the bed.

"I had all the important people in my life write 'I love you,' so I could tattoo it in their handwriting."

*Oh that's beautiful.* It wasn't the first time I realized that Liam Hennessy had layers. He wasn't just the hot, funny doctor that the world saw. He had depth and emotional strength running within him because etching people's love into your skin like that wasn't something a shallow man would do.

I touched one. "Who's this?"

He looked down. "That's my mom." He pointed to others. "My dad. My grandmother. My brother. Shaen."

Jax walked back into the room holding three shots of tequila, and I realized, guiltily, that I hadn't even heard him leave. When he handed me mine, he slapped my ass.

"Happy New Year." Jax held up his shot. "To new experiences, new friendships, paying off student loans, and passing the boards."

We clinked our glasses and tossed them back. The alcohol burned, making me cough, but it also sent a hum of anticipation through me.

*How do we start? What do we do first?*

Before I could overthink it, Jax reached over and unclipped my corset, peeling it off. I watched Liam peruse my body, then flick to Jax, who nodded and gently pushed me toward him.

I went willingly.

I gasped as Liam kissed down my neck and around each nipple. As he sucked on one, Jax bent and took the other into his mouth. My head fell back in pleasure.

They kissed their way across my chest, meeting at my sternum, where their lips fused. They licked their way into each other's mouths with groans and heavy breaths.

I was still on my knees when Liam's hand hooked around my back, smoothing down my ass. Jax sat back against the headboard and watched. Liam's fingers played in the strings of my thong, then yanked them up into my ass, pulling a surprised, "Oh!" from me.

He bent and licked my clit through the sheer material of my

lingerie, making it soaked in seconds. The contrast between the warm, wet heat of his mouth and the silky fabric pulled up against my skin was driving me wild. I could barely stay upright. I lifted my eyes from where Liam's mouth was working me to where Jax sat, gazing at us, enraptured and focused. I was going to come. When my knees gave out, I'd collapse onto the bed.

My hands curled into Liam's hair and I held his head steady, my hips moved against his mouth, finding exactly what I needed. Jax had his cock out now, slowly stroking it.

"Ohmygodohmygod," I chanted. Liam yanked the thong aside and his mouth—hot and bare—enveloped me. Three swipes of his tongue and I exploded on his face.

I held Liam's hair like an anchor because I couldn't keep myself up anymore. I was making sounds I didn't recognize, and apparently my boys liked them, because they groaned in response.

"Fuck." I was on my back now, completely boneless. The orgasm had lit up every nerve ending in my body.

"Let me taste her on you," Jax growled.

Liam pulled down his boxers, tossed them off the bed, and crawled over to straddle Jax. With a moan that sounded like satisfaction, they were kissing again. Liam asked, "Can you taste her?"

Jax groaned in response, hand wrapping around Liam's cock, jacking him as they kissed. Liam was fucking his hips against Jax's palm, breath hitching between their mouths.

"D-don't make me come," he gasped. "I want more than just a hand job."

Jax stopped moving his hand and reached for the prescription bottle on Liam's nightstand. "If you take one of these, you'll stay hard all night—even after you come."

Liam inspected the label, his cock still bobbing against Jax's stomach. "Okay." He seemed satisfied with the ingredients.

I grabbed a water bottle and opened it.

"Feed it to me," Liam said, his voice husky with need.

"Huh?" I blinked.

"He wants the water from your mouth, not the bottle," Jax said, sounding steady, but his cock stood at attention.

"Do you want some?" I offered the bottle to Jax.

"I already took one." He grinned.

*Well, here goes nothing.* I took a mouthful of water, and Liam popped the blue pill onto his tongue. I pressed my lips to his and let the water flow into his mouth, pulling away quickly to follow Jax's no-kissing rule.

Liam swallowed, his eyes gleaming in the dim light.

"I want to kiss her," he declared.

Jax shook his head. I reached between them, wrapping my hands around both of their cocks, stroking them together. Their moans filled the room, chests heaving against each other. Liam stayed seated on Jax's thighs, his ass resting against Jax's knees.

I leaned down, still holding them pressed together, and enveloped my lips around both of their heads at once.

"Holy shit," Liam breathed.

Jax's hand was on my neck, holding me steady as I blew them. My jaw started to ache, so I pulled off, saliva sliding down my chin. I spit on them and picked up the pace with my hands.

Their pants built, their movements shook the bed. Jax came first, erupting all over my hand as I continued to move, using his cum to slick up Liam's cock. Liam followed moments later with a shout of, "Fuck me!" and "Goddamn."

They collapsed on the bed, sweaty, sticky, and spent.

Letting them rest, I got up to wash my hands and returned with a warm, wet washcloth to clean them up.

"Are you still hard?" I asked.

Liam's voice was muffled in the pillow. "Make me hard again, baby."

A flutter sparked in my chest. Had he meant to say that? I

looked over at Jax, unsure how he'd respond to Liam's use of the word baby—but he just grinned. "I'll do it."

Moments later Liam was fully erect again, thanks to Jax's mouth on him.

"Get a condom," Jax instructed. I did, handing it to him, and watched as he rolled the latex onto Liam's cock.

Liam groaned. "Why is that so hot?"

I half-giggled, half-groaned. Because it was.

"On your knees, sweetheart." Jax pulled the wet thong from between my legs and turned me to face the headboard. "Get her ready for me, doc."

"I'm gonna need a second," Liam muttered. "Who knew the quiet guy in construction had such a dirty mouth?"

Jax chuckled and slapped my ass as I wiggled it, ignoring the tickle of self-consciousness trailing up my spine and instead focused on feeling tempting and wanted.

I'd gotten comfortable with Jax over the years. I went to bed with my hair up, retainers in, wearing one of his T-shirts—and he still wanted to fuck me. I didn't have to try.

But with Liam it felt different. I felt like I had to be sexy. It was very obvious that he liked what he saw when he looked at Jax, he had even admitted to being attracted to Jax last week but a small voice whispered, wondering, was I here because he wanted me or because I was part of the Jax package? I hated that it even crossed my mind. But it did.

"Put me in her," Liam rasped.

I felt him behind me, and turned to watch as Jax guided his cock up against me and felt as he began to inch his way in. Jax was a little longer but Liam was quite a bit thicker, and I felt the stretch as he bottomed out, his thighs meeting the backs of mine.

His hands gripped my hips, pulling me back against him.

"Fuck, you feel good."

One of his hands slid around my waist, fingers dancing across my clit, drawing a whimper out of me.

"How tight is she?" Jax wanted to know.

"So fucking tight," Liam gasped.

His thrusts were slow but so deep. He kept hitting that spot inside of me that made everything go fuzzy. I heard the sounds of them kissing again and it had me grow even wetter.

"She's soaking down my balls."

"Can I feel?"

Liam must have nodded at Jax's question because I felt his hips falter as I assumed Jax had moved his hand between Liam's legs.

"She's soaked. Taste it."

I turned to watch Jax put his fingers in Liam's mouth. He pushed them in so far Liam gagged briefly before Jax pulled them out.

Then Jax put his hand back, probing around where Liam entered me, touching my skin and encircling Liam with his fingers so he had to thrust through Jax's grip.

He kissed him once more and Liam moaned out a strained and guttural, "Jax."

Then Jax moved in front of me, tapping the head of his cock against my lips.

"Make her come," he told Liam, breaching into my mouth.

I had never been so thoroughly fucked. My mind emptied. I blew Jax in a mess of saliva, moans, and pleas. I was brought to the edge over and over until finally Liam let me come—and I shattered.

I called out for a God I didn't believe in, choked out Liam's name around Jax's cum, tears springing to my eyes as Liam grabbed onto my hips and grunted his way to completion.

We fell asleep tangled in each other—bodies sticky, condom used, sheets barely clinging to the mattress.

"I love you," Jax murmured.

"I love you too," I whispered, and Liam's hand moved to rest on my hip as we all drifted off.

"Liam." I was shaken awake.

"W-what?" Where was I? What was happening? Was I on call? I looked down, I wasn't wearing anything. Where were my scrubs?

"Can you page the other resident? I need a minute," I murmured, turning back over.

I heard a soft laugh and was shaken gently again.

"Liam, you need to wake up. Your phone keeps ringing."

My phone? Where was my pager?

*Holy fuck that's Charlee.* I was laying next to Charlee. Jax was sleeping next to her.

Last night's events replayed in my mind as I picked up my phone and squinted into the bright light. I had seven missed calls, starting from an hour ago—four from Remi and three from Shaen.

"Fuck." I sat up fast, my heart now hammering as I tried to search for my boxers in the dark. I called Shaen back with trembling hands. She picked up on the third ring.

"Liam?" Her voice was raw and pitiful. She sounded like she had been crying.

"Shaen, baby, I'm so sorry. I was sleeping." I located my boxers in a heap and tried to pull them on with one hand.

"I think I'm in labor."

I froze.

"You're only thirty-seven weeks. Are you sure they're not just Braxton Hicks?"

I was met with heavy breathing followed by a low groan of pain.

"She's in labor." Remi had taken the phone. She must be having a contraction. I had done this so many times with so many patients, yet as I listened to my best friend breathe through the pain, my body began to shake slightly.

"How many minutes apart and how long are they?" I whispered.

"About five to six minutes apart, lasting for about forty-five to fifty seconds," Remi informed me.

"Are they bad?" I knew what she would have to go through, and I braced myself to deal with watching her, especially since she was adamant she wanted to do it naturally. No epidural.

"She can't talk when she gets one."

Shit.

"Okay, I'm getting in the car. When they get to sixty seconds or longer, head to the hospital. Call your doctor and let them know you're coming." I was using my doctor voice doing what I could to calm them.

"Okay. Drive safe. See you soon."

"I love you, Shaen."

"I love you too."

She sounded scared, and that scared me. I could deliver a baby in my sleep, but this was different. *This was someone I had loved nearly my entire life.*

I ended the call and looked over. Charlee was fully sitting up now.

"Shaen?" she asked, already piecing it together.

"Yeah. I gotta go. I'm gonna have to call out tomorrow. Good thing I still have a few measly vacation days left."

I stood and realized that my boxers were on inside out.

"Good luck. Let us know how it goes." Charlee smiled sweetly. I bent down to hug her goodbye.

"Thank you. I will."

I was grateful at how easy it was for me to transition from being the man who had done all those dirty things to her last night back to the man who was her friend.

I took a quick and quiet shower, careful not to wake Jax, and packed a bag of essentials by feeling around in the dark.

It was freezing outside, my hands like ice as they curled around the steering wheel. The sun wouldn't be up for another two hours, so I let my car warm up for five minutes before pulling out, my breath still fogging the windshield, and heading toward their hospital in New Jersey. *Please let me make it in time.*

Though the timing couldn't have been better. All the party-goers were asleep and no one was up for work yet, so the streets were empty, and I made it to the highway in record time.

I was ten minutes out when Remi called again.

"They got worse and closer together, so we left. We're almost there."

"Same. I'll meet you at admitting."

"Kay." He sounded like he didn't know what to do.

"It's gonna be okay, Rem. And soon you're gonna be holding your baby."

"Yeah." He breathed. I heard Shaen cry out in the background.

"Drive safe, I'll see you in a few." I ended the call to let him focus on driving as I pulled into the hospital's guest parking lot and found a spot.

Ten minutes later, Remi and Shaen walked through the electronic doors. He was holding her hospital bag in one hand and a giant pillow in the other. She was barely holding it together, hunched over, her face pinched and gray. When she saw me, her eyes brimmed with relief—or maybe pain—and I swallowed hard, trying to keep it together.

I had a wheelchair waiting and quickly helped her into it while Remi went up to the admitting desk to sign her in.

"Who's he?" the receptionist asked, gesturing at me.

"I'm her doula," I responded smoothly. "And I need to get her upstairs now."

Shaen was folded over in pain as another contraction took over. Her second one since arrival.

"Her doula?" She raised an eyebrow, clearly skeptical. I stared back, irritation snapping at the bit inside of me until she finally handed me a guest sticker, which I slapped to my chest. Like what—*a man can't give a damn about birth?*

"Let's go."

I wheeled her to the elevator, Remi followed close behind.

Up on the maternity ward, I was recognized immediately by a nurse who used to work at my hospital.

"Yes, nice to see you again. Can we please get her into a room?" I asked quickly. Seeing Shaen in so much pain made my chest tighten. Although a bed wouldn't fix it, I knew it would help, even if only a little.

"Of course," another nurse said. "Follow me."

I turned around while they helped Shaen put on a gown. Then the questions started. One nurse was typing in the chart while a second nurse came in to prep the IV.

"Can you check her? I'd like to know how dilated she is," I asked.

"Sir, I'm gonna need you to let me do my job." She seemed horrified that I'd even asked.

"He's an OBGYN," Shaen spoke up weakly.

"Well great." The nurse sounded the opposite of thrilled but she did move the laptop aside and put on gloves to do a cervical check. I stood by Shaen's head to give her privacy.

"It's not super comfortable," I warned. "But it should be quick."

"Okay."

"That's my brave girl," Remi said as he sat on her left side and took her hand.

"She's at a seven," the nurse informed. "And about ninety percent effaced."

"That's great, baby!" I turned to Shaen. "You're so close and you're killing it!" I leaned down to kiss her cheek.

"I still have so much more to go." She looked like she was going to cry again.

"Honey, I get patients in at one or two centimeters. You can go from seven to ten so quickly. I promise."

Remi propped her pillow behind her head and gently pulled her hair back in a ponytail. The nurse started the IV and strapped a monitor to her belly. Then she asked about the epidural.

"No-no." Shaen moaned through another contraction.

"Okay, well let me know if you change your mind."

"I won't." She was gripping Remi's hand so hard, his knuckles were turning white.

"Call if you need anything. The doctor will be in shortly." The nurse left.

I watched the monitor, satisfied with the baby's heart rate with each contraction. Then I helped Remi unfold the dad cot.

"This is quite literally the worst thing I've ever sat on," he said.

"I know, it's like they had a meeting one day and decided to make the fathers miserable." I laughed.

Remi went back to Shaen's side. The contractions had lulled, allowing Shaen to close her eyes. I wasn't worried about it. They'd be back with a vengeance, I was sure, but I was glad she would be able to get some rest before they did.

I checked the IV bag, inspected the equipment around the room, adjusted a monitor that didn't need adjusting. Paced to the door. Looked into the hall. Nothing. The world outside felt oddly still, like the hospital had pressed pause *just for her*.

When I stepped back in, Shaen was still sleeping, her breathing steady. Remi had his head down on the bed beside her, one hand tangled in hers. They looked peaceful—finally—like a moment suspended in time. I didn't want to disturb it. I took a few quiet photos, wanting to capture it all. Not just for them, but for me too. Just as I was slipping my phone back in my pocket, a text popped up in the We chat.

JAX:

Made it there okay?

LIAM:

Yes, here now

JAX:

How is she doing?

LIAM:

She's at a 7. She's resting now but I think it will be soon

JAX:

Keep us posted

LIAM:

I will

I sat down on the dad cot, which was really as uncomfortable as Remi had said. If I closed my eyes, I could almost pretend Jax was my boyfriend checking in on me. I felt warm and somehow whole in my delusion and I drifted off to sleep sitting up.

We slept about two hours before the contractions picked back up and I was woken up from the sound of Shaen crying out. I was back by her side in a flash helping her sit up so I could apply strong pressure to her back.

Remi gave her two combs that she was pressing into the palms of her hands. She said it was a technique she learned in birthing classes. An hour later, her doctor finally made it in to check on her again and he seemed confused to find two men in the room.

"Who's the dad?" he asked.

"I am," Remi identified himself.

"So who are you?" He turned to me.

Before I could answer, Shaen's water broke all over the bed.

"Fuck, that's a lot." Remi seemed concerned. "Is that normal?"

"Yep," I assured him, stepping closer to inspect for any meconium. The doctor looked over at me again.

"Sir, can you step back please." His tone was dripping with disdain. I finally understood why doctors had such a bad rep sometimes.

"He is my best friend, my cousin, and he's an OBGYN. So please leave him be," Shaen snapped through grit teeth.

I shrugged when the doctor looked back at me.

"Dr. Liam Hennessy, nice to meet you." I smiled broadly.

"I need to use the bathroom," Shaen panted, sounding frantic.

"Do you feel like you have to poop?" I asked. She nodded, then let out a guttural yell as her body began to shake. I looked over at her doctor who was gowning up and pulling on gloves. It was time.

Two nurses came running in. I helped her sit back against the bed while the nurse adjusted the lever on the bed to detach the foot section and click the handle to raise the stirrups.

"What's happening?" Shaen looked at me, fear lining her face, her neck taut with it. Her voice shook.

"It's time to have your baby, darling." I smiled as I took a cool washcloth and wiped the sweat off her forehead.

Remi was trying to stay strong for her, I could tell, but I knew him well enough to know that watching her suffer like this was driving him crazy. He was encouraging her, telling her how much he loved her and how proud he was. I videoed it—I knew that later they would cherish these memories.

I checked the monitor again. Everything still looked good. The nurse came over to position her legs.

"Okay honey, Dad and I are going to each hold one of your legs and on the next contraction I want you to take a really deep breath and push."

Shaen looked over at me, glassy eyed with fear and pain.

"I can't do it. It's too much. I can't do it," she sobbed. Her eyes locked on mine, searching for permission to fall apart—and I couldn't give it to her. What she'd said echoed in my chest, sharp and heavy, shaking something in me that I hadn't even realized was fragile. The words in my throat felt thick but I was quiet for a beat, considering what to say. What to do.

Remi was already holding one of her legs so I dropped down beside her and pressed my forehead to hers.

"You can do anything, baby. You always have. You are the strongest woman I know. This baby is so lucky to have you as its mother. Do you know that?" I felt a lump grow in my throat as I saw her panic start to subside and my adoration for her well up inside me in droves. "Your baby is coming. You need to push, Shaen. You can do this honey, push."

She nodded, renewed determination apparent as she grabbed hold of my hand.

"Now. Deep breath and puuush." She listened and her face contorted as she put all of her strength into the push.

"Okay. Stop. Deep breath and push again." She pushed three more times until Remi said, "I see the head!"

"Okay one more, Shaen," her doctor instructed. She squeezed my hand again, then let out a guttural groan from deep within her and she pushed with everything she had left. And then—stillness. A single suspended breath. The room held quiet like it was bracing for something sacred. My chest tightened as I watched Shaen's face twist between agony and something almost holy.

Her body trembled. Remi's eyes were wide and wet. Then—the cry.

Sharp and beautiful as her baby was born. The most alive sound I'd ever heard.

The baby was immediately placed on her chest and in a flurry of movement the nurse suctioned the mouth and another beautiful cry filled the air.

"What is it?" Remi looked over trying to get a glimpse himself.

"It's a girl!" the nurse announced, her voice cracking through the silence like a light switch flipped on.

Laughter and sobs spilled out of all of us at once. Shaen was crying as she watched them wipe her daughter down. Remi was bent over the bed crying with them and I snapped another photo of their very first moments as a family.

"Happy birthday," I told my goddaughter with my own tears welling in my eyes and dropping down my face.

ONCE THEY MOVED her to the mother-baby unit, I was told I would have to leave soon but I could come back during visiting hours. Remi had gone to fill out paperwork. It was just me, Shaen, and this impossibly, beautiful baby who had already rearranged the shape of my world.

The room had quieted. The baby was swaddled tight, asleep on Shaen's chest, her little mouth making soft sucking motions in her dreams. She had nursed like a champ and Shaen seemed to intuitively know what to do.

The nurse had dimmed the lights. The chaos of labor had given way to a sacred stillness, and I stood in it, trying not to cling.

"She's so beautiful, Shay Shay. You did amazing." I kissed her forehead gently, not wanting to wake the baby, and took another look at their gorgeous daughter. She had a ton of hair, chubby cheeks, a tiny pert nose, and little rosebud mouth.

Shaen looked up at me, her skin pale with exhaustion, her eyes soft and glowing—ethereal.

"Thank you for coming," she whispered.

I gave her a look. "Of course I came. I would have never missed this."

"I wouldn't have been able to do it without you." She said it simply, like it was a fact. And maybe it was.

I squeezed her hand. "I love you."

Before I could say goodbye, she blinked at me, then said, "Do you want to know her name?"

I smiled.

"Fuck, I mean frick, of course I do. Tell me." I was already messing up not swearing in front of the baby.

She took a breath. "You know how the name Liam comes from the name William?"

"Okaaay." I wasn't sure where she was going with this.

"Well I couldn't name my daughter Liam or William. But we wanted to name her after you. So we named her Billie." Shaen's eyes shone with emotion.

The air left my lungs. I stared down at the tiny bundle on her chest, and the name hit me like a second heartbeat.

"After me? You named her after me?" My voice cracked.

Shaen nodded. "The best gift I can give her is you. As her godfather. As her friend. Because I know how much it changed my life." Shaen was smiling through her tears now.

"Shay Shay… I don't know what to say." I ran a finger down the side of Billie's swaddled body. I tried to say more, but my voice wouldn't come.

"Ah, fuck." I turned away as my tears really began to run and I wiped them away with the back of my hand. "Stop it," I choked, trying not to laugh. "You're turning me into a pussy."

Shaen laughed. "Ouch. That made my vagina hurt."

"Way to ruin a moment," I joked. "I love you. Thank you. I'm honored. I'll see you soon."

I leaned down and pressed a kiss to the top of Billie's head, one hand cupping her tiny back. She smelled like fresh baby skin and something pure. Then I let go and with one more goodbye, I left.

I didn't go home.

I just kept driving north, Billie's photo still open on my phone like it was lighting the way. I hadn't planned on going to my parents' house, but somehow, I ended up there anyway, parking in the driveway. By now the sun had fully brightened the sky, signaling a new day.

I almost backed out and left, my heart banging behind my ribs, palms damp. But then I remembered Shaen telling me she named her daughter after me and I finally felt accepting enough of myself to share my secret. I felt safe. So I called through my open window to my mother as she left the house to head to work. She cried when she saw pictures of Billie. When I told her the baby's name. And again when I finally told her the truth I'd been holding onto for so many years.

There was a beat of silence. My stomach twisted. I couldn't breathe. Bracing myself for… I didn't know what.

But then I felt her fingers wrap around mine, soft and sure.

"My love for you will never waver, my darling," she said, her voice low and certain. "I will love whoever you love. I just want you to be happy."

She held me while I finally cried for the little boy who'd believed for so long that all he brought to the table were the things people told him he did. The realization that love was love —no matter how society perceived it—felt like something new was emerging.

Later, as I drove down the highway toward home—toward Jax and Charlee—exhaustion burning my eyeballs, I opened the window a crack to let the biting air hit my face and keep me awake.

I felt different. Like something had shifted—not just in my life, but in me.

For the first time in years, I wasn't bracing for impact. I wasn't hiding behind a laugh. I just was. Raw. Honest. Seen.

It was almost like two people were born that morning. Little Billie, for the first time.

And me, Liam—for the second.

Charlee and I had washed Liam's sheets, remade the bed, and cleaned up his room because God knows he wouldn't want to come back to a sex den after attending his best friend's birth. Charlee had gone to work, but I finally had a day off and had spent the morning restocking the fridge, deep cleaning the apartment, and had just sat down to play some video games when I heard him come home.

My heart skipped a beat, tossing me back to when I was sixteen and had my first crush on a guy. Then my mind flew to Charlee, and for the millionth time today, I straddled two realities—one where I was madly in love with my wife and desired nothing but her, and one where I couldn't get the image of Liam's mouth against my skin out of my system.

Last night had been... unforgettable. Dangerous. Impossible to get out of my mind.

I watched as Liam hung his coat on the hook next to Charlee's and turned when he heard the sound of my video game. His eyes were bloodshot. From crying or from exhaustion—or maybe both?

I wanted to shift over on the couch and offer him my lap and

the sherpa blanket next to me. I wanted to make him breakfast and listen to him tell me about the birth. I wanted to kiss him.

I was wading into dangerous territory. My body desiring him was one thing, but my heart wanting to take care of him and feed him was more than just a physical response. And it was what I was most afraid of.

"Hi." Liam's face was unreadable. I couldn't tell if he was also thinking about last night and if he was uncomfortable with it—or if he, too, couldn't scrub the images from his mind's eye in a good way.

"Hi," I said back. "Tired?"

He nodded and yawned. "Exhausted."

"We washed your sheets."

"Oh, you didn't have to do that." He walked further into the living room.

"We kind of did." I chuckled. "There were questionable fluids on them."

My insinuation hung thick in the air between us.

"They're just gonna get dirty again." He said it quietly as he sat down on the couch next to me—not too close but close enough.

I felt myself grow semi-hard in my pants at his deep voice saying the word *dirty*.

"That's—that's how it works," I stammered. "Sheets need washing at least once a week." I kicked myself as I said it.

Liam laughed at my awkward response as he took out his phone and showed me photos of Shaen and the new baby.

"Adorable." I leaned over to get a good look. "Was it different helping her than your patients?"

"So different. I was calm, of course, but it was much more emotional for me. I was surprised at how physically affected I was from watching her be in pain."

I nodded.

"I'll be a wreck one day when it's my wife giving birth," Liam added.

I looked over and saw that his eyes were closed, head leaning back against the couch at an awkward angle.

"You want kids?" I choked out.

He cracked one eye open. "Oh definitely. I want a bunch." The corners of his mouth lifted in a small smile, like his whole body was delighted at the thought of being a dad. "Do you?"

I shrugged. "Maybe one day. Charlee said she'll let me know when the time is right."

Liam let out a soft snore.

With a sigh, I took a pillow and put it next to me, half covering my right thigh, then tugged on Liam's shoulder, pulling him down till his head rested on it. He murmured something as I pulled the blanket over him but he stilled right back into a deep sleep.

His head was warm against my leg, and something soft, unfamiliar started building inside me. The same feeling I got when I hit every green light on the way to work, or spotted a cute puppy at the grocery store. I couldn't name it, but it grew slowly as he gently snored in my lap. A muscle twitched in my thigh and my fingers curled tighter around the controller, but I didn't move. I didn't want to wake him. He lay like that for three hours while I played multiple rounds of my game and pondered all of my life's choices.

Eventually my stomach growled, forcing me to move, startling Liam awake.

"Shit, I'm sorry."

"No, I'm sorry—did I fall asleep on you?" Liam sat up, the blanket falling off his shoulders. The embroidered design on the pillow had left a red imprint on his cheek and his hair was smushed up in disarray.

"It was fine."

I went to the kitchen, trying not to overthink the intimacy of him napping half on my lap. Was that considered cheating?

*Should I tell Charlee about it? Should I not have let it happen at all? What is wrong with me?*

I heard Liam walk down the hallway and the door to his room shut. I'd been holding my breath as if bracing for impact, but I let it slip free in a shaky rush of air.

*Get it the fuck together,* I chastised myself.

I made grilled cheese sandwiches and tomato soup for lunch, stopping only to answer a text from Charlee when she messaged me on her lunch break.

After Liam had left so abruptly last night, I'd felt awkward—as if we were overstaying our welcome in his room. But also I didn't want to run through the chilly air of our apartment to try to fall back to sleep in our own bed.

"You okay?" Charlee had whispered.

I'd turned to look at her, making out her beautiful features in the dim light through the window from the streetlamp below.

"Are you?"

The heady high from our climax and the thrill of experiencing something slightly taboo together had worn off, leaving me feeling confused and strung out. On one hand, I was more than okay. I'd never known how satisfying it would be to watch another man pleasure my wife. It felt weird to admit, but it was true. I'd felt no jealousy as I watched Liam fuck her. Instead, surprisingly, I'd felt like I'd given him a gift—a gift I myself cherished.

On the other hand, I felt selfish letting it happen. I'd made my choice when I married a woman, and who was I to compromise that decision? My father's voice rang in my ears, *"Why can't you just choose one and stick to it? Why do you have to be such a glutton?"*

I knew no matter how many times we reiterated our boundaries and verbalized that this was just for fun and that my marriage and our friendship had to come first, this situation had the potential to get horribly messy.

Not only because feelings could get entangled in the web—

something I dreaded even acknowledging because I didn't know if I could handle Charlee loving anyone but me—but also… what if I could never go back? What if now that I knew how good it could be with three, that two wouldn't be enough?

I'd physically shaken my head to rid myself of the blasphemy of ever thinking Charlee wouldn't be more, way more, than what I could ever fathom needing. I was being an idiot. A selfish, horny idiot. And as much as I regretted letting myself be spontaneous and pushing outside my little box, I also couldn't help but revel in how hot it had been. How I couldn't wait to see what else we would come up with.

*We.*

The word clunked around inside my head as Charlee leaned over to kiss me on the lips. Softly.

"I'm perfect," she'd said and fell back to sleep, head on my chest, body curled around mine.

Without thinking too deeply into it, although a nervousness I wasn't used to feeling shook my fingers slightly, I'd texted Liam to make sure he'd arrived safely. Once I was sure he was okay, I'd fallen back to sleep surrounded by my wife's hair and Liam's musky, masculine scent.

I was flipping through the choices of movies when Liam came back into the room. He'd showered and changed into a pair of grey sweatpants and a soft sweater.

"Lunch is on the counter," I offered, pretending I didn't notice how blue his eyes were next to the blue cashmere of his top.

"I worry I will get used to this," he joked as he sat back down next to me, pulling the blanket back over him, letting some of it rest on my lap.

"Days off?"

"No, you cooking for me." He bit into the sandwich and shook his head. "So. Damn. Good."

My cock thickened in my pants as I watched him enjoy the sandwich I had made for him. My throat tightened as desire and guilt flooded my senses again. I forced myself not to look at him—because somehow, even him chewing on a sandwich was doing it for me.

"That one is good." He pointed to the movie I was scrolling past.

"*Savages?*" I sounded dubious as I read the description. The plot sounded decent, but it was the two men dating one woman part that had me interested. I looked over at Liam, who winked and said, "I can only watch a little because I have to study."

With that, I pressed play and started the movie.

Halfway through, both of our phones buzzed as a text arrived in the group chat.

CHARLEE:

Just helped deliver twins. Vaginally. No epidural. Fucking hero mom. How are you guys doing?

LIAM:

Damn girl all I did today so far was nap, shower, and eat a sick grilled cheese sandwich.

I never took selfies, but I felt compelled to turn the camera to selfie mode and leaned in next to Liam, snapping a picture to send in response. I texted it over to her without overthinking it. We looked good together. My dark hair next to his lighter counterpart. He was smiling, his smattering of freckles making him appear younger than he really was. I had my usual somber look—Charlee always teased me that I had resting bitch face.

I watched as Liam saved the photo onto his phone. My breath hitched in my chest.

CHARLEE:

(Hot panting face emoji)

CHARLEE:

(Eggplant emoji. Water emoji.)

CHARLEE:

Gif of Paris Hilton saying "that's hot."

CHARLEE:

Wait for me! I'm not off till 7. (Sad face emoji)

LIAM:

We're watching a movie.

CHARLEE:

Is that what the kids are calling it these days?

JAX:

What do you want for dinner, babe?

CHARLEE:

Chicken tortellini. Send me a lil preview… (wink
emoji)

I heard Liam take a deep inhale as he shifted next to me.

"She's…" I started, my breath catching. His face was right next to mine.

"What Charlee wants, Charlee gets." His tone was seductive, his chest was resting against my arm.

I leaned back. "Liam. I—"

"She asked for a little preview, Jaxon." His smile was naughty, his eyes shone with mirth as he lifted up his phone to record us and planted his lips against mine.

"Mmph." I gasped against his mouth as he dove right in—kissing me, licking against the seam of my lips, forcing me to open and allow his tongue to dance against mine.

When he pulled away, he winked at the camera and then stopped recording. A second later, the video had been sent.

I sat there in stunned silence as Liam settled back in his spot on the couch and took a drink of his water.

"Cat got your tongue?" He sounded like he was on the verge of laughter.

"Shut up," I growled.

He cracked up, but we both sobered when Charlee texted back a minute later.

CHARLEE:

Holy.fuck.me.

CHARLEE:

Gotta run. Wait for me, I'll be home soon. (Kiss emoji.)

We finished the movie without any further shenanigans and then I began making dinner while Liam studied on the couch. I had my headphones in and was listening to music as I began to slice up sundried tomatoes for the sauce when I felt Charlee hug me from behind.

"You're home early." I turned to kiss her.

"Dinner smells delicious. I'm starving."

"It's almost ready," I promised.

"I'm gonna set the table and then I'll help Liam study," she informed me as she took three plates out of the cabinet. I nodded and took my headphones out, tucking them back in their case.

The rumble of Liam's voice, broken up by Charlee's laughter, had me feeling *warm* inside. I tried to focus on whisking the parmesan into the bubbling sauce instead of on the cozy, satisfied feeling creeping up around me. *What does all this mean*, my brain wanted to know. I didn't know what to tell it, so I just added spinach and the cooked tortellini to the chicken in my skillet and watched the leaves wilt and curl as they cooked, deepening in color.

When I left the kitchen, I found Charlee sitting on the couch with her legs crossed beneath her, holding a bunch of flash cards —and Liam on the carpet in front of her.

"What is the most likely cause of infertility in a couple with normal HSG and monthly menses?" Charlee read. "A— anovulation, B—luteal phase defect, C—male factor, or D—tubal factor."

I watched as Liam responded confidently and Charlee clapped when he got the right answer.

"Okay, two more and then you take a break to eat dinner," I interrupted.

"Let's break now." Liam sniffed, the aroma wafting off the plates pulling at him.

"Two more," Charlee insisted. Liam sighed but acquiesced.

"Which of the following is a risk factor for endometrial ablation failure? A—age older than forty, B—history of dyspareunia, C—parity greater than 5, or D—prior use of oral contraceptives?"

"C." Liam didn't miss a beat as he gathered up his study supplies.

Charlee beamed. "You're so smart; you'll definitely pass."

Liam smiled. "Why, thank you. I hope so."

"Okay, last question." Charlee held the card up in front of her. "Where is the clitoris?"

My hand shook as I poured water into everyone's glasses and ended up spilling some onto the table.

"There's no fucking way that's a question on the boards." I looked at Charlee and the devious grin on her face cracked me up.

Liam gently pushed her back on the couch and grabbed the flash cards away from her as she giggled and squirmed away from him.

"That question is definitely on the oral certifying exam," Liam teased, tickling her with one hand and holding the cards up away from her with the other. "After dinner, I'll be sure to show you that I know exactly where the clitoris is."

His tone grew heated and his words held promise.

"Oh yeah, Doctor Hennessy?" Charlee's voice turned flirty,

her body language made it clear that she was enjoying every second. "I hope you don't fail. This is your entire career, after all."

"I will pass," he all but growled as he peeled himself away from her. He walked to the table, and as he passed me, I saw his glassy eyes—turned on by Charlee—I could see the flush on his cheeks and the suspicious bulge in his pants. I was sure I looked the same with a stupid dazed expression, face heated and half-hard, like a teenager with a crush and no idea what to do with it.

"Tortellini, anyone?" I said, my voice hoarse.

Charlee sat up and rearranged her hair, a faint pink blossoming on her face. Tonight *should* be interesting.

Dinner was surprisingly normal, despite my little clitoris question. After we ate, Shaen FaceTimed Liam and we all got a close-up view of baby Billie.

"How was it?" I asked Shaen.

"So much worse than I imagined," she said without sugar-coating it. "But I'd do it again in a heartbeat."

Billie started to cry, and I watched as Shaen opened her robe, latched Billie onto her breast, and turned back to the phone.

Jax shifted in his chair at the sound of the baby gulping.

"You're already so natural at being a mom," I told her, genuinely impressed.

"That's because I have Liam. He educated me on everything." She smiled at her best friend, who just shrugged it off.

"Motherhood becomes you," was all he said.

She beamed under his praise. I was struck by their obvious adoration for each other, and for a moment I wondered what their lives had looked like to create such a deep bond.

Growing up, my friend group had always been small. Now, the friends I stayed in touch with didn't even know each other. I was friends with them individually, which meant no group chat,

no girls' vacations. Other than Jax, I didn't share a connection with anyone like the one Liam and Shaen had.

It made me respect Liam even more. It spoke volumes about his loyalty, his kindness, and the way he showed up for people so wholeheartedly.

Guilt surged in my chest with my next heartbeat. I excused myself from the call and headed to the shower.

Jax knew I was attracted to Liam, and I'd seen the same pull in my husband. But we had an unspoken boundary. This was meant to strictly be physical. Emotions weren't a part of the deal.

I wasn't supposed to look forward to both Jax's dry responses in our group chat and Liam's teasing jokes. I wasn't supposed to notice what a solid and good man Liam was.

And I definitely shouldn't have been cognizant of the fact that he gave off serious daddy vibes—cooing to baby Billy, asking Shaen what size her clots were, and explaining the difference between colostrum and milk.

If I let my thoughts run unbidden, they'd spiral into fantasies of what a life with the three of us might look like. I reeled them back in before they became anything more than a quick flicker in the matrix and doused them in a cold dose of reality.

As I shampooed my hair, reality struck me square in the chest and lodged there, heavy and sour. I had to gulp it down as it manifested as nausea.

Between the two of us, Jax was definitely more relaxed. I didn't usually spend too much time in my head. But now, I couldn't shake the feeling that I was doing something wrong. *Being bad.* I'd always been the girl who mostly behaved. I had my share of fun, but I also made sure to get good grades, kept my curfew, worked every summer, and definitely didn't do anything scandalous—like sleep with two men at the same time.

One was my husband. The other, the hottie doctor turned friend turned roommate… who was literally down the hall.

"Fuck, what am I doing?"

Gone was the casual, open-minded Charlee who had told Jax that this would prove how strong our love was. The girl who stated she may be down for some DP was nowhere to be found. The girl who sucked dick with Liam who? She was most certainly not in the room with us anymore.

I slid down the shower wall with a sticky squelch of skin on tile that would definitely leave a mark on my ass, and folded my arms around my knees. I sat on the shower floor, panicking under the spray. The water ran cold way sooner than I was ready to leave the foggy cocoon of steam and stress I'd created behind the shower door.

Shivering, I finally turned it off. I wrapped myself in a towel, brushed my hair, and for the first time since getting married, I went to bed under the pretense of having a headache.

Jax offered to bring me tea, I told him no thanks and curled up under the covers with a heavy heart and no one to unpack it with—not Jax, not Liam, not anyone. Not without making everything messier.

I must've fallen asleep, because the next thing I knew, Liam was calling a soft good night from the door, and Jax was climbing into bed next to me.

"Everything okay?" he asked gently.

I nodded, eyes still closed, and let myself drift back to sleep without saying anything.

THE NEXT MORNING I was relieved to find that by the time I got up, both Liam and Jax had already left for work. My relief quickly turned into guilt, again. I let myself cry while I got dressed but I pulled it together by the time I sat down to do my makeup.

I knew I could call it quits on this little rendezvous anytime I wanted to—but I didn't want to steal the experience away from Jax. And if I was being honest with myself, I didn't want to stop for my own sake either.

I *wanted* to touch Liam. I wanted *him* to touch me. I wanted Jax to watch. To guide us. To tell us how. No, I didn't want to stop. Not even close.

And *that* was the crux of the problem gnawing away at me.

I was afraid of how much I liked it. Of the rhythm we'd already fallen into. Of how natural it felt. Not just physically… but in doing life as well. The fun we had embarked on had started to feel more real for me and I was as afraid of letting it go as I was of holding on.

What the hell did I do with *that*?

When I arrived at work, it was mayhem. A female prisoner was in labor, which meant we had police in the halls and extra security protocols to follow. Three emergency C-sections had already been rushed to the OR, and we had sixteen other laboring moms on the unit.

Immediately, every bit of chaos in my mind vanished. I no longer felt like crying. I wasn't confused. There wasn't an ounce of guilt left.

All I could think about was doing my job—and doing it well.

It was a relief, honestly, the way my brain could just switch into nurse mode. There was no space for feelings or uncertainty when I was in this environment. Just focus. Just instinct. Just babies who needed my help coming into this world.

Halfway through my twelve-hour shift, I finally got a break. I headed to the lounge to eat the lunch Jax had packed for me.

I unzipped my bag to find a buttery croissant, a toasted turkey sandwich, a side salad, a chocolate bar, and a can of lemonade.

And a note that said:

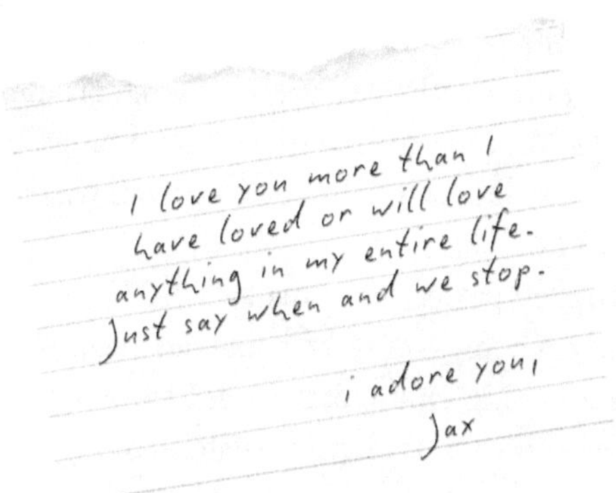


My man knew me so well.

A smile pulled at my lips as I reread his words, a warm calm settling in my chest. Just that, knowing he saw me, knew me, was thinking about me—soothed the turmoil I hadn't realized I was still carrying.

I felt my freak out start to fade.

When Liam walked into the break room for a coffee, I let my heart skip a beat. I didn't feel guilty about it anymore. I even let myself enjoy the warmth of his hand brushing across my shoulders as he passed me and said hi.

"You okay?" he asked, and I nodded.

Because suddenly—I really was.

LATER THAT NIGHT, after my shift, I said good night to Liam, who was staying in the hospital, and headed home to my husband.

Jax had run me a bath. He gave me a long, grounding massage. Then, after making me come—twice—he braided my hair while we watched one of those trashy reality shows we only watched to make fun of.

Everything felt perfectly normal.

It was only when Liam texted *miss you two* in the group chat, followed by a kissing emoji, that I was reminded of the hot man that we were both very obviously crushing on.

"Just say when," Jax whispered in my ear as I hesitated, fingers hovering over my keyboard, unsure of what to text back.

"What do you want?"

"I want what you want. Always." He smoothed my hair off my face, and grasped my hands between his.

"I just had a minor freak out. I think my period's coming," I admitted. As a labor and delivery nurse, you'd think I'd be on top of my own cycle, but I couldn't be bothered to track it. It just came when it wanted to—sometimes I was prepared, sometimes I had to scramble for a tampon. It never really phased me enough to mark it in my calendar so I'd know exactly what day it was due next.

"Baby, a minor hormonal freak out is one thing. Regret or anything more than that is something else." Jax peered up at me from where he lay, his chest bare, concern clear in his eyes.

"I love you," he said softly. "And I'll admit, watching you with him is so fucking hot." I could hear how hot it was for him in the rasp in his voice. "It's like watching a gift I've always had, now being unwrapped in a new way. It makes me love you even more."

He propped himself up on one elbow as he said it. I'd never thought of it like that, and I told him so.

"Yeah, this only makes me feel closer to you." He stroked his finger over my cheek.

"But you also like it?" I asked.

He laughed. "I like it. He's hot. It's good." His voice softened as he leaned forward to kiss my forehead. "But it's not worth it if it will make you get all up in your head. I don't like seeing you like that, sweetheart."

Tears pricked my eyes. *Yup, my period was definitely coming.*

"I'm okay, I swear. It just felt like... a lot," I admitted. "I guess my brain realized he's not just some random guy we hooked up with. He lives here. He's my friend. He's *our* friend. And he's so nice. And smart. And sexy. And saying that out loud makes me feel... weird."

Jax sighed and pulled me against his chest.

"Do you think that'll be a problem?" he asked gently.

"Never," I said without hesitation.

"Then he's sexy and smart. So are you. Nothing wrong with that in my book." He shrugged like it was obvious.

"And nice," I added.

"So fucking nice," Jax grumbled. I burst out laughing. Still smiling I picked up my phone and texted back a reply.

*We miss you too.*

A few seconds later, Liam hearted the message.

I fell asleep in my husband's arms.

Before Charlee and Jax, the winter would've dragged on and on. But with the distraction of them in my life—and my bed—paired with busy shifts and nonstop studying, January, February, and March flew by, bringing the welcome thaw of April in what felt like the blink of an eye.

Somehow, Billie was now three months old and had started cooing and smiling, which made me melt every time I saw her. Shaen called me at least three times a day with baby questions or sent photos of poop to ask if it looked normal. I had to remind her that while I was a doctor, I was not, in fact, a pediatrician. Her usual anxiety had doubled during pregnancy, but it had practically tripled postpartum. I found myself reassuring her that her baby was perfectly fine multiple times a week.

I'd spent the last three months on the gynecologic oncology service. I knew how important it was to learn the basics of radiation and chemotherapy, to perform advanced laparotomies, to get really good at doing colposcopies, and perfect my surgical skills before graduation—but it wasn't where my heart was. I was excited to get back to L&D.

Residents were allowed an elective month, which had to be

approved by the program director, and of course, I had chosen L&D. I'd also be spending the final two months before graduation on a night float rotation where I'd continue the responsibilities of chief resident. Which overall included managing the L&D patients, and the emergency gynecological department, as well as teaching the junior residents. I was close to the finish line, which couldn't come soon enough—but I was physically and emotionally depleted.

At this point I could recite every flashcard by heart, but Charlee still studied with me every chance we got. I smiled to myself as I thought of her while scrubbing in for a C-section. We had a set of triplets coming, so the OR was packed with nurses, an anesthesiologist, neonatologists from the NICU, and someone from peds.

"Why you smiling, Hennessy?" I heard from behind me. Jason Shaw was onto me. He could tell I had a little extra pep in my step lately, even though I was falling off my face at the end of every shift. He kept trying to figure out why. At this point, he was convinced I was getting laid—but he clearly hadn't figured out *who* it was.

He wasn't wrong about the getting laid part; that was for sure.

I felt myself begin to harden in my scrubs at the memory of Jax pulling me out of Charlee while she was above me, reverse cowgirl. He sucked me into his throat, swallowing me down, pulling a groan from deep in my chest. Then he'd slid me back into his wife and gone down on her while I fucked her.

Goddamn.

The vision had me so hard I had to recite the different kinds of yeast infections to make it go away.

"Candidiasis, trichomoniasis, cryptosporidiosis," I murmured to myself as I walked into the OR, hands held up in front of me, ready to be gowned and gloved.

"ARE ALL THE BABIES OKAY?"

When our schedules aligned, Charlee and I had taken to eating lunch together in a rarely used supply closet. It mainly housed broken machines waiting for repair and some shelves stocked with boxes of catheters, sterile bandages, and sharps containers. We'd rearranged the space to create a small nook—private and quiet. The break room was always busy, and I was paranoid someone would notice us being a little too familiar. It wasn't against the rules but it would certainly cause unnecessary drama. But more than that, I just wanted these stolen moments with her. They came way too infrequently for my liking.

"All perfect. Tiny, but perfect," I told her, chewing a mouthful of pepperoni fried rice.

"That's amazing." She beamed, and I was struck, yet again, by how incredible she was. She'd probably attended close to a thousand births by now and still she was excited for each one. New life gave her joy.

I watched as she took a sip of her seltzer, and the overwhelming desire to kiss her punched through me. At this point, we'd shared so much intimacy that it almost felt cruel of Jax to keep kissing off-limits. I wanted her mouth on mine so badly sometimes I felt like asking for an exception. Just once. But I didn't want to disrespect the trust between Jax and me. The friendship we'd built mattered to me. So I never said a word.

I reached into my bag to see what else Jax had packed and my fingers closed around a folded piece of paper.

"No fucking way."

Charlee looked up, a bit of sauce smeared at the corner of her mouth. I reached out with a napkin and wiped it away.

"Thanks." She sounded breathless. I let myself hope it was

because of me. That I made her flustered. That being this close to me did something to her body, the same way she affected mine.

I looked down at the note in my hand, my heart flipping in my chest at the sight of Jax's rounded handwriting.

"Have a good day." I sounded out the simple words out loud. It meant nothing, absolutely nothing. But to me it was everything.

"You got a note?" Charlee's eyes widened, surprise bloomed on her face.

"I finally got a note." I could barely hide my excitement as I carefully folded it, and slid it into the front zipper pocket of my lunch bag. Jax had written me a note. Glee filled my veins. Quiet, reserved, yet-bossy-in-bed Jax, had taken the time to write something just for me. I liked it way more than I had any right to. I liked it way more than I should have, especially sitting next to his wife.

"What does your note say?" I finally asked, desperate to distract myself from my growing crush. Not that talking to Charlee would help me squash those feelings because she too was the object of my affection and desire. She never let me see her notes. She would just giggle, blush, and hide them but today she surprised me by sliding closer until our knees touched and she turned to show me her note.

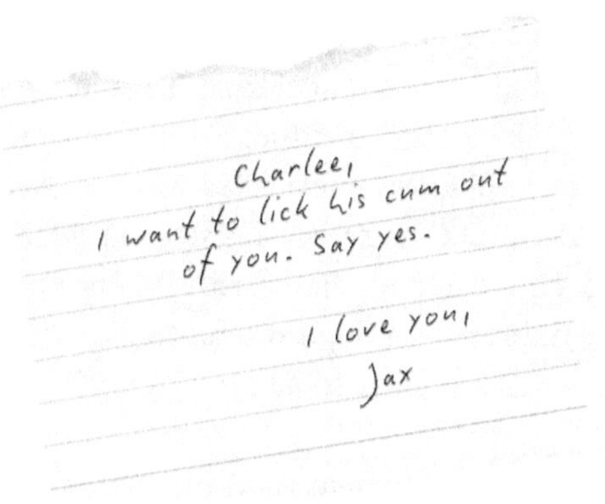


Holy fuck. *Did I just moan? Jesus. Get it together.*

For the second time today, my dick was threatening to split the seam of my scrub pants.

"Are all of his notes this graphic?" I managed, my voice

hoarse.

She shrugged. "Often enough."

"Shit." I was finally out of words.

She laughed and began putting the note back in her bag, but I caught her hand between mine.

"I need to make you come." It was my turn to sound breathless. My voice sounded wrecked.

"Here?" Her pupils dilated, and she shifted slightly.

"Ask him if it's okay." I reached behind me and locked the door. The click echoed in the small space, and she startled. Then as if in slow motion she reached for her phone.

It only rang twice before he picked up.

I could hear Jax's deep voice, low and steady, and it sent sparks of desire for him down my spine. I had known a lot of good men in my life up until this point and he was a good man. He loved his wife so much that it made me believe a love like theirs might exist for me too. He was reliable and dependable. Thoughtful in quiet, unexpected ways. He kept my favorite foods stocked in the house. He insisted on washing my sheets every week. Laminated my flashcards. He once heard me telling Shaen that I didn't have a single day off to go help Remi fix something with her dog kennels so he drove up on his next day off to repair it.

He was everything I could want in a friend—and everything I'd imagined in an ideal partner. But he wasn't mine. Not really.

I was shaken from my daydream of the husband I could never have when I heard Charlee whisper, "Can Liam make me come?" I heard Jax say something back and Charlee glanced at me.

"He wants to talk to you." She bit her lip and I had to look away so as to resist the urge to follow her teeth with mine. She handed me the phone.

"Hey."

"Last night wasn't enough for you to take the edge off?" Jax chuckled.

Relief swept through me. He wasn't saying no.

"I saw your note." My voice was husky in response.

He was silent for a second and then said, "Yours or hers?"

"Both."

He cleared his throat at what could only be considered some sort of a confession on my part.

"No one will find you?"

"We're locked in a supply closet. No one will be looking for us for at least ten more minutes."

"I want you to video it for me."

I nodded even though he couldn't see me.

"And Liam." He almost sounded sad.

"Yeah?"

"Promise me, no kissing."

"I promise." The meaning of the moment hung in the pause of our silence until he grunted, "have fun" and told us he had to get back to work.

"I love you," Charlee whispered before ending the call.

We sat there, quiet, the only light in the room came from the temporary glow of her phone screen. I reached for her as the darkness closed in around us.

"Do you want to let him…" I gestured vaguely at the note she had hidden away.

"Eat you from me?" Her voice was almost a purr, and I bit back a moan.

"Y-yes." *Look at me, big strong Liam, Dr. Hennessy. Stuttering like a damn teenager.*

She slid closer until she was practically in my lap. Her breath tickled my cheek.

"If you both want it so bad, then I want it too," she whispered.

Visions of Jax lapping up my warm cum from her pussy flooded my mind, and my erection turned painful. I fumbled with my phone, setting up the camera, then hit record.

"Do you want to come?" I asked, tugging the bow of her scrub pants loose and easing them down.

"So bad."

"Fuck me," I breathed when I found her soaked.

I brought my fingers to my mouth, tasted her essence, then slid them back down and circled her clit.

She gasped.

"You need to be quiet. Be a good girl. Don't make a sound," I told her.

She rocked her hips in response.

I slipped two fingers inside her, curling them in a come-hither motion, hitting her G-spot. Her head dropped back. One hand flew up to cover her mouth, stifling the cry building up in her throat.

Holy shit, she was so hot.

Her breath came in little pants around her hand, her hair cascading down her back, her hips grinding on my fingers as I fucked her deep, my thumb moved erratically over her clit. The slick sound of her arousal filled the small room, and I had to fight every instinct in my body not to pull my pants down and thrust inside her.

I leaned in and rested my forehead against hers. Her warm pants warmed my face. I pulled away before I was tempted to kiss her.

"Come baby. Come," I urged her in a whisper.

She started moving faster, at this point she was fucking herself on my fingers. Her body was shaking with the effort.

"Mmph." Her hand muffled the sound, and then her entire body went rigid. I felt her gush around me, soaking my palm.

"So good?" I asked, at a loss for words.

"So good." She exhaled, rising up slowly, easing my fingers out. I looked down. She was flushed and tight. I already missed the feel of her.

"More tonight," she promised.

I licked her off my fingers again. Her eyes gleamed in the dark.

"Delicious."

She looked like she wanted to say something but didn't. Instead, she reached out and ran a hand down my cheek, resting it briefly over my lips.

"Bye, Liam," she whispered.

"Charlee."

I watched her unlock the door and disappear, the door making a soft whooshing sound as it closed behind her.

That's when I remembered the recording. I reached over and ended it. Without watching it, I sent the video to Jax. Not in the group chat—directly to him.

It was the first text I'd ever sent him.

The video sat there, mocking me, until I deleted it from my phone and stood to return to my shift.

F *uck, I'm so hard I'm aching in my jeans.* I shifted in my seat in the forklift that I'd commandeered to watch the video Liam sent me. I was supposed to be overseeing a delivery of some very expensive pavers right now, and instead, I was here reminding myself that jerking off in public—even if hidden in a forklift—was most definitely frowned upon.

The room was dark, but his camera had brightened it just enough that I could see my wife pleasuring herself on his fingers. *Him. Liam. My friend.* But sometimes, when my mind dared to disobey me, he felt like more than that—but I couldn't go there. I'd been avoiding that conversation in my mind for weeks.

I didn't know what compelled me to write him a note this morning, but something about last night had pushed me to do it. Maybe it was way he'd gasped Charlee's name against my mouth, or the way he had watched me fuck her as she lay sprawled across him, my hand gripping his knee. Or maybe it was how he'd slept next to Charlee, his arm flung across her body to hold my hand.

My heart leapt to my throat at the thought of my hand curling around his, rubbing my thumb against his palm as I drifted off to

sleep. The catch in his voice told me that my note had meant something to him, and I worried I'd opened a door that couldn't be closed. A door that would have to be closed in two months' time.

That door was why I wasn't surprised to find that not only was I not jealous at the thought of my wife coming without me there, but I actually found that I was frantically anticipating the video. When it finally dinged on my phone, my whole system seized up, and I immediately found somewhere halfway private to watch it.

I pressed play again, but this time I watched Liam. I was enthralled by the way his body was primed to take her, the way his fingers disappeared into her scrubs. I couldn't see what he was doing, but I could *hear* it. At one point, I thought he'd ignore me and kiss her, but he pulled away, a pained look of desire clear on his face.

I almost felt guilty, but I couldn't let go of this need to have one part of Charlee be wholly mine. One day, soon, he'd leave, and I wanted there to be something left of her that he'd never touched. Something for us to build back off of when we went from three to two. From *we* to just *us*.

I shook my head to release the intensity of my thoughts and closed out of the video. What did I even text back? *Thank you?* That felt like an odd thing to say to a man who had just made your wife orgasm. So instead, I said nothing and waited until my body calmed down before climbing out of the forklift to go find the delivery guy, who was probably already waiting on a signature.

Liam was on day shift in April and would then switch to night shift for all of May and June until graduation, so he and Charlee were already home when I got back.

"We made dinner, baby!" Charlee called as she came over to take my lunch bag and laptop.

"'Made' is a bit of an exaggeration," Liam added, poking his head out from the kitchen.

Charlee laughed and corrected herself. "I ordered burgers and washed the lettuce while Liam chopped up a salad."

I chuckled as I pulled her toward me and placed a kiss on the top of her head. "How was everyone's day?" I rubbed the back of my neck as the exhaustion of my day hit me. The wrong pavers had been delivered which was going to push everything off and we were already a week behind due to bad weather last week.

"The usual. Hectic, with an obscenely packed schedule—but everyone stayed alive this shift, so that's a win." Liam squirted a generous amount of ketchup on his plate and swatted Charlee's hand away when she tried to dip her fries into it.

"Get your own ketchup, girl." He playfully stole one of her fries and then looked at me. "Control your woman, Berman." He laughed and took a bite of his burger.

"She's your problem too, Hennessy."

The words slipped out of my mouth before I could rein them in. Liam looked up quickly, and our eyes met. I walked away under the pretense of grabbing napkins, but really, I just needed to gather myself.

When I came back, no one mentioned what I'd just said, and no one mentioned the video either. Between the good food and a beer, I finally found myself starting to relax until Liam announced he planned to go look at apartments tomorrow after his shift and asked if we wanted to come with him to see baby Billie.

"Are you kidding me? Of course we want to come see the baby," Charlee said, already in planning mode as they began to discuss whose car to take and what time we'd leave.

I knew it was happening soon, and honestly, I didn't want to think about it. But I thought about it all the damn time. Charlee and I would be fine—I knew that. It wasn't just the end of our sexual arrangement, though I'd definitely miss that. It was more than that. I'd gotten used to having Liam around.

I liked knowing that sometimes he was here with Charlee when I had a late night at work. I enjoyed playing a video game with him or shooting the shit about sports. It had become second nature for me to buy his favorite foods just like I did for Charlee. If I was being honest with myself, I hadn't just gotten used to having him around—I *liked* having him around.

The apartment would feel quieter without his sarcastic jokes and his deep laugh. I'd miss seeing his stethoscope on the counter and packing his lunch in the morning. We'd both have to get used to it being just the two of us again.

"Jax?"

I was shaken from my thoughts.

"Huh? Sorry, I drifted off there."

"I'm off tomorrow, and Liam gets off at five, so if we leave right away we can see three apartments by seven, and then stop at Shaen and Remi's for dinner." Charlee began to clean up the table.

"Sounds good to me." I forced a smile, but didn't relish the idea of helping Liam find the apartment where he'd move on from us in. Where he'd find a beautiful wife and start the life he so clearly deserved—leaving the two of us behind as a beautiful memory.

"I went on the pill," Charlee announced as I pulled off my shirt, and dropped it on the bathroom floor, getting ready for a much-needed shower.

"Something wrong with condoms?" We had always used condoms and never had an oops moment.

"I'll just be on it till Liam moves out," she explained. "I figure if you both want to finish in me, I need a better form of birth control."

The note I'd written her flashed in my mind, and I felt myself start to harden.

"Mmm," I grunted my agreement.

"I'll go back off it in June." She sounded wistful. She lingered in front of the mirror, her fingers faltering as she undid the braid her hair was in, her mind obviously wandering to him leaving.

"It'll be weird not having him around." I turned on the water and got in so she wouldn't see my face and pick up on how I was *really* feeling.

"Yeah, you'll have to fuck me overtime to make up for him not being here anymore to do it." Her tone was teasing, but it made my heart jump uncomfortably.

I poked my head out from behind the shower door. "That's never been a problem for me," I all but growled.

She winked and popped her retainers in as she left the bathroom.

After my shower, I pulled on plaid PJ pants and found Charlee and Liam in the living room. She sat on the couch, scrolling on her phone. Liam lay on the couch with his head in her lap, holding a study guide in front of his face. Charlee was running her fingers through his hair, absentmindedly.

At one point she laughed, showed him a meme, and then jokingly slapped his cheek when he said it wasn't funny.

Was it crazy to think something like this could work more long-term?

I had no idea how. I didn't even know if I really wanted it. But I couldn't say the thought hadn't crossed my mind.

"Oh hey." Liam glanced over at me. "Good shower?"

I nodded and walked across the room. The rug was thick and soft under my feet.

"I need a break." I dropped into the oversized chair across from them.

Charlee looked startled. Liam sat up, concern clear on his face.

"Is something wrong?"

"I mean a vacation. A break from work—not a break from *this.*"

I'd picked the wrong word, and I almost laughed at the visible relief on their faces.

"What the fuck, Jax?" Charlee threw a potato chip at me.

"Okay, simmer down." Liam grinned as he moved the bag of potato chips out of her reach.

I plucked the chip off my chest and ate it. "Okay, hear me out. I checked your schedules. At the end of April, Liam has a rare three days off before he starts the night shift. I have tons of vacation days saved. Charlee, you're off the same days because of your back-to-back shifts at the start of the week. I found really cheap red-eye tickets from Westchester to Puerto Rico. I figure we can eat dinner at Shaen and Remi's and then head straight to Westchester airport. What do you think?"

"You want me to come on your family vacation?" Liam almost sounded confused.

Charlee pushed him with her foot. "Duh."

She said it so nonchalantly that my thoughts from earlier returned. *He fits in so effortlessly.*

*He never took anything from our relationship—he only enhanced it.*

Could I ever see us actually navigating a real relationship? God help me, maybe.

For what felt like the hundredth time this week, I wondered if he'd even consider it. I was almost getting sick of my brain repetitively bothering me with these thoughts.

"I have so much studying to do, but fuck it. I haven't been on a vacation in literally years." Liam was in. Charlee didn't need any convincing.

"We won't know anyone there, so we can all just be together."

"I'm not fucking you in public, Charlee," Liam joked.

"Hilarious." She rolled her eyes. "No, but we can definitely all make out on the beach."

She was practically bouncing with excitement. "I'm gonna go make sure I have enough bathing suits. Buy the tickets, Jax."

She bounded out of the room and I took out my phone to pull up the flights.

"You sure you want me to come? I know you two haven't been away alone in a long time." Liam's voice was quiet.

I peered over my phone at Liam and frowned. "Do you want to come with us?" I volleyed back at him.

"A weekend away from the hospital, on the beach with two of my favorite people? Obviously I do. But I don't want to interfere. I worry I've done enough of that already."

I didn't respond with words. Instead I just bought the tickets and texted the flight details into the group chat. Then I leaned over and kissed him.

"You haven't interfered at all," I murmured against his lips. *You've only made everything better.*

"Promise?"

I nodded.

"Okay." He kissed me back.

JAX:

Is everyone fully packed?

CHARLEE:

I just need to put my makeup bag in but
otherwise I'm good to go

LIAM:

Omg ur such an airport dad. Are u gonna hold
my ID for me, Jaxon?

JAX:

Is that your way of saying you're not packed,
Liam?

LIAM:

By the time we leave tonight - I will be

CHARLEE:

Can you pick up my next pack of birth control
babe? I'm skipping the period week so I need to
refill early.

LIAM:

Which one of us are u asking?

JAX:

I'll do it. You're elbow deep in a vagina right now

LIAM:

Not the vagina I want to be in either

CHARLEE:

Did you just make a joke, Jax?

JAX:

(Middle finger emoji) don't forget to download a movie, we're flying cheap- there are no screens on our flight. And make sure to pack light, I think we only have 35 lbs each

LIAM:

Honestly don't bring clothes- I plan on having u both naked for most of the trip

CHARLEE:

One of the moms from earlier just delivered a stillborn and this pill is making me so emotional- so I'm a mess

JAX:

I'm sorry, love

LIAM:

Aw honey. Meet me in the supply closet in 10, I'll kiss it better

JAX:

Hey

LIAM:

(Middle finger emoji, suspicious face emoji, crying emoji, kissing emoji)

CHARLEE:

Can't, going into another delivery. I'll see you both tonight. (Alcoholic drink emoji, palm tree emoji)

As promised, I was fully packed by the time Jax pulled his truck up to the front of our apartment building. I took both mine and Charlee's suitcases and made sure all of the lights in the apartment were off before closing the door behind us and locking up.

"You have everything?" Jax met my eyes in the rearview mirror. I was sitting in the back seat, since I had insisted Charlee sit up front.

"Yes, babe, stop worrying." It slipped out. "Sorry I—" A flash of panic cooled my sternum. The word felt too intimate—but also too natural to regret.

"I like it," Charlee interrupted, smoothing right over my anxiety. "Call him that again later."

She didn't say anything else, but for the rest of the drive, the air between us was thick with the promise of what *later* would bring.

Shaen had cooked up a storm, of course. She'd learned the behavior from my mother. The scent of garlic and roasted chicken had washed over me the moment we walked in. During dinner, somehow Jax ended up holding Billie, and it did something to me to see him cooing to the baby and then eventually rocking her to sleep. It hit me in the chest—how unfair it was that it felt like I might never get to do this. Not like that. Not with someone who looked at me the way Charlee looked at him.

"He's a natural," Remi declared. "Not to be intrusive but do you two want kids?"

Charlee sighed. "We do, but I dunno when. Not yet. I want to pay off my student loans first—and maybe switch to a less hectic hospital."

That was the first I'd heard of this. "But you love NYU."

"I do," she agreed. "But if I'm going to be taking care of a baby, I'd rather work in less of a fast-paced environment. Somewhere I can maybe take fewer shifts so I can be home more." She shrugged. "It's a long-term plan. I haven't even discussed it with Jax yet, but I know he'd love to get away from the city."

"Move here," Shaen piped up.

"Yes. Move here." I loved that idea. "I can get you a job in my new practice."

The night I'd come up here with Charlee and Jax to choose an apartment, I'd been officially offered a job at a local practice. No twenty-four hour shifts. While I'd still have nights on call, the day office hours were a very manageable nine to five.

"What about your job, Jax?" Remi asked.

"My uncle's been wanting to branch out to more residential areas anyway, so I'm sure he'd be cool with it. Or I'd just drive into the city every day. I'll do whatever makes you happy." He said it with his usual mellow ease.

I pretended that when he said *you*, he was also referring to me—not just his wife. I liked to fantasize about a life where we bought an extra-large bed and furnished my new apartment together. Where we christened every surface. Had my family over. Built a life. Built a family. I knew it wasn't in the cards for us. That Charlee and Jax would move on to the rest of their life without me once I moved out. But sometimes, I let myself indulge in the thought of a future with them. It made me feel happy and peaceful—even if it wasn't real. The fantasy was dangerous, too tender, too tempting—but it was mine.

"I made that viral Dubai chocolate," Shaen told me. "I'm gonna go change Billie, but it's in the garage fridge if you want to get it." She turned to Charlee. "Oh, and those clothes I told you about are in a blue bag in the garage. Throw them in your suitcase real quick."

Apparently when Shaen found out about our trip, she'd gone through her closet and put aside some clothes for Charlee that didn't fit her freshly postpartum body just yet.

"Thanks, Shay Shay." Charlee stood to follow me to the garage.

"Aww that's cute, that's Liam's nickname for me," Shaen said sweetly as she gently took Billie from Jax. He went outside with Remi to check out a 1965 Ford Mustang he'd bought at an auction to rebuild.

I took the plate from the fridge. "Oh shit, this looks good. Here—taste this."

I turned to Charlee and held out the delicate dessert. The pistachio cream dripped onto my thumb. She bit into the corner and closed her eyes as she chewed.

"Damn that is good." I took a bite myself, letting the flavors of chocolate and pistachio flood my tastebuds.

"You have a little something…" I wiped a smear of chocolate off the corner of her mouth, and Charlee caught my finger between her lips. I grunted as she swirled her tongue around the tip.

"Later, I'm…" I started, but then felt my heart fall out through the bottom of my feet when I heard Shaen's, "what the actual fuck," from behind me. I spun around and found my best friend gaping at me, shock written all over her face.

"Shaen, I can explain." My heart thundered in my ears,

whooshing as my panic rose. I couldn't move. Couldn't breathe. Everything I had kept secret for so long was now imploding in front of me.

"Get the fuck away from him." She immediately took my side —and I loved her for it—but she had it all wrong.

"Do you have no shame? Your husband is right outside. And you…" She spun to look at me, disgust clear in her eyes, her voice thick with contempt. "You are better than this, Liam Hennessy. You really are. How could you?"

Was she crying? God, I needed to shut this down fast.

"Shaen, stop." I stepped closer to her, and she backed away.

"No." She held up her hand. "I love you; I'll always love you. But right now, I don't respect you. I need a minute to process."

"You didn't even see anything," I defended myself.

"She was sucking on your finger. Giving you a *look*."

The disdain in her voice had my stomach churning.

"Okay maybe you saw something," I acquiesced. "But I swear —it's not what you think."

Shaen laughed in my face. "Don't act like I'm stupid, Liam."

"He's not. Just let him explain," Charlee finally piped up.

"Do not speak to me." Shaen whirled on her like she was filth. "And to think I liked you when you're just a slut."

"Don't talk to her like that. She doesn't deserve it." I loved Shaen but I wouldn't let her talk to my… talk to Charlee like that.

Shaen glared at me but stayed silent.

"Jax knows." *This was not how I wanted her to find out but the universe had forced my hand.*

"Knows what? That his wife is cheating on him?"

"No, Shaen. Charlee is not cheating on him." The chocolate was already melting in my hand. I felt it oozing between my fingers.

"So he lets you guys…" She gestured vaguely in our general

direction because she lacked a better word to describe what she presumed was going on between us.

Charlee nodded, a flush rising on her cheeks. I wanted to gather her in my arms and hold her—but I stayed put.

"I don't understand."

I opened my mouth to explain, but then Billie's cries suddenly came through the baby monitor in Shaen's hand. She turned away abruptly and stalked off without another word.

"Fuck." I set the remains of the chocolate back on the plate.

"I'm sorry—I shouldn't have done that," Charlee whispered, eyes glassy.

"Baby, no. It's not your fault." I reached for her hand, but thought better of it.

"I mean, it is. I know you didn't want anyone to know, and now I've put you in a difficult position."

"I'm gonna go talk to her. Tell Jax I'll be ready in ten." I squeezed her shoulder and turned to follow Shaen.

I found my very irate best friend in the nursery, sitting in a rocking chair, breastfeeding Billie. She opened her mouth, but I cut her off.

"Not a word out of you. I'm going to speak and you're going to listen."

"Fine," she muttered.

"I'm..." My heart was racing and my hands started to get clammy. I hadn't imagined the moment I'd tell her that I'm bi looking anything like this—her furious at me, the sound of a baby suckling in the background—yet here we were.

"I'm bi, Shaen. So is Jax. And the three of us have kind of been..." I tripped over my words. "Charlee's not cheating on Jax. She's a good person. So is he. I..."

My mouth was so dry I couldn't even finish. She handed me her water bottle wordlessly, and I took a long gulp.

We stared at each other for a second. Neither of us said anything.

"Please say something," I whispered.

Shaen switched Billie to the left side, and I averted my eyes as she tucked her other breast back into her bra.

"You're bi?" She too was whispering but her words rang out like a shout in my chest.

I nodded, and to my horror, I felt my eyes fill. Tears stung at the corners and threatened to fall. Her bottom lip trembled as she opened her arms. Relief washed over me so fast it almost knocked the wind out of me. I dropped to my knees next to her and let her pull me in close, careful not to squish the baby between us. Her chin rested against the side of my head. I caught a drift of the warm smell of Billie mixed with the scent of Shaen's shampoo and the faint trace of breast milk. I didn't even try to hold the tears back anymore. They broke free as I turned so my head was on her shoulder, and they rolled down my cheeks.

I'd finally let my ten-year-old secret into her light, and while I felt as though a heavy weight had been lifted off me, I also grieved for the younger version of myself—the scared twenty-year-old who had decided to keep the secret from her in the first place.

Billie kicked at my chest and let out a squeaky grunt. I leaned back and gave a watery laugh.

"How long have you known?"

"Since college."

"Why didn't you tell me?" She looked genuinely hurt.

"It's complicated. I wanted to tell you, but for a long time… I wouldn't even acknowledge it myself."

Usually, I'd make a joke in heavy moments like this. Pretend it wasn't a big deal. But I couldn't joke this away.

*It was a big deal.*

"Liam." Shaen sniffed. "I'm sorry. You know I accept you and love you no matter what."

I nodded. I knew she meant she was sorry for how she'd

reacted earlier, for how she spoke to Charlee—but also for the ten years that I felt like I had to keep this secret.

"I'm sorry for not telling you." I wiped my eyes with the sleeve of my hoodie.

She gently shifted Billie to her shoulder and began to burp her. "So like… are they your boyfriend and girlfriend?"

"I really like them, Shaen." My voice cracked and the need to cry resurfaced. "But it's not like that. They're happily married. And we all agreed at the start that this was just… fun. An exploration kind of thing."

She gave a little "hmph," her classic I-don't-believe-you noise.

"They should be so lucky to have you as their boyfriend."

I laughed through my tears at her immediate defense of me. "Thanks, babe."

She looked at me and squeezed my hand. "Don't get your heart broken. I couldn't bear to see you like that."

That knocked the breath out of me more than anything else had tonight.

"I won't." I forced a grin. "It's just fun."

I winked, trying to lighten the moment. "A lot of fun."

"Okay ew." She giggled.

I laughed with her, but in the pit of my stomach, something coiled tight.

In two months, I'd move out. Life would go on. They'd be fine. I was the one who'd be left wondering if any of this had meant more than just fun because my heart would be broken and for what? But it was what we had all agreed to and therefore I just had to brace myself for the inevitable. Because this had always been temporary. But my growing feelings for them? That part never felt like it had an expiration date.

We got some weird looks from the airport personnel as we checked in together, but other than that, our travel went smoothly. We landed in San Juan about four hours after takeoff, at three a.m., and finally checked into our room at four. Check-in took longer than expected because the woman behind the counter kept insisting that we needed two beds but finally, Jax told her, "*Nosotros necesitamos una cama,*" in broken Spanish, and she laughed, "*Oh, señor, está muy enamorado.*"

"*Sí, sí,*" Jax replied, grateful to finally get our room keys.

We all collapsed into the one king bed.

After sleeping for six hours, we ordered room service for breakfast and then took a shower before getting into our bathing suits.

"Damn, sexy." Liam slapped my ass in appreciation of the black bikini that I wore that crisscrossed across my waist and ribs.

"You're looking pretty hot yourself." I ran fingers down his abs. His hand caught my wrist before I could cup his package.

"Not now, sweetheart. First sun, then sex."

I pretended to pout.

"Is everything squared away with Shaen?" I packed up my beach bag with sunglasses, a book, and snacks.

"Well, I told her that I'm bi."

"Was that hard?"

"I feel relieved that she knows." Liam slid his feet into his flip-flops and sat on the bed to wait for Jax to get out of the shower.

"And what about us? Does she still think I'm a slut?" The word burned on my tongue. I didn't blame Shaen for a second, for saying it, but I'd be lying if I said it hadn't burrowed its way under my skin. It lingered, an echo that made me question whether the world would always see me as less than for living outside societies rules.

"I'm sorry she said that. You know that's not true." Liam pulled me toward him until I was standing between his legs, his knees holding me close.

"She wanted to know if you were my girlfriend, but I told her we're just having fun."

I nodded. Being someone's girlfriend while also being someone's wife wouldn't work, would it? Then I reminded myself—he was moving out. In fact, I had helped him choose his next apartment, the one with the beautiful kitchen and huge bathtub that I'd fallen in love with.

"You'll have to use it when you come to visit," Liam had told me.

I'd wanted to ask if he'd get in with me, but I knew that wasn't possible, so I just nodded and said something about bath oils.

Jax walked across the room butt naked, and Liam gave a short whistle.

"Nah, don't put that on," he protested as Jax pulled on his bathing suit.

Jax looked over at us and winked. "Who's ready to get wasted and tan?"

He didn't have to ask us twice.

I was roasting in the sun and had never felt better—especially after a piña colada, two shots of chichaito, and a Puerto Rican soda called Good-O Kola with rum in it.

"Should we get some food?" Jax asked from behind me. He was sitting in a lounge chair on the beach, my back pressed to his chest. Liam sat sideways in front of me, sunglasses on, face turned up toward the sun. His freckles were already more pronounced.

"I could eat."

"I have something you can eat," Jax said without missing a beat.

I laughed as Liam looked over at him. Drunk Jax had entered the chat.

"I bet you do." Liam leaned forward, his chest brushing mine, and gave Jax a kiss.

I began to turn to join them, but my blood ran cold when a man standing about a foot away—with his modestly dressed wife—hurled a slur at Jax and Liam. At first I thought I must've misheard him, because who in the twenty-first century would say something like that out loud? But then Liam said, "What the fuck did you say?" and the man repeated it, really dragging out the f and the g in his thick, southern accent.

I pointed to the cross hanging around the woman's neck.

"Doesn't your religion tell you not to talk to people like that?"

The man laughed. "My religion tells me that people like you are an abomination and a sin."

"Well, your religion isn't our religion. So you can live whatever homophobic life you'd like, but you don't have to shove it down people's throats," Liam retorted.

"I'm not the one kissing a man in broad daylight. So who is shoving what down someone's throat."

"I'll be shoving something down Liam's throat later," Jax murmured, making me laugh through my discomfort and anger.

"Miss, you should really choose better company to surround yourself with," the woman added, addressing me.

"It's not like it's catchy," I snapped, pushing my sunglasses up to sit on top of my head. "And I don't know why it bothers you so much. It's kind of weird how fixated all you Bible-thumpers are on what men do in the privacy of their bedroom."

"Well, it's a good thing Jesus died for your sins with you out here dressed like a whore," the man ignored what I said and insulted me instead.

"I didn't ask him to die for me, so like thanks but no thanks," I hurled back.

"Don't talk to my girlfriend like that," Liam growled, striding toward them. They backed up fast, kicking sand up with their shoes. Jax got up and followed, physically stopping Liam from doing anything he would regret once he wasn't so angry.

"Keep walking," Jax told them firmly. "Have a good day."

They finally left, scoffing as they went.

"Don't let them rile you up. They're nobody." Jax had his arm around Liam's shoulders and was leading him back to our beach chairs.

"They may be nobody, but their opinion is held by millions of people around the world." Liam sat back down next to me and downed the shot in front of him.

"Yeah, but who cares. It doesn't affect you. Let them be ignorant."

"It will affect me if it stops me from being able to just live my life," Liam grumbled, though his anger seemed to be fading.

"Girlfriend huh?" I peered up at him.

"Yeah, sorry… I was just trying to make a point." He was looking at Jax now, like he wasn't sure if he'd overstepped some invisible boundary.

"I liked it," Jax said, surprising us both, and then walked off to find our waiter to order food.

I lay back on the chair to continue tanning. Liam's hand found mine, curled around it, like he needed an anchor as much as I did. He gave me a small squeeze.

I closed my eyes and smiled up into the sun.

We stayed on the beach until the sun went down. The boys played volleyball while I finished an entire book—something my work schedule never let me do. We ate lunch, drank more, and swam in the ocean. The sunset was gorgeous, streaked across the sky in vibrant reds and golds and I said so as we walked back to our room to get ready for dinner.

"*You're* gorgeous," Jax told me, taking my hand.

"Thanks, babe."

"You are," Liam added, taking my other hand. We walked that way, connected, every step pulling at my heartstrings. My heart galloped in my chest at this make-believe moment that felt a little bit too real.

Jax made us each drink an entire water bottle before we changed.

"He's so bossy," Liam pretended to complain as he chugged his water. His cheeks were pink from the sun and his hair was a mess from the salty sea water.

"You like it." I winked at him. Liam chuckled as Jax raised an eyebrow at us.

After finishing my water, I slid into a light pink, flowy boho-style dress with thin straps and a high waist. As I reached for my thong Jax said, "Uh uh."

"What?"

"Don't put that on."

"This?" I held out my underwear. Liam snagged them from me and tucked the gauzy material in his pocket.

"Hey, if the wind blows the wrong way everyone's getting an eyeful," I protested.

"We'll make sure that doesn't happen," Jax promised.

*We'll.* That word startled me and then comforted me in the same breath. They had become a unit. In the way they cared for me physically, but also in the way one carried my suitcase, the other fetched my shoes for me after going through security. One made sure I had eaten enough at lunch; the other moved my phone into the shade so it wouldn't overheat. I had always enjoyed how Jax was so in tune with my needs, but now that he had a partner to do it with, it felt like a puzzle piece I hadn't even known existed had clicked into place.

"Fine, but if anyone else sees my pussy it's on you. I think two men seeing it is more than enough," I joked.

"Two is perfect," Jax corrected, taking my hand as we went to find the restaurant that we had made reservations at.

Jax requested a booth, instead of a table, so I could sit between them. It was as if the sun had stolen my appetite. I wasn't very hungry from the heat, but I ordered soup and a fruit platter. The boys had steak and potatoes and of course we ordered more drinks.

Halfway through my soup, I felt hands sliding up my thighs under the table. I startled and clenched my legs shut but Jax's hand pulled them apart as Liam's hand began to rove under my dress.

"Boys," I hissed, scanning the room to make sure no one was around and could see what they were doing.

"Shush," Jax quieted me and then murmured something to Liam that made him laugh.

"Are you wet?" Liam's mouth brushed my ear, sending a shiver down my spine.

"Why don't you check and see."

Sassy, thanks to the alcohol. It earned me a soft pinch, from Jax, on my inner thigh. Liam's finger slid up through me, and I jolted, letting out a slight whimper.

This could not possibly be happening right here, right now.

But it was.

"Is she wet?" Jax asked.

"Soaked," Liam confirmed.

Jax's finger joined his, and together they danced around, one inside of me, one circling my clit.

I clenched the napkin in my hand, trying to stay silent.

"Can you take both of us?" Jax asked, sliding his finger in beside Liam's.

I wanted to take both of them and I said so. They both stilled for a second, presumably picturing what it would be like for me to actually take both of them, before they doubled their efforts. I came hard, my face hidden behind the napkin, biting my lips to stay quiet, my body trembling.

When I looked up, the couple from earlier was walking by. Liam casually sucked his finger clean and then flipped them off. My face felt flushed, and I was sure I looked exactly how you would expect me to look after what had just happened. I ducked behind my napkin again, and stayed there until they disappeared from view.

Back in the room, Jax answered some time sensitive emails while I got ready for bed. Liam FaceTimed Shaen, who insisted on apologizing to me.

"It's okay," I brushed it off.

"It's not okay. I feel terrible."

She looked like she felt awful about it. I reassured her again.

"If fuck-face over here would have told me what was going on sooner, I wouldn't have said it," she grumbled, glaring at Liam, who laughed.

"Fuck-face is sorry."

"Well, I'll leave you to whatever shenanigans you're up to." She winked. "Have fun."

"Love you," Liam said before ending the call.

"I should've told her years ago. It's like I knew she'd be cool about it, but I still worried. And the longer I waited, the harder it got to just say."

"Sometimes we think things will be easier to bear alone." Jax didn't look up from his phone as he said it.

I nodded in agreement as I flopped back on the bed. Liam lay down next to me and lifted up his phone to take a selfie. We looked good next to one another, tan and flushed, his blondish hair bright against my brown.

He turned and placed a kiss on my temple as he snapped another photo, then lay back, eyes closed, his face serene and content.

"Let's stay here forever," he murmured.

"Yes," I said. "Let's."

Even though we all knew we couldn't.

By the time I finished answering the important emails in my inbox, Charlee was in pajamas—a frilly tank top and shorts—and Liam was under the covers next to her, stripped down to his boxers. I shut off the main light, leaving the one in the bathroom on, and crawled in next to them. My mind was hazy from lust, sun, and remnants of alcohol, so I leaned over and kissed Charlee as I reached into Liam's boxers, waking them both up with my touch.

"Hi, baby." Charlee smiled up at me and kissed me back. Liam hovered close, and I turned to kiss him too—his lips so close to Charlee's, but never quite meeting. I knew that it drove him crazy, but I couldn't bring myself to relinquish my no.

Liam groaned as my grip on his dick tightened and I began to jack him till he was fully stiff in my palm.

"Do you still want to take both of us?" I asked Charlee. Her eyes flitted from me to Liam, who was hanging on by a thread, waiting. She bit her lip and finally nodded, I heard Liam's breath hitch and I felt my own breath get stuck in my throat. I smoothed some hair away from her face and kissed my way down her neck until she was panting and writhing beneath me.

"Make her come, get her slick for us," I heard myself say and Liam didn't need telling twice. In seconds, her shorts were gone and his face was between her legs. I hovered above her, watching her expression. Her eyes stayed on mine—wide, glassy, focused. God, watching her fall apart like this... nothing made me feel more like a man.

"Is it good, baby?" I knew it was but I wanted to hear her say it. She nodded frantically, letting out a yes as her head strained back, neck bared to me. I bit the side gently.

"Do you like his mouth on you?"

"Yes." Just a breath.

"Do you want him to come inside you and I'll clean it up?"

She whimpered. Liam slapped the bed with his hand, startling me.

"Do you want that, doc?"

"Fuck." His mouth sounded full. I crawled and kissed him, tasting my wife's tang on his tongue.

"You're so hot," I told him.

"I—"

I pushed his face back to her before he could speak. Then I slid Charlee's tank top off, and unhooked her bra while he ate her until she was shaking and begging. I lay down, with my head on the pillow, my cock jutting up. I showed Liam how to lay so our legs intertwined and his pelvis was up against mine, our cocks pressed to each other, lengthwise.

"Go slow." I caught Charlee eying how thick we looked together.

"You'll stretch," Liam encouraged. She hovered over us, holding each of our hands as she slowly sank down, enveloping us in her tight warmth. She moved so achingly slow that by the time her body got used to the girth of us and she was halfway down, I was already at the edge.

"Fuuuck." She was soaked and hot, and I could feel Liam pulsing against me. Just the idea of her taking us both had me feeling feral. *So that's what that feeling half out of my mind is like.* I hadn't really known this kind of intensity until now. Something animalistic clawed under my skin, demanding more. I wanted to grab her and thrust up inside of her, but I held steady.

"You feel so good," I murmured, gripping her hips. "So fucking tight." I looked up at her and encouraged her to ask Liam if he felt good too. He confirmed that he did, his voice shaky.

Finally she was fully seated, and both Liam and I groaned with satisfaction. It had me gripping her hips and lifting her up off us so I could slide us back in, gently. Just a little.

"Is it too much?" *Please say no. Please don't be too much, I never want to stop.*

"It's a lot… but it's not too much." She was looking down, watching us gliding in and out of her, thick and throbbing.

*Thank fuck. I needed this. I needed them like this.*

"Oh god." Liam's hands were tight on my thigh and her waist. "I'm never gonna last. It's too good." His eyes were closed, his jaw tight. His muscles were straining as she let us fuck her in tandem.

"I'm gonna come," Charlee gasped into the air fraught with the tension of our shared pleasure. I reached for her clit and strummed, tipping her over the precipice. Her body locked up as she exploded around us, walls clamping down. Moments later, hips bucking, muscles tense, Liam spilled inside of her with a stuttering curse.

"Oh f-fuck."

I felt it and heard it and it almost made my eyes roll back in my head. His abs strained as he lifted his shoulders off the mattress to get a good look at what had happened.

"It's so good. It's too good." He collapsed back, slipping out of her, I could feel his warm cum smeared along my length, dripping down my balls. Not even my wildest fantasies could have prepared me for this.

I pulled out and gently laid Charlee back against the pillows.

"Can you come again?" I kissed her, needing to anchor myself in what was real, because I was half out of my mind at this point and barely felt tethered to reality.

"I'm sensitive… but I can go again." Her nipples were peaked and tight, so I sucked them before kissing down her stomach.

I hovered over her pussy. In the dim bathroom light, I saw Liam's mess spilling out, shining on her inner thighs. I lapped that up first, tasting him—salty, slightly bitter—and then went wild. I licked and sucked every last bit from every crevice until she was crying out, pulling my hair—pushing me away and pulling me closer at the same time—begging. Still, I didn't stop. Not until her legs trembled and her voice gave out.

"How many was that?" I wiped my mouth with the back of my hand and looked up at her from between her legs.

"Two more."

"Damn." I was proud of myself.

"Water?" Liam offered me a cup and we all took a refreshing sip. Then Liam revealed something else in his hand—a small bottle of lube. My heart skipped a beat.

"What would you like to do with that?"

"I'm not ready for… well… more…" he said. "But I thought maybe.you.could.fuck.her.while.I.finger.your.prostate?" He said it so quickly, rushing the words, that I almost didn't catch them.

"You want to fuck me with your finger?"

He nodded quickly.

"It's been a while. You'll have to go slow."

"I will. I promise." He seemed eager to try.

"Kiss me," I demanded. He did—messy and hungry. He said something against my mouth but Charlee was suddenly asking me to fuck her, so I turned, and slid into her warmth.

The lube was cold, but Liam's fingers were gentle as they breached my ring of muscles. I pushed out to ease the burn. It had been a really long time and I quickly grew overwhelmed by the stimulation both on my cock and in my ass. I let out a loud moan when Liam added a second finger, then a third. When he found my prostate, stars exploded behind my eyelids.

"Shit, shit—" A few more strokes in Charlee, a few more slides of Liam's fingers and I broke. Exploded into a million pieces, pouring myself into my wife, while also backing myself up against Liam's fingers as he fucked me. I cried out, tremors shook me, every sensation colliding until there was nothing left of me but the feelings themselves.

"Oh my god." I flopped onto the bed, unable to move, barely able to think, my eyelids felt heavy, my arms were weights at my sides.

"I have never—I don't know..." I trailed off, and heard the tinkle of Charlee's giggle. Then Liam whispered in my ear, "I got you, babe." *And damn if he didn't.*

A warm washcloth cleaned me up and I drifted off into a trance-like sleep.

THE NEXT DAY, we toured the island, swam in the pools, and played more beach volleyball. We spent so much time in the sun that by the time we got back to the room to get ready for a night out at a dance club, we were all golden and bronzed.

Charlee wore a sleeveless black bodysuit, the upper half a whisper of sheer panels, broken up by the opaque strips that concealed her nipples. Thin straps exposed her back, leaving no room for a bra... which I didn't mind one bit. The shorts she paired it with hugged her hips, short enough to be mistaken for underwear. I watched her button them, completely taken by her thighs, already imagining them wrapped around my neck later.

"She's so hot." Liam's voice broke me from my thoughts, his breath warm against my neck.

"You both are."

He wore black linen pants and a white button down, dress shirt. The sleeves were rolled up, the top few buttons were left open, revealing a good amount of tan skin. I licked my lips as I let my eyes rove over his body, ending on his face where his mouth was lifted in a mischievous grin.

"I like when you look at me like that."

"I like looking at you," I admitted. He beamed as Charlee approached.

"Ready?" she asked.

I was. Not just for the night ahead—but for everything I dreamed of that I wished could come after.

The club was packed, loud and alive. Music throbbed through my chest, the dance floor was a pulsating crush of people. Liam grabbed some shots that we all downed before we made our way to the dance floor and began to move. It was fluid between us. Somehow, we all managed to dance without leaving anyone out. First me and Charlee, then Liam and Charlee, then me and Liam and then all three of us. Hips moving, arms grasping, sweat beading, my heart thrumming in my chest as we danced. Charlee melted against me as I recreated that night I had met her. I danced in front of her, my hands on her waist, our bodies fused together. Liam behind her, moving to the beat, his hands on mine, which were on her. I pressed forward and kissed him as Charlee danced between us.

"Fuck yes," she breathed. I kissed him deeper, his tongue against mine, his taste overwhelming my senses, his groans vibrating against my lips.

"Can you feel that?" I whispered to Charlee, then pulled away. She watched me with eyes clouded with lust.

"How much we both want you?" I knew she could feel my hard cock against her stomach and I was sure she could feel evidence of Liam's desire against her back. She nodded, biting into her bottom lip.

"Good, because we do." I spun her so she was facing Liam. He nuzzled her neck, kissing her right above her collarbone before he grasped my hands, one on her waist, the other right against her ribs, under the swell of her breast and we spun together, fused as one, across the dance floor. There was something so right about this. Like we were exactly where we were meant to be.

LIAM:

Okay lovers wake up, I just finished working out and I found the craziest shit

LIAM:

Are u still sleeping or fucking without me? We have a flight soon

LIAM:

Okay just ignore me. It's cool. Anyway I found a vendor on the beach selling friendship bracelets but guess what. They had options that came with 3 matching bracelets, not just 2. So I bought us a set

LIAM:

I'm coming back to the room now. Wake the fuck up

JAX:

<Photo of the bracelet on> (heart emoji)

When the night shift got exhausting and overwhelming, I'd revert my brain back to the three days of paradise that we spent together in Puerto Rico. The sandcastles we built, the jet skis we rented, the seashells we collected. The sex—so much sex—and the depth of the conversations we had. Charlee had shared stories about her childhood and showed me pictures of her brother. Jax told me more about his parents and his sisters. They both opened up about their dreams, their goals, and their struggles. I felt so much closer to them now that I understood where they came from and what made them who they are today.

One night, we sat by the ocean and I told them about my own childhood. Meeting Shaen. What it was like growing up with so many brothers. How Remi came to live with us. Charlee had fallen asleep on the blanket beneath us, so Jax and I lay there, holding hands and watching the stars.

In any other scenario, I would've told him I liked him. That I could fall in love with him if he let me. That I could see myself growing old with him.

In any other scenario, I would've told him that I was obsessed with Charlee. That making her happy made me happy. That I wanted to give her my babies. That I felt like I'd finally found my home—with them.

In any other scenario, they would be mine and I would be theirs.

But I wasn't. They weren't. We were now only six and a half weeks away from graduation. My official start date for my new job was July first. Somewhere in between, I had to move out and say goodbye. I wasn't sure if my heart could take it. I'd just discovered where I belonged. And now I had to leave it.

My pager buzzed, shaking me from my pathetic thoughts.

*Saved by the hemorrhaging placental abruption,* I muttered in my head as I ran toward the OR, calling out for units of blood.

Being on night shift kept us apart more than I liked—especially with me moving so soon. We only had sex a few times in May, but every time, Jax had us both come inside of her, making a mess that he had quickly become obsessed with. Charlee joked that Jax would miss me because she would be going off the pill soon and would make him use condoms again.

"Why don't you stay on it? You're loving skipping your period," I'd asked.

"I don't like how emotional it's making me, and I've gained like six pounds already. It's not for me," she'd explained.

As an OBGYN I wouldn't argue with that. I understood the negative side effects of the pill and I would never tell a woman that she was—or wasn't—experiencing something.

"Then condoms it is," I said with a nod.

I was practically falling off my face as I punched in the code on the front door. Charlee was already at work. She'd texted in the group chat that she would miss me and that she was jealous of Jax being home with me on his day off. I'd texted back that I would probably just sleep and study all day, that she wasn't missing much. She'd sent back a winky face emoji in response, which I hadn't understood.

Jax was washing dishes when I came in. He took my lunch bag

from me and laughed when I mentioned his note. I'd almost choked on my dinner when I'd unfolded it and read:

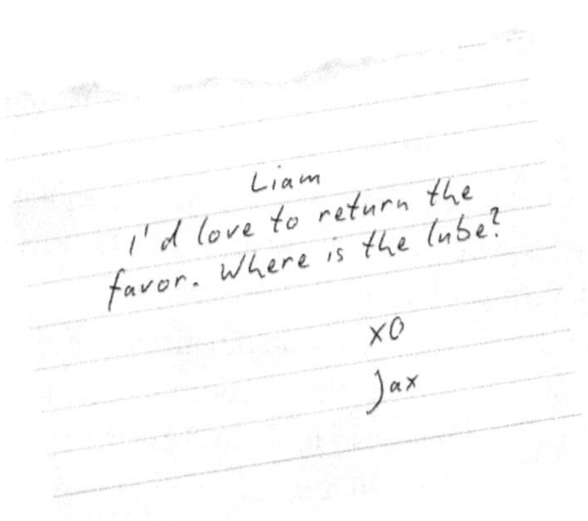


"You look exhausted," Jax said as he dried his hands on a towel and walked over to examine my face.

"Just get it over with and tell me how ugly night shift's making me," I joked.

"You could never be ugly." He shut me up with a chaste kiss that quickly turned into more. He pushed me against the wall, his hips pinning me, our tongues dueling, both of us gasping into each other's mouths.

"Are you too tired to let me return that favor? I already got Charlee's blessing."

Suddenly, her winky emoji made sense, and my cock stiffened. The exhaustion disappeared. I must have looked hesitant because Jax practically begged.

"Please, Liam. We're running out of time and I can't stop thinking about it."

I nodded, afraid to speak lest I burst into tears at the mention of our limited time.

How would that even work? We just say goodbye and never talk again? Stay friends? Did we disband the group chat? Could we be friends-with-sometimes-benefits or would that be too messy? What's the plan?

He had no idea how loud and chaotic my thoughts were as he led me down the hall toward his and Charlee's room. My bottle of lube sat on the pillow.

It hit me then—this would be our first, and maybe only time together without Charlee there. As much as I adored her, as obsessed as I was, I was also looking forward to seeing how this would play out. Just Jax and me.

"You're thinking too much." Jax pulled off my scrub top and ran his finger over my nipples, making them bead up.

"Sorry," I grunted as his tongue circled one of them.

"You can say no. I'll put you to bed myself."

"I'm not saying no." I pushed him away, then pulled him closer again to grip the sides of his face and kissed him until my lips felt swollen.

Somehow we ended up on the bed, clothes strewn across the room. Jax straddled me, his hard dick pressing into my abs. I strained my hips, trying to buck up and get some much needed relief.

"I'm gonna try to make you come without touching your dick," he said—and in that moment, I knew I was in for it.

"You're a virgin here, right?" Jax was pouring lube onto his fingers. It spilled all over my ass.

"Well, I tried once myself, but no one else has been in there," I admitted.

"Fuck, that's hot."

"What is?"

"Picturing you trying to fuck yourself. It's got me so hard."

I looked down. He was already leaking precum.

"Taste it."

I did and he groaned his approval.

"Okay stop—I don't want to come yet."

I pulled off his cock with a pop.

"You've gotten so good at that."

"I had a good teacher." My mention of Charlee hung between us, but then all thoughts fled as his finger began to breach me.

The lube only did so much. I groaned at the burn of the stretch.

"Well, that's unpleasant."

"It'll get good, I promise."

He seemed intent on going slow, but kept going deeper as my body allowed it. He poured on more lube and introduced a second finger. I fought the need to tell him to stop.

"You're doing so good." His praise relaxed me. "You look so fucking hot with my fingers in you." His next words buzzed through me and made my cock twitch.

Suddenly, his fingers curled—and a feeling I had never experienced before zinged like electricity all the way from my ass straight to my dick and I let out a shout.

"Fuck, Jax. Yes."

He smiled knowingly and leaned down to kiss me.

"Don't stop," I begged.

"Never," he promised.

"I need to jerk off."

"Don't touch yourself," he warned.

"Fuck." I was in a frenzy of frustration, but I followed his orders and left my cock alone. His fingers picked up speed. Every time they brushed my prostate, it felt like all my air was gathering in my pelvis, and I needed to come just to breathe again. I rocked my hips backward, chasing his fingers now, begging for more with my body.

"More baby?" His breath was hot by my ear. I nodded frantically. *I wanted to be his baby. I wanted to give him this. Maybe if I did, he'd keep me. Maybe he'd let me stay.*

My thoughts were scrambled. He added a third finger, and pain turned to pleasure so fast that I was half-crazed from it.

"Come, Liam," he ordered—like he wanted my orgasm as much as I did. My body obeyed. Every nerve ending misfired, and I clenched around his fingers as I came with no direct touch. My cock jerked, cum streaking my stomach and the towel beneath me.

"Holy shit."

Jax flipped me onto my back and knelt above me, on his knees, jerking himself with an almost too tight grip. He came moments later, his release joining mine across my skin. He ran a finger through the mess as his breathing slowed.

"Don't move—I'll get a wet towel."

I couldn't have moved even if I wanted to. My ass ached, cum was drying on my chest, and my heart had ballooned with how beautiful it had all felt.

*I want to keep this. I want to keep him. I want to keep her. Please let this be real.*

"Fuck," I muttered.

"Right." Jax came back with a warm washcloth. He cleaned me up, then climbed into bed next to me. He hooked his leg over mine and pulled me close. I fell asleep with my ear pressed to his chest, listening to the steady beat of his heart.

I woke up a few hours later to my phone buzzing.

"Hey, Rem," I mumbled.

"We're at your door."

I rubbed my eyes. "What do you mean?"

"I mean—we're at your door," he repeated slowly, like I was impaired.

"I'll get it," Jax said from beside me.

I hung up, trying to acclimate myself as I swung my feet over the side of the bed. The sound of voices floated down the hall.

First order of business was to toss the sex towel into the laundry and hide the evidence. Once that was done and the lube was shoved under a pillow, I grabbed one of Jax's sweatshirts and pulled it on with my scrub pants. Bleary-eyed, I made my way into the living room and found Shaen, Remi, and Billie sitting on the couch. Jax was in the kitchen assembling a snack platter.

"Sorry," I mouthed to him.

He shrugged, relaxed as always.

"Can you—" I started.

"I already put the watermelon gummy candies and a can of seltzer on the coffee table for you."

Damn. I wanted to hug him. He winked like he'd heard the thought.

"What brings you to the city?" I asked, popping a candy in my mouth. I was still half asleep as I chewed.

"I went to a car auction nearby," Remi said. "Shaen and baby tagged along so we could surprise you." He tossed some pretzels into his mouth as Jax sat down in the chair beside me.

"Is that my sweatshirt?"

I looked down. "Oh—yeah. Sorry, I just grabbed it. I can take it off."

"Nah. I just thought I recognized it. Looks good on you." He cracked open a seltzer and took a sip. I turned and caught Remi and Shaen staring.

"What?"

"Wait. You guys are so cute together."

I groaned. As a teenager Remi had always been quieter and more reserved but since getting married and working with other mechanics all day he had grown bolder. He now just said whatever came to mind. I worried he would say something that would make Jax uncomfortable.

"Look at you sharing clothes. Were you just fucking? Sorry if we interrupted." Remi was laughing now.

"First of all you said 'fucking' in front of Billie," I pointed out. "Second—we weren't just fucking, so cut it out."

"That ship has sailed. We tried not swearing in front of her, but it didn't work out." Remi turned to his daughter. "Isn't that right, princess?" She babbled back as he reached over to take off her little jacket and hat.

"So when are you gonna tell everyone your little life update?" Shaen asked.

"Well, my mom knows."

"You told your mom? That's huge, Liam." Jax sounded genuinely happy for me. Shaen watched our exchange, smiling.

I wanted to tell her to knock it off. That this little thing she was getting excited about was not going to last that much longer. But, instead, I just smiled too.

"I'll tell everyone else in due time. When I feel ready."

"It's nothing to feel ashamed of, Liam," Remi said enthusiastically. "Honestly it's cool for you. Gives you more options, y'know." He turned to Jax. "No offense."

"None taken," Jax said easily. "With a face like that, he'll always have options."

*I don't want options,* I wanted to say. *I just want you and Charlee. Take me off the market.*

Instead, I just shrugged.

"I'm focused on graduation and moving. We'll figure out the rest after that."

"I got Billie the cutest dress for your graduation," Shaen said, bouncing the baby in her lap. "Are you coming to the party his mom's throwing the week after?" she asked Jax.

"If he wants me to, I'll be there." Jax smiled at me, and Shaen shot me a look that said *oh my god he's so cute, you guys are adorable together. You better figure out your shit and lock this down.*

I shot her a look back that meant—*it's complicated, stop making it weird.*

Her eyebrows raised—*I'm not making it weird.*

My chin tilt responded, *yes you are.* She laughed and stuck out her tongue.

"Here, hold your goddaughter. I have to pee."

Suddenly I was holding Billie, and as I breathed in that soft baby scent, I looked over and found Jax watching me. There was something in his gaze. Something soft. Something that almost made me believe we could have more than a moment.

"Hey."

"Hey," he said back.

I leaned back in the chair, talking to Billie, feeling his gaze linger on me for the rest of the afternoon.

"**I**'m officially going off the pill today. I've gained another five pounds, it's giving me brain fog and making me tired. I hate it." I announced it at dinner.

Liam looked up from where he was twirling spaghetti around his fork.

"Go throw them out," he encouraged. "We're both cool with condoms, babe."

Jax grunted his approval from the couch, still focused on his video game.

"You'll probably get your period in two to four weeks. Just give your body time to acclimate."

"Thanks, doc. Do you have time for an exam?" I joked.

"That depends on how thorough an exam you're looking for." He waggled his eyebrows at me as I got up to take the pack of birth control from my bag and toss it in the garbage.

When I returned, Jax's phone buzzed and he sighed, paused the game, and muttered a soft, "Fucker," as he read the message.

"Work?" Liam asked.

"No, it's my sister."

"What's wrong?" I sat down next to him.

"Apparently my father saw the photo you posted from vacation. He told my sister to make sure I'm 'behaving myself'."

"The photo of us at dinner?"

He nodded.

"That's the tamest picture ever. Liam couldn't have looked more like a platonic, straight friend if he tried," I protested.

Jax sighed. "Yeah, well, you know my dad. Always assuming the worst."

Liam cleared his throat. "What would your dad do if he found out about…" He waved his hand vaguely, the friendship bracelet that he bought us shifting on his wrist.

"He'd probably mock me. Tell me I'm a glutton. Ask me why I always have to cause problems. Why can't I just be normal?"

"Well, I don't think you're any of those things." Liam picked up his plate and brought it to the sink. "I'd say your dad's missing out, because clearly he doesn't know you very well."

Jax's eyes softened. A smile played on his lips.

"Thanks, Liam."

Liam nodded and disappeared into his room to continue packing. His last shift was tomorrow, and his graduation ceremony was only days away. I was silently beginning to unravel. Every item he packed felt like another piece of him I'd never get back. We had yet to have a conversation about what came next, even with the reality looming large over our heads. It was like pretending it wasn't happening somehow made it less real.

Six months ago if someone would have told me that inviting my doctor friend to rent our spare room would lead to this, I'd have laughed. If you would have told me that it felt like my love for Jax had doubled as my heart expanded to make room for my feelings for another man I would have said you were insane. But here we were.

If we could all be honest—if we all laid our cards on the table —I had a feeling we'd all admit this wasn't just fun and physical. That if given room to allow whatever this was between us to naturally take its course and grow, I could imagine a life where we finally admitted that this was a relationship. Unconventional, sure. But a real relationship nonetheless. Maybe if we could wear our hearts on our sleeves and weren't so scared, we could admit that we cared for each other. *Deeply.* But maybe we were all too afraid of what we'd lose if we did.

I heard Jax turn his game back on.

"I'm sorry about your dad." I kissed him on the cheek.

"I'm used to it."

"Yeah, but you shouldn't have to be. You deserve better."

"What matters now is that I'm gonna be better for our kids." Jax eyed me.

"Yeah, about making that happen. What do you think of moving out of the city? Me getting a slower-paced job?" I curled my feet onto the couch, Jax shifted to make room for me.

"If it means having a baby, I'll do anything." Jax paused his game again to look at me.

"You really want one that badly?" I'd never heard him talk about having kids this emphatically before.

"I'd never ask you to do something you don't want to do but if you're down, I'm down." He started massaging my feet.

"I feel like I'll never really be *ready* to shove a watermelon out of my hoo-ha, but I'd say I'm comfortable starting to look for a job outside of the city. In the meantime, you can talk to your uncle about expanding the business there. Once we move, maybe we can start trying."

"I'm gonna be so good at the trying part." Jax had a huge grin on his face.

"I know you are."

He laughed.

"I guess we can rent out the apartment." I looked around our living room thinking of all the memories we had made here.

"Or we can sell it."

"My mom would probably kill us if we did."

"True." Jax turned his game back on for the third time. "Whatever makes you happy, Charlee. That's what I want."

"Anything?" I asked.

"Anything," he promised.

"Deal." We still hadn't talked about the elephant in the room. The six-foot-one, light brown with a mix of blond-haired, blue-eyed, freckled elephant. And we were rapidly running out of time.

"YOU GUYS DIDN'T HAVE to do this," Liam said, looking genuinely touched by the goodbye party we had thrown for him at the nurses' station.

It wasn't much, *party* may be stretching the truth a little bit, but for us busy nurses—sushi, cake, and balloons was a full out ball.

"We're gonna miss you." One of my co-workers handed him a slice of cake.

"I'm gonna miss all of you too." He took a bite. "Damn, this is good. I've gotta eat fast, I've got so much to do today." He took another huge forkful and then turned to hug several of the nurses.

"You better stay in touch."

"I can't believe you're leaving us."

"Save me cake," Dr. Shaw called, passing by on his way to perform an epidural.

"Don't save him any cake," Liam told us conspiratorially. We all laughed.

"I can't handle change. No one else is allowed to leave," Patty, the sixty-five-year-old nurse who'd been in our department the longest, announced.

"I can't promise anything," I told her.

Liam gave me a look—eyebrow cocked as if to ask, "what do you mean by that?" I shrugged. He tilted his head toward the hallway that led to the storage closet. I nodded. Later we would have our last storage closet lunch together. It felt fitting.

"Thank you, guys." Liam put his empty plate down. "But I've got to run. So much to do, so little time." As he walked away, the group of third-year residents he was training followed him. He had to transition care, hand off patients, and attend last minute meetings to wrap up. This handover period was making me emotional. I almost felt tears well up in my eyes before I straightened my back and went to check on some new admissions to distract myself. That damn pill had really fucked me up. I was looking forward to it fully leaving my system and getting back to my less teary-eyed and less bloated self. That's all this was, it had nothing to do with the fact that Liam was leaving and a piece of my heart would be leaving with him.

Liam and I ended up doing one more delivery together. It felt like the perfect way to end our last shift.

I was finishing my charting when my phone buzzed.

LIAM:

I can get away for twenty. Meet me?

Twenty minutes with him suddenly felt like the best part of my day.

CHARLEE:

I'm coming

LIAM:

I wish u were (winking face emoji)

CHARLEE:

We should probably all finally talk about this

LIAM:

Blah blah. I don't know what ur referring to

I laughed at his blatant denial of reality. I stuck my phone back into my pocket, sat my iPad onto the charging station, and announced that I was taking lunch.

"Enjoy," Patty told me as she picked up the ringing phone.

I grabbed my lunch bag from the fridge and walked toward our closet. I was looking forward to reading Jax's notes in our bags.

As I approached the door, I heard a loud pop. It sounded like a car backfiring, followed by silence. I hesitated, then shook it off and pushed the door of the closet open.

Liam was on FaceTime with Jax.

"I'm pretty sure it's in the front hall closet, top shelf, behind the grocery bags Charlee saves."

"What's up?" I asked.

"He lost his measuring tape," Liam explained.

"I didn't lose it, it's just not where I last saw it," Jax grumbled.

"Isn't that the same thing?" I laughed.

"According to Jax, it's not." Liam grinned. That *oh isn't he so cute* look on his face made my stomach twist.

"Oh, here it is." Jax located his Stanley measuring tape and held it up to the camera.

"See, not lost. Just not where it was supposed to be."

"Isn't..." I started to speak but then another loud *pop* rang out. Three in a row. My heart began to race as it dropped into my stomach.

"What the fuck was that?" Jax asked sharply. One look at his face confirmed that he knew exactly what he had just heard.

I spun toward Liam. He stood super still, head cocked, eyes squinting. His body shifted. I could practically see the moment his mind began to race.

"Liam..."

"Shush."

He moved closer and pressed a finger gently to my lips. The contact made me feel worse because it confirmed that I was real. *This is real. Not a bad dream.*

Liam looked down at the phone that he held loosely in his hand. I watched as he and Jax shared a silent moment—no words spoken, their eyes said everything.

We all jolted as the overhead speaker crackled. **Code silver.** Liam's pager buzzed. A robotic voice announced, "All departments, please refer to your emergency flipcharts."

"Is code silver an alarm for an…" Jax whispered.

"Active shooter," Liam confirmed. "Yes, yes it is."

Another announcement came over the loudspeaker, "All staff, patients, and visitors, please seek shelter or remain in a room with the door closed and secured."

Liam's pager buzzed again. He turned to stare at the door, looking like he was debating something.

"Do not be a hero, Liam," Jax ordered sternly. "Please."

Liam looked back at me, then away. I was frozen in my spot until I heard more shots and my body began to shake.

"Liam," Jax repeated. Liam wouldn't look at him.

"Baby please…" Jax was begging now. Liam finally looked at the screen.

"Please protect her. Please. I need you two to hide."

I was going to throw up. My arms felt like lead. My hands were shaking so bad that I dropped my lunch bag. Liam caught it right before it hit the floor.

"Charlee, I need you to breathe," Liam whispered. *He's whispering. That means the shooter could be close.* The thought slammed into me like a blow. I didn't know where to run. Or even if we'd have to, or could. I started to feel like I was going to have a panic attack because now all I could think about was how close the shooter was. I couldn't move. I was frozen.

Liam turned off the light and quietly locked the door. Terror engulfed me as he pushed an old, metal, sterile supply cart in front of it, jamming the door handle in place.

More shots sounded out, echoing around us. It felt like they were moving closer. Reflexes had my hands rushing up to protect my head. Adrenaline had its hold on me and it was running cold and ruthless through my bloodstream. I jumped as Liam's hand grabbed my arm but he just gently guided me toward the back of the closet, behind a set of filing cabinets, and motioned for me to hide behind one of the metal doors.

"Don't make a sound. Promise me." Liam's hushed words echoed in my ears as I began to rock back and forth trying to will myself to stay calm.

"Charlee. Sweetheart. Listen to Liam. Please baby."

Was Jax crying? *I'm so scared. What about everyone out on the floor? What about all the moms? The newborns?*

We heard someone run by, down the hall, followed by an, "Oh shit!" and then more shots rang out.

*I.dont.want.to.die.I.dont.want.to.die.I.dont.want.to.die.*

"Oh my god." A whimper escaped me, and Jax let out a frustrated huff from where the phone sat against the cabinet. I could only imagine how terrified he was—completely helpless, forced to watch us hide for our lives, unable to do anything.

"I'm scared." Panic surged through me, flooding every limb. My fingers felt cold, my body stiff with fear. Liam crouched in front of me, and when another cry pushed its way out of my throat, his lips were suddenly on mine. And just like that, I was kissing the man I'd been steadily falling for over the last six months. If this was our last moment—I wanted it to be this. Us. Together.

I was driven by the trepidation clawing at my insides and the need to keep her quiet, but once my lips touched hers for the first time, I got tunnel vision. Nothing else existed. Just her sweet taste, the tiny gasps she was making and the way her mouth felt beneath mine. The eerie silence, between gunshots, had my brain buzzing inside my body, and I suddenly remembered where we were. I pulled away, whispering, "You need to stay quiet honey, I love you, I love you—you can't make a sound."

She stared at me for a second, eyes wide with shock at my admission, or fear, or probably both. Another buzz from my pager made her tug me back down, and our mouths fused once more. My tongue danced against hers, and I could feel her terror fueling her. Her heartbeat beneath my hand was way too fast, yet I did nothing to calm her down. I just kept kissing her.

Another shout and more gunshots had us springing apart. Those were way too close. If I died here, at least I'd have tasted what I'd been starving for. I stood, placing myself in front of Charlee, and grabbed an IV pole, the only semblance of a weapon that I could find, ready to do what it took to keep her safe. My eyes fell on my phone, which had dropped to the floor. The call was still connected, but I didn't have time to worry about what Jax had—or hadn't—heard. I was the only thing standing between Charlee and whatever madman was outside that door with a gun. Just me and my IV pole.

My mind raced, and with a jolt, I tried to remember the last thing I had said to Shaen. Remi. Billie. My parents. My brothers. The thought of dying here, like this, had bile rising up in my throat, acrid and burning. In a nanosecond, everything about being alive had re-shaped. All the stupid things I'd stressed about suddenly felt so insignificant compared to this desperate need to stay alive.

The door handle jiggled.

I heard Charlee suck in a strangled breath from behind me.

I couldn't look at her. If I was going to die like this, I wanted the last thing I saw to be her face as I told her I loved her—not her eyes etched in terror and dread.

Someone kicked the door, but the cart I'd wedged under the handle didn't budge. My heart was no longer beating. Was it? I couldn't feel a single movement as everything around me slowed. I felt stuck in Jell-O—unable to breathe, unable to do anything but wonder how hard I could swing this pole.

It felt like I'd stood there for an eternity when I heard shouts.

"NYPD!"

"Drop the fucking gun!"

Then six shots rang out, fast and final, and a heavy thump hit the other side of the door. Whomever had been trying to get in slid down, the sliver of light beneath the doorframe vanished. I watched in horror as blood began pooling slowly beneath the crack, creeping its way into the closet.

I was a doctor. I saw blood every single day. Yet the sight of it now made me nauseous.

"Liam." Charlee stood in front of me, trying to loosen my intense grip on the pole.

The police were shouting, asking if anyone was in the closet.

The loudspeaker announced an all-clear. We were being told to come out with our hands up. Charlee scooped up my phone—Jax's call had been disconnected, probably because the cell towers were inundated with calls.

The door opened. More shouts met us. The hallway felt blindingly bright. Hands guided us around a body.

"Don't look," someone instructed. But everywhere I looked, there were more bodies. So many bodies in the hallway. I couldn't avoid seeing them.

Pattie lay haphazardly across her desk, her cheek resting in the leftover cake, eyes wide and unblinking. The balloons around her danced grotesquely. Blood splattered the wall behind her.

I heard Charlee sobbing behind me, but I couldn't do anything but walk. I followed the police officer, wondering if there was something else I had to do before my shift ended. Was it already over? Were they just going to send us home?

*I can't think.*

My legs barely moved as I trudged forward, wondering how the fuck this happened.

They gathered us in a lobby near the ER. The hospital had diverted all incoming emergencies, and now the place was crawling with police. I even saw someone with a jacket that said **FBI** on the back. Doctors from psych joined us, one of them said I was in shock—did I want something to take the edge off?

I shook my head.

They wrapped me in a blanket. I thanked them, my teeth chattered. The police began their interviews, asking what we heard, if we saw anything. Charlee answered for me. She seemed to have shaken off her freeze response, and her voice was clear, no tremor.

"Can we go now?" I asked. Despite the blanket I was still shivering.

"Yes, doctor. You can go."

We were finally released, and exhaustion hit like a wall. The adrenaline had drained out of me, and all that was left was disbelief. *This really happened.*

After we retrieved our belongings from the bins they'd set up on tables, Charlee led me outside.

That's when I saw him.

Jax was leaning against his truck, arms crossed against his chest, his face thunderous.

At that moment, I finally snapped out of it. It wasn't the police shouting, or the hallway of bodies that did it. It was the way he didn't move when he saw me.

The rushing in my ears quieted. The fog in my brain cleared. My muscles unfurled and released their tension. My shivering began to ease.

Reality slammed into me with a force I wasn't ready for.

I'd fucked up.

Jax barely nodded at me before gathering Charlee up in his arms as she sobbed.

"Baby. I got you," I heard him murmur. He practically carried her to the car and buckled her in himself.

I told myself he hadn't embraced me because we were at my work and I didn't want anyone to know. *But deep down, I knew that wasn't it.*

The Jax from this morning would've said, "fuck it," like one of the heroes in Shaen's BookTok books, and kissed me in front of everyone. But tonight's version of Jax did no such thing.

He barely waited for me to buckle before tearing out of the parking lot, tires screeching.

I kept my eyes fixed out the window, listening to Charlee speaking softly and hearing the rumble of Jax's low responses. I didn't look at them. I didn't want to interrupt.

For six months, I hadn't felt like an outsider.

But tonight I did.

Tonight I felt awkward in my own skin—like I needed to unzip myself, step out, and leave this version of me on the side of the road. The one that was traumatized, shaking and unraveling inside.

Jax revved the engine, speeding us away from the mayhem, the flashing lights, the crowds of reporters, from the memories of the place I'd devoted the last four years of my life—now left ripped to shreds in that parking lot.

Back at the apartment, I stumbled up the stairs, and waited for Jax to unlock the door. Once inside, I started for my room, but he held out an arm and stopped me.

"I'm glad you're okay," he said, not quite meeting my eyes. "And I'm thankful that you kept my wife safe."

*My wife.*

The two words cracked something open in my chest. My heart thudded painfully behind my ribs.

"But when I get back from work tomorrow… I don't want you to be here anymore."

A lump grew in my throat as Charlee stepped between us.

"Jax! No. What are you doing?"

"He loves you?" Jax's eyes burned with resentment, his voice was raw. The words came out like an accusation. "He *loves* you."

I watched as he pulled his arm out of her grasp.

"You kissed her."

His voice broke. The words were brittle, hissed. Anger radiated off him.

"He was trying to keep me quiet!" Charlee snapped. "He saved my life, Jax. He stood between me and the door as the shooter tried to get in."

"And I said thank you. I'll be forever grateful." Jax was sounding slightly calmer, but he didn't back down.

"Then what the fuck? After everything, how could you tell him to leave?" Charlee's voice cracked as she began to cry.

"He was already going," Jax muttered. "Now he'll just do it two days early."

He turned and walked away without looking back, leaving us

frozen in the hallway, mouths open, hearts breaking, minds still trying to grasp what the hell had happened today.

"Liam…" Charlee reached for my hand.

But I pulled away.

She followed me to my room as I took in the mess of packing tape, clothes, and half-filled boxes. Most of my belongings were already packed. Still, it felt overwhelming.

"I'll fix it," she promised, sobbing, sounding desperate. "He's just in shock."

"No, Charlee. There's nothing to fix."

I wanted to hug her. I wanted to ask if she had seen Pattie. I wanted to go punch some sense into Jax. I wanted to scream. I wanted to call my mom.

But instead, I pulled out my suitcase, packed up the essentials, and left a message for the moving company asking if they could come pick up the rest of my stuff a day early. I planned on taking an Uber back to the hospital to retrieve my car and then hoped I wouldn't be too exhausted to drive… *home*. I had no idea where that was anymore.

When I finally left the room, Charlee stood by the front door watching as I grabbed some of my odds and ends from the hallway closet.

"Keep the coffee maker. I know how much you like it."

I tried to smile, but I couldn't—not when she had tears running down her face.

"Liam…" she hiccupped.

Wordlessly, I opened my arms, and she fell against my chest, wrapping herself around me.

"You did so good staying quiet," I told her gently, running my hand down her cheek. "I'm sorry. So sorry."

"Please." She shuddered against me, her tears leaving my fingers wet.

I could feel my own tears and swallowed thickly, pushing them back down.

"For what it's worth, I do love you," I whispered against her hair as I unwrapped her arms from around me. I had to let go even though I would never get the chance to hold her again. I grabbed my suitcase and left without looking back. It was like being evicted from a life I was still desperately trying to belong to.

It wasn't until much later, when I sat in my car in Shaen and Remi's driveway, that I finally broke.

I wasn't exactly the kind of guy that cried a lot, but today had sawed me into tiny little pieces, and I'd lost some of those pieces while trying to gather them up and put them back where they belonged. I wasn't sure if I was still in shock from the shooting, was irrecoverably sad from the biggest non-break up of my life, or angrier than I'd ever been at the way Jax had calmly, essentially, told me to fuck off.

Physical intimacy aside, he had begun to feel like a best friend. And now the backstabbing bastard had pulled the rug out from underneath me—literally and figuratively.

We may not have made any formal promises to each other. We definitely hadn't had the much-needed conversation about what we meant to one another, or what would happen in the future—although we should have. Even so, I'd expected more loyalty from him. I thought I meant enough to him to at least talk it out.

I knew I'd disrespected his one request, but the circumstances had been dire and catastrophically unique. I thought he'd be intelligent enough to understand that.

I wanted to beat my head against the steering wheel—do something, anything—with all this pent-up frustration inside of me.

But instead, I turned to get my suitcase from the back seat and saw the lunch bag that I'd forgotten in my car this morning. I could've left it, I should've. But like a masochist, I opened it up, searching for Jax's note.

It was written on a bigger scrap of paper than usual, and as I opened it, the lump in my throat grew to the point where it felt like I was choking on the disbelief of today.

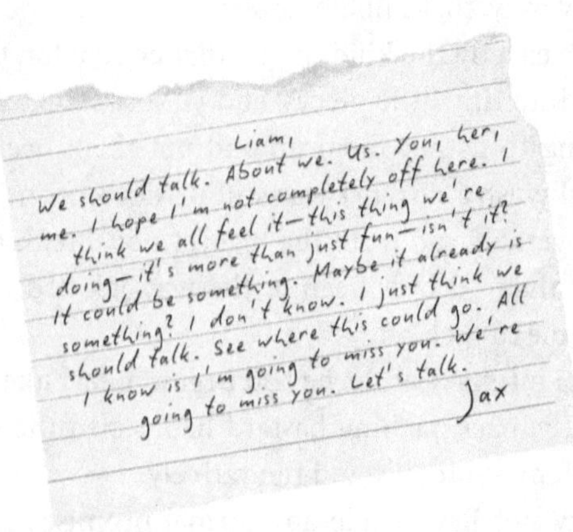


I took in a shuddering breath and pressed the screen on my phone to open our group chat. Maybe I could talk some sense into him. Clearly he felt something, as did I, maybe there was still hope.

*Jaxon Berman has left the chat.*

We no longer existed.

At that, the tears finally came in abundance. That's where Shaen found me—practically shaking, snotty, with bloodshot eyes.

"What happened?" she demanded.

I couldn't even answer right away, so she climbed into my car and held me while I sobbed—for Pattie, for my lost last shift, for Charlee's fear, for Jax's anger… but mainly I cried for the love I'd been forced to leave behind. I was mourning everything that might've been.

Remi helped Shaen guide me inside, and once I'd showered and crawled into bed, Shaen brought me a bowl of potato soup.

The two of them listened as I finally unloaded every detail of what had been going on for the last six months.

Remi kept gasping and Shaen kept slapping his arm as if to tell him to stop being so dramatic, but when I finally got up to the part of the shooting—and me telling Charlee I loved her— Shaen began to cry and Remi looked shell-shocked.

That quickly changed when they found out that Jax had told me to leave.

"I'm gonna fuck that motherfucker up," Remi promised.

I was exhausted from how emotionally taxing the day had been. I curled up under the blanket, torn between wanting to get my anger out on Jax and begging him to take me back.

I felt lost without them. Like I had been a piece of a puzzle that made a whole picture. And now I was just a piece again. Just a part—of absolutely nothing.

"GET UP, DARLING." My mother pulled open the curtains, letting the sun scorch my eyes.

"Fuck," I groaned.

"That is precisely what I thought when I got a whiff of your stench. Get up and shower."

"Mom," I protested. "Please…"

"Liam."

She sat down on the bed that I hadn't left in three days and pulled back the blanket. My apartment was ready, and all of my furniture and boxes had been moved in, yet I hadn't been able to bring myself to go there.

I could barely exist here with Remi and Shaen. I couldn't imagine doing this alone. So I stayed.

"You worked way too hard to let a fucking psycho and a little heartbreak stop you from attending your graduation today."

My mother had her no-nonsense look on her face, and I knew I was never going to win.

"It's not little," I mumbled into the pillow.

"What?"

"My heartbreak isn't little."

She tutted and ran a hand over my bristly cheek.

"I know it isn't, my sweet boy. But even so, I want you up, showered, shaved, and dressed in the next hour. I will drive you to the ceremony, and you will tell me more about your heartbreak. If I can fix it, I will. Okay?"

I nodded.

"That's it, sweetheart. Mom's got this." She kissed my forehead so tenderly that for a moment, I truly believed that she could fix this.

The sweat-soaked nightmares of a jiggling doorknob, shots ringing out around me, and the silence emanating from the two people I needed to talk to the most.

An hour later, I almost felt human again. I'd showered and shaved and donned a suit that I'd wear under my black gown with its green hood.

When I came out to the living room, my whole family sat there.

"There's my beautiful boy." My mother came up to brush some non-existent lint off my lapel and straighten my tie.

My dad clapped me on the back and pulled me in for a long hug.

"I'm so proud of you, son."

"Thanks, Dad." Why did everything make me feel like crying?

I felt too open and vulnerable. My unrequited love had ripped everything in me, leaving me raw, my emotions chafed and ruined.

"We'll meet you in the car," my mom told me and I watched as all of my siblings followed her leaving the living room empty except for Shaen.

"Thanks for letting me crash here." I hugged her. She snorted.

"Are you stupid? After everything you've done for me, I'm almost grateful I was finally given the opportunity to do something for you."

"It still hurts, Shay Shay." My voice was hoarse as I tried to hold back the tears I'd been plagued with for the last three days, but they came anyway, wetting my lashes and streaking my cheeks.

"Oh babe, I know." She was so tiny next to me, but she hugged me with everything she had, and I felt her love so strongly that it made me cry even more.

"Fuck, I'm such a pussy." I tried to laugh it off, but she wouldn't have it.

"It's okay to be sad. I'll do the furious part. 'Cause I'm still in the rip-their-limbs-from-their-body phase, so you can stay sad for as long as you need." She squeezed my hand. "You finally felt what love is, and it got stolen away from you. Of course you're heartbroken."

I nodded, not trusting myself to speak.

We'd done a lot of talking as I languished in bed, and now I felt like I didn't have anything left to say. Shaen reached up and wiped my tears away with the sleeve of her shirt. I tried to protest, but she wouldn't hear it.

"Don't even. I have a baby now—I clean everything with my clothes."

That made me laugh, and she ushered me out the door to go graduate. Her hand never left mine for the entire car ride.

I knew it was naive to look around the crowd to see if Jax and Charlee had shown up. But I looked anyway. They didn't come.

I tried to focus on the speeches, to allow myself to bask in the huge accomplishment I'd looked forward to for almost ten years, but all of it was shadowed by my broken heart. I felt fake as I shook hands. I had to force so many smiles I worried I was starting to look a little insane.

As we posed for photos, I was certain that you could see the shock and grief in my eyes.

Later, at the celebration dinner, I drank so much wine that I finally felt the pain numb a little—but I ended up vomiting it all up in the bushes outside Shaen's house.

Yet again, Shaen and Remi had to help me into the house, where I collapsed on the bed still in my suit, my phone falling from my grip onto the floor.

The noise startled me into thinking it was a gunshot, and when the panic finally abated, I found that I was crying myself to sleep yet again.

It really wasn't giving the smart, accomplished doctor vibes that I had been hoping for—and it most certainly wasn't how I had imagined my graduation night would look like.

LIAM:

I'm so sorry. Please, please forgive me. I never meant to disrespect u. U know I would never do that purposely.

LIAM:

Did u block me? I hope u didn't block me.

LIAM:

My heart hurts, Jax. I can't do this without u both

LIAM:

I keep hearing gunshots in my sleep. Is she okay? I just wanted to keep her quiet and safe.

LIAM:

u blocked me didn't u?

LIAM:

I'm going to miss u

LIAM:

fuck u Jaxon Berman. U ruined my life

LIAM:

I'm so sorry I was really drunk last night. I won't message u again

I'm an asshole. Even thinking the words made my chest burn. But there was no denying it. Not only did I know it, but Charlee had told me so at least ten times in the last three days.

I tried to explain it to her, but she was so angry with me I didn't really think she'd truly listened. I didn't know how to properly describe the helplessness of watching your wife—and the man you cared deeply about—literally hiding, hoping that their lives would be spared.

If I was being honest, watching it play out had broken something inside of me. Being a bystander to a near-catastrophe that I couldn't even put into words, something that had almost been the worst single moment of my life, it had me unable to sleep properly. Every time I closed my eyes, I saw Charlee's trembling hands over her mouth, trying not to scream, and the dread clear in Liam's eyes. It was like my soul was screaming, but my body couldn't move on from that moment.

I was good at fixing things. I was the calm, dependable one. I was Mr. Nice Guy. Oh look at Jax, he's so nice and sweet. Yet the last three days had me losing my phone everywhere I went and

dropping expensive tools at work. I'd even organized the spice cabinet twice today, and I still couldn't breathe right. It was like my brain had short-circuited and was still trying to reboot.

I was Jax, whose Dad verbally beat on him simply for liking boys, yet who never talked back. Jax who finally decided to be brave and venture outside his window of tolerance—who tried to have his cake and eat it too—but it had come back to bite him in the ass.

All of that resentment had boiled up inside of me, and hearing Liam profess his love for my wife—while knowing a shooter could break in and kill them at any second, and being unable to do jack shit about it—destroyed something inside of me I'm not sure I'll ever reclaim. And how could I after I'd been forced to stand there and just watch and wait, my nails digging painfully into my palms, not a word able to leave my mouth.

It wasn't even that I was mad Liam loved Charlee. In fact, it made sense. She was lovable, and she deserved to be loved by the important people in her life.

I wasn't stupid. I knew he was important to her—hell, he'd become important to me. *Special even.* But he had kissed her, and it just wrenched my heart out of my chest.

Because we hadn't talked about anything. Because he was leaving. Because he had kissed her. Because they could have died.

It had all just been too much. My nervous system had been torn the fuck up. When I drove to the hospital—ready to force my way in if I had to—my legs were shaking, and even now my jaw ached from how hard I'd been clenching. I recognized telling him to leave was a direct result of the adrenaline coursing through my body, but once the words had left my mouth, I couldn't bring myself to take it back.

He'd already been packed to leave. He was already set to start his new life. Not once had he said anything to indicate he felt something, or wanted more. That he'd miss us. And then, to make matters worse, he had gone and fucked it all up.

I was also self-aware enough to know that I was being a pussy by focusing the blame on him. But it was easier than facing the fact that he loved Charlee... But he didn't love me.

Liam's texts on my phone taunted me. I wanted to call him. I wanted to say I was sorry. But I also wanted to shake him and ask him why he'd profess his love when he knew he was leaving? Why hadn't he said anything sooner? I wanted him to punch me —just so I could feel something other than the fear of losing those that I loved most and the shame of how I'd acted. But mostly, I was wallowing in regret because I could have avoided this entire thing if I'd just stuck with one—just like my dad had always said.

I'd fucked up from the very start. Now my wife was mad at me, Liam probably hated me, every time I thought of him my heart jolted painfully, making me flinch from the physical ache. I didn't know if I could fix it. This might finally be a mess too big even for me.

I wanted to scream. But instead I packed up Charlee's lunch— because of course, even after a shooting and some major life upheaval, she refused to take off more than three days.

The hospital was open and L&D was back to admitting patients. So she was going to work to do what she did best.

I sighed as I uncapped my pen to write her note.

There was nothing I could say that would be "right", but I'd been writing her a note for four years, and I wasn't about to stop now. My hand shook as I pressed pen to paper. Like somehow the ink might bleed forgiveness into everything I'd broken.

LATER THAT NIGHT, I found her crying in bed. She was curled up under the blanket, fists clenched, breath coming out in hiccups. She'd gone back to work, but so many others hadn't. Like Pattie, a security guard, a receptionist, and a sonography tech who had all lost their lives that day. They couldn't return with her.

All because a man had lost his wife during birth in a completely different hospital, in a totally different state, and had chosen NYU to let out all his rage.

I whispered to her, brushing her hair off her face, handing her tissues as needed. She finally let me hold her. I rocked her because I couldn't do a damn thing else but hold her while she cried over the people who couldn't be saved.

The whole time all I could think about was Liam's texts and wondering if he was still being woken up by gunshots that weren't there.

"You need to fix this," Charlee finally said, once her tears subsided.

"How do you suggest I do that?"

"You go and apologize."

"And then what, babe? We stay friends? How am I supposed to hang out with a guy who knows what my dick tastes like, oh, and is also in love with my wife?"

My exasperation slipped out. She sat up, pulling away from me.

"Don't do that, Charlee. I know I'm an asshole, and you both hate me, but please try to understand why I was upset in the first place."

"We don't hate you." Her face softened.

"He probably does."

"No, he loves you."

My heart jolted. I hated how much I wanted her to be right.

"He told you that?"

"He didn't have to. It was obvious."

"Yeah, well, if he did, he had an odd way of showing it," I grumbled.

"By what? Standing in front of your wife to make sure if anyone got shot, it would be him?" Charlee was back to being mad at me.

"Babe..."

"No. Don't 'babe' me. You need to fix this. Not for anything other than because he deserves an apology. He's a good man, and we acted like we were all in a relationship for six months—then you kicked him to the curb after he went through the most traumatizing thing of his life."

I hung my head, the shame returning in droves.

"You're just mad because you love him too," she added for good measure. I didn't acknowledge what she said. I couldn't.

"Do you love him?" I was afraid to hear the answer. She snorted.

"I love *you* and I'm married to *you*. And maybe what I feel for him *is* love but it really doesn't matter anymore, does it. I know that I hate that he's hurting right now. I miss him. I miss us... And before you ask, no—I haven't spoken to him. I want to, but I haven't, and I hate that I haven't but I respect our vows, I respect you, I respect your boundaries. I plan on talking to him once we've made things right between all of us, but I need *you* to fix it first..." Her arms were crossed against her chest and she looked disappointed in me.

"Say he forgives me, what does after that look like?"

She shrugged.

"I don't know. But to be honest, I can't focus on that. What matters is that he hears you say you're sorry. Even if it changes nothing. So take a day. Take a week. Take a month. But at some point, you're gonna have to talk to him."

"When will you forgive me?" My heart ached as I asked, because deep down, I was afraid I'd lost her too.

Charlee crawled back over to me and kissed me—deeply, slowly. And when she pulled away she said, "I love you and I understand why you did it. I do. I get it. There is nothing that I have to forgive you for. We are solid—forever. With or without him. I am yours, and you are mine."

The anxiety knotted in my chest loosened, and for the first time since the shooting, I felt like I could take a deep breath. My chest rose, actually rose, showing me I hadn't really inhaled properly in days.

"I love you too."

She smiled at me.

"I know."

But the thought of *without him* bothered me more than I cared to admit.

Not once in my entire marriage had I questioned my love—or my adoration—for Jax. Even now, my feelings for him didn't waver. I was his wife, and I would remain so, no matter what the future had in store. While I understood what had led to him reacting the way he did, I still didn't like it. I didn't like not seeing Liam at work. I didn't like grappling with my feelings of missing him—of my anger toward Jax, my guilt over the kiss, my fear that I somehow betrayed my marriage. That maybe Jax would start to question everything. I didn't like the cacophony of chaos inside my mind every day. Like a thousand voices shouting at once, none loud enough to make any sense. I also didn't like watching our group chat sit frozen in silence. I opened it again to see the last notification.

*Jax left the chat.*

I hated that after six months of living with Liam, fucking him, falling for him, eating most meals beside him—in a moment he had become a memory. A ghost thirty miles away. I had so much to say to him.

*Thank you for saving me. I love you too.*

But my fierce devotion to Jax kept me silent. I couldn't reach out to Liam—not before Jax fixed this chasm between us. One he had created.

I most certainly couldn't check on him even just as a friend—not when my sleep was fraught with memories of his lips on mine, our tongues tangled, his breath hot and heavy across my mouth. Kissing him had been nirvana. Everything had started and stopped in that moment. A very clear realization had sliced across my adrenaline-drunk brain. I could chalk it up to fear, to heightened tensions, to the game of denial we had been made to play for six months... but I knew better. The kiss had been so good—so delicate yet so messy, so full of emotion and things unsaid—because he was my soulmate. How a girl could have two was beyond me. But it was true. I needed them both. Liam's soul had spoken to mine through that kiss, as clearly as his whispered confession of love had spoken to my heart.

Even if no resolution ever came, I knew I'd never be the same.

On one hand, I hoped he was healing. I wondered if he'd unpacked his apartment yet. If his new job had started. How his graduation went. I hoped he was sleeping better than I was. That that grisly scene of bloodied balloons and crushed cake didn't haunt his dreams like they haunted mine. On the other hand, my selfishness hoped he wasn't okay. That he was pining for me. For us. That he couldn't stop thinking about me. That he picked up his phone ten times a day to call me—like I did—but stopped himself each time. I hoped that was why my phone stayed silent. Silent the way I wished my mind would be but wasn't.

On break, at work, I stalked Shaen's social media. Pathetic, maybe—but it was the only window I had into his world now. Liam didn't post much, but Shaen did. Her stories were full of Billie, rescue dogs, Remi showing the baby his new car project, and whatever she'd baked that day. But today she posted what I'd really been wanting to see.

Liam.

He was sitting in his mom's backyard, shirtless, holding Billie. A real smile lit up his whole face. His hair looked wet, messy— like he'd just gotten out of the pool. His freckles were clear in the summer sun. His bracelet, our bracelet, still on his wrist. My heart caught in my chest. Fuck, I missed him. The way you miss air when you're drowning. Tears welled up in my eyes for what felt like the hundredth time this morning. I screenshotted the picture before shutting off my phone.

If I let myself be delusional, I could picture a life where it was our baby he was holding. In our backyard. While Jax manned the grill and I pretended to toss a salad. I snorted. Definitely delusional if my fantasies included me *cooking*. I shook my head, trying to physically dislodge all of the sadness and longing that burrowed into the crevices of my mind. My break wasn't over, but I got up anyway. I'd rather busy myself with restocking the L&D supply cart than sit here spiraling.

I passed *our* supply closet on my way back. There was no bloodstain on the floor. No echo of gunshots in the hall. A new nurse sat at the admissions desk. All visible traces of what had happened just a few days ago had been erased. But the memories lingered. Haunted me. I could feel it in my bones. In the way I flinched at loud noises and counted every exit. The long shifts no longer held the allure they once had. Everything I had loved in this department was now gone and I realized, with trepidation, that I no longer wanted to work here.

WHEN I GOT HOME, Jax was still at work. He'd left a carefully wrapped meal in the fridge with a note.

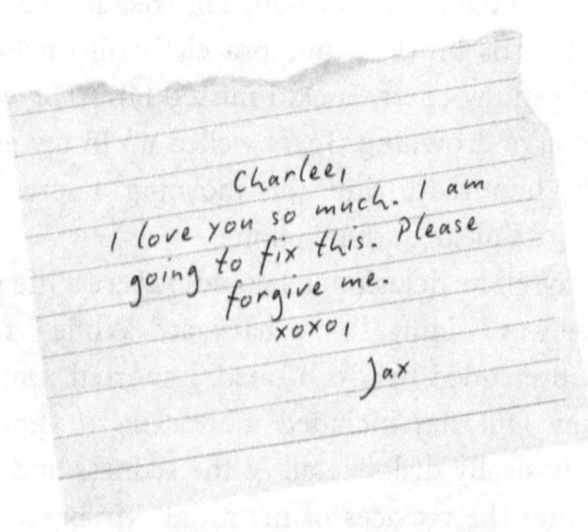


He kept asking for my forgiveness when I had already told him he didn't need it. We had all been through trauma that night. His trauma may have looked different than ours but the cut—it bled just the same. Me pushing him to talk to Liam wasn't about trying to rekindle anything physical, or explore what his, I love you, meant. What the kiss had meant. It was simply because Liam deserved it. Not only because of the good man he was, or what we had all shared over the last six months—or because he had quite literally saved me in that supply closet—but because of who *Jax* was. Jax embodied kindness. He was loving, loyal. Good. I didn't want this sitting on his conscience, weighing him down. I wanted him to clear the air, no matter the outcome. Say what needed to be said. To feel unburdened from the shame and pain he was carrying. I wanted to see the color return to his cheeks. I wanted to stop catching him watching me like I was going to leave. We had talked but I still felt like not enough had been said. My heart had made space for Liam, yes—but the very first love my heart knew was for Jax and that was sacred to me. Something I would never give up, never tarnish. Never disregard.

Even if it hurt to bandage up and soothe the place in my heart that beat for another… it's what I would do.

Garlic steak and potatoes were usually one of my favorite meals, but grief and shock sat heavy in my stomach making me nauseous. I wrapped the food back up and settled for toast with cream cheese and jam.

I could almost hear Liam fake-gagging.

*Don't knock it till you try it, Hennessy.*

*Over my dead body, babe.*

I sobered as I looked around the kitchen—silent and empty. The coffee machine mocked me from the counter. Unused. Untouched.

While I ate, I looked for jobs. Anywhere but here. Somewhere slower-paced. Somewhere I could still love what I did… but maybe feel settled enough to have my turn to grow and birth my own baby. I rested a hand against my flat stomach as I came across a listing for an L&D nurse at the hospital Liam's new practice delivered.

*Would that seem like stalking? Awkward? I hoped not. Maybe.*

But it didn't feel sinister. It felt like searching for home again.

I filled out the application and hit send before I could overthink it.

**Thank you for your application**. The screen blinked at me. I stared. The universe owed me one after all this shit it had put me through recently. Maybe it would pull through for me. I was scared to even hope because it all seemed so perfect. It was shockingly higher pay. Only three twelve-hour *day* shifts a week.

Day shift. Practically unheard of. I guessed the post-2020 chaos had changed the industry more than I had realized.

I didn't want to question it. I just whispered good vibes into the air.

I had no idea where we'd live. No clue how we'd rent out our current place. I wasn't even sure Jax's job would allow him to relocate. But I'd deal with all that later. For now I was ready for change. I didn't want to ignore the pull calling to me. To force me to recognize that I couldn't stay doing the same things when I was no longer the same. The shooting, Liam, my sadness—it had all changed me. Permanently. It had carved new shapes into who I was. Ones I hadn't asked for but couldn't ignore.

Something about applying felt like relief. Like tentative hope. Not because I thought we'd go back to what we had been—but because maybe I was stepping toward something new. Something necessary.

I rinsed my plate and set it on a towel to dry. The toast helped, a little, but my stomach still churned with the weight of too many emotions stacked on top of one another like bricks. I found a cluster of pimples on my chin this morning. Later when I went to pee and wiped, I'd seen a smear of red, telling me that my period was not far off. I'd felt a wave of relief. Between the stress and my hormones swirling so hard I'd been on the verge of unraveling.

I curled up on the couch, pulling the throw blanket over my body, sinking into the warmth, as I opened my phone and went straight to my photo app like a lovesick idiot.

There we were. A selfie in bed. I lay in the crook of Jax's arm, Liam wore a soft smile, his eyes fixed on me instead of the camera.

Jax and Liam walking toward me on the beach. Skin glinting, hair wet from the ocean, their laughter frozen in time.

Jax kissing my cheek.

Liam twirling me around the kitchen.

A picture of one of Jax's notes. *I still taste him on you.*

Jax and Liam kissing.

The memories hurt, but they were warm. They didn't sting like a burn or a cut—no they hurt the way sweet nostalgia ached when my brother, his wife, and my nephews left after a weekend visit. When the kitchen went from being full of laughter and beautiful chaos to an empty quiet only another visit could remedy. It throbbed the way my heart did after reading a gorgeous book with a sad ending. There was no regret in my pain, just a yearning that echoed in my bones. Nothing about our arrangement had been perfect, but it had been real. *Ours.*

I closed my eyes. I was out of tears. They'd come back, I was sure. But for now, I was too tired even for grief.

So instead of crying, I whispered into the silence, "I miss you."

To who—I wasn't sure.

Maybe to him.

Maybe to the version of me who once thought it would just be simple. Fun. Uncomplicated.

Jax came home, opening the door carefully, quietly, like he didn't want to startle me. He sat down on the edge of the couch, his hand brushing over my hip, tentative. I didn't move.

After a moment, I reached for his fingers, and laced mine through them. Our matching bracelets clinked together. That tiny thread of hope said more than any words could in the dark.

"SHOWING up at his graduation party at his mom's house sounds like the least subtle thing you could do, babe." I was anxiously watching the cars fly by as we drove.

Jax shrugged. "The universe is sending us a sign. You had a job interview today, which just so happens to be near his mom's house. And we *know* he'll be at the party. Any other day, we have no idea where he is. His apartment? I don't remember the address or even which one he chose. And I'm certainly not showing up at his work."

"You could just call him," I insisted.

"He deserves more than just a phone call."

I didn't argue. He wasn't wrong. He did deserve more.

"How was the interview?" Jax changed the subject.

I smiled, a real one. "So good. I think they liked me."

Jax snorted. "Of course they liked you. You're the fucking best."

I laughed softly. "They said they'll let me know by Monday because they need to make a decision ASAP. I told them if I get the job that I'll need to put in two-weeks' notice."

"They were good with that?"

"Yeah. They said that's fine."

"It'll give us two weeks to find somewhere to live," he murmured.

I nodded slowly, the weight of it all pressing down. "At least the rest of it fell into place," I told him. My heart began to gallop as we turned onto Liam's parents' street. Cars lined both sides of the road, indicating just how many people were attending this party.

"That it has," Jax agreed, looking for a parking spot. He found one right in front of the house. The universe was toying with us.

His uncle had jumped on the idea of Jax moving and expanding the northern division of the construction company. He even wanted to make Jax a partner and let him run it. Then my brother had called out of the blue asking if we knew anyone renting in the city—his firm was transferring him to the NYC office. I'd told him we might be moving and offered him our place if we did. The puzzle pieces of life seemed to be falling into place, snapping together like fate.

But I wasn't ready to hope yet. Not yet.

I still needed to get the job. We still needed a place to live. And Jax still had to face Liam.

I glanced out the window as Jax shut off the car. My stomach soured and bile rose in my throat. Shaen was by the front door, re-fastening a sign that had fallen. Her head turned. She saw us. Her expression hardened instantly. She looked furious as she stormed the stairs and down the big, curved driveway, toward our car.

Jax stepped out. Didn't say a word. Didn't flinch.

Shaen's voice cracked, "You have got to be kidding me." Her jaw clenched as she got right up in Jax's space. She was tiny and if it wasn't so serious I would have laughed at her yelling at Jax, who towered over her.

"Get the fuck out of here," I heard her yell through my open window.

He didn't move.

"I need to talk to him."

"No." She pointed toward the street as if she expected him to just tuck his tail between his legs and leave. "You don't get to show up here. Not today. Not when he just started smiling again. Eating again. Not after what you did to him."

Guilt gnawed at my insides, my anxiety flaring like nausea again.

"I know. I'm sorry," Jax said quietly.

"You don't get to be sorry." Her voice trembled. "You don't get anything when it comes to him anymore."

"I am not asking for anything but a few minutes. To apologize. To explain." He remained gentle. Not moving. My love and respect for him flared up behind my ribs.

"No." Shaen pressed her lips into a firm grimace. "No. He loved you. Both of you. And you—you just broke him. Like it meant nothing. He didn't deserve that... he's..." She was fully crying for her friend now, and it made me want to get out of the car and console her—but I stayed put. Jax shifted, then reached over awkwardly, and patted her on the back. I watched, stunned, as all the energy drained from her body. The sharp edge of her anger softened into sorrow, and she leaned into him, letting him hug her. I couldn't hear what he said, but she nodded, wiping tears from her cheeks, as she finally stepped back.

Even faced with her wrath, he still knew how to be kind. How to make people feel safe. My admiration for him continued to burn bright.

She glanced at me briefly, then turned fully as the front door opened and Liam stepped outside.

Time slowed.

He walked down the front steps, expression unreadable, his presence hitting me in the chest like a wave. He wore white pants and a thin, cable-knit, blue collared shirt. He was just as beautiful as I remembered. But the circles under his eyes were more pronounced. Was he thinner? I swallowed audibly.

Liam's gaze shifted. First to Shaen's tear-streaked face, then to Jax standing quietly behind her. Then to me.

Back to Jax.

His Adam's apple bobbed as he swallowed, and we all watched as he strolled down the driveway. A breeze ruffled his hair, a drink held loosely in his hand.

Unsurprisingly, he went to Shaen first. He leaned in close, speaking quietly. She nodded, her shoulders falling with the kind of release that only came from finding acceptance. He pressed a kiss to her hair, and she turned to walk away. Just before disappearing into the house, she looked back.

"Please don't hurt him, Jax." Her voice cracked—just slightly. More plea than warning.

"I never wanted to hurt him," Jax replied softly.

It seemed to pacify her, because she gave a small nod and shut the door behind her.

The two most important men in my life stood there, eying

each other. Neither speaking. Liam seemed hesitant, uncertain. Jax's shoulders were squared, steady with resolve.

I drew in a breath.

"Don't cry," I murmured to myself as Jax finally opened his mouth to speak.

I knew I was drunk, but I couldn't possibly be drunk enough to have conjured Jax and Charlee at my graduation party. I wanted to reach out and touch his bicep just to confirm that he was really here, but I stopped myself. He wasn't mine to touch anymore. Sadness rose again, and I took a long gulp of my drink to push it back down. I stared at the spot just behind Jax's shoulder because if I looked directly at him, I knew I'd cry. I definitely couldn't look over at Charlee—even knowing she was just a few feet away in the car—because if I did, I'd break.

I could hear the music coming from the backyard and the bubbling of the fake waterfall by the pool. It was ironic how many people were back there eating and celebrating my biggest accomplishment while I stood here letting my heart shatter. Again.

"Hi." Jax's voice rumbled through my chest, deepening the fissure of pain and want inside me.

"Hi." I cleared my throat. *Do not cry.*

"I'm sorry for showing up like this. For upsetting Shaen. I would've called, but we were in the area…"

I tilted my head, silently asking, *what do you mean?*

Jax answered my unspoken question.

"Charlee had a job interview."

Hope flared in my veins, dangerous and fast, but I quickly doused it with more alcohol.

"I hope it went well." I tried to keep my voice neutral, but I failed. I know I did.

"It did. I'm sure she'll get it." Jax was watching me with those deep eyes of his. Almost like he could see all the pain inside of me. I looked away.

"I'm so sorry."

My eyes snapped back to his.

"I should've never done that to you."

Heat prickled up my neck at the pain in his expression. The rawness in his eyes. The wetness behind his lashes.

"I could explain… tell you why I said it. What it felt like to watch you… helpless…" He swallowed. "I know it doesn't make it okay, but at that moment… I…" He trailed off, shaking his head. "Well, what I mean is I never meant to hurt you. But I did. And I'm so sorry." A single tear escaped, rolling down his cheek, disappearing into the beard that had grown out since I last saw him.

"Please don't cry," I choked out. "I don't want you to cry."

He shrugged.

"I can't help it."

He was earnest in his honesty, no defense in his tone, just truth. It made me want to grab him, pull him close to me, lick the tears off his face and beg him not to leave me. Instead, I just stared as he wiped his face with the sleeve of his shirt and took a few steps back.

"You don't have to forgive me, but please don't hold it against Charlee for not reaching out. She wanted me to talk to you first." He licked his lips, shuffling in place, like he was nervous. I took another chug of my drink.

"And thank you—for saving her. For saving yourself. I don't

know what I would've done if—" And just like that my big, beautiful man began to sob.

"Fuck, Jax." Before I could stop myself, I had him in my arms. His body trembled against mine. "I understand," I whispered against his ear. "And of course I forgive you. How could I not?" His body stilled as I nuzzled into his neck, breathing in his familiar scent, setting my own body on fire.

"Thank you." His breath was hot against my skin. I still held on to him and slowly, his arms circled me, pulling me in until I could feel his heart hammering against my chest.

"I read your note, Jaxon." The words slipped out.

He froze. I felt the slight turn of his head, his beard tickling my cheek. He let go, and I let my arms fall too. He stepped away, his nose was running, his eyes still wet with unshed tears. The car door opened behind us, soft footsteps nearing. *Charlee.* Wordlessly she handed us both a tissue and if I wasn't swimming in emotion, I would've laughed at how perfect she was for us. Always thinking ahead. Always prepared. As we were for her.

*We.*

Charlee took Jax's hand as he blew his nose. She looked at me, her expression unreadable but her presence grounding. Her beauty twisted in my heart.

"Hi, Charlee." I smiled.

"Hi, Liam." She smiled back, softly, carefully.

Jax cleared his throat as I repeated myself.

"I read your note, and maybe I'm being reckless saying this, but I agree—we should've talked. Because this was always more than fun. You know I love her but what I never got the chance to say was, I love you too."

Jax's body jolted. His eyes snapped to mine in disbelief. Charlee made a soft, strangled sound.

"I didn't want to disrespect you, telling her when I did, kissing her how I did... but I was so scared..." My throat tightened, voice catching. I drained my glass, hoping the alcohol would dull the

sharpness of the memory. "I was so scared we were going to die…
baby…"

I didn't get to finish.

Jax's lips crashed to mine. I grunted against his mouth as he
kissed me—deeper, rougher, and with more emotion than I ever
remembered feeling from him. His hand gripped my waist,
yanking me flush against him. He tasted like himself—familiar,
raw, real—and of the saltiness of his tears. His kiss felt desperate
like he needed to feel something. Needed to prove something.

His other hand, the one not holding Charlee's, slid up to
anchor the back of my neck, holding me in place like he was
afraid I'd vanish if he let go. A part of me *wanted* to vanish—to
escape the risk, the heartbreak—but most of me… most of me
wanted to disappear into *them*. The safest place I'd ever known.

We kissed like two men who had almost lost everything.

Like people still piecing themselves together.

When he finally pulled back, he kept his forehead pressed to
mine. Our breath tangled, erratic.

"Please say it again," he whispered.

"I forgive you?"

He shook his head.

"I read your note?" I teased, knowing what he wanted.

He huffed.

"I love her. I love you," I acquiesced. His eyes fluttered closed,
breath catching. For a second, neither of us moved. The air
between us felt too full—of pain, of love, of forgiveness.

"I love you too."

Jax's admission hung there. Charlee sniffled. I felt the enor-
mity of his words slice deep, humming almost painfully into all
the sad and empty places that had carved into me this past week.

"So does she." Jax gently moved Charlee toward me. She
smiled at me, almost shyly, nodding to show her agreement with
what he'd just said.

"I do."

She grabbed hold of my shirt, rose up on her toes as she pulled me down toward her, and at the first touch of her lips to mine I began to cry.

I cried for the pain, the fear, the absence of them on graduation day. I cried for being allowed to *feel* this—to *be* this. A man who loved another man. A man who also loved the woman whose lips were moving against mine, whose hands were on my face, who whispered comfort against my mouth. I pulled away, breathless.

"I'm so drunk right now I think I might be imagining this." I sounded worried.

Charlee laughed. "This is very real."

I pulled her closer, and Jax wrapped his arms around both of us and said, "So real that I don't give a fuck where we go from here, as long as we do it together."

"If you get the job here, will you move in with me?" I figured if we were throwing out life-altering declarations, what was one more?

Charlee grinned, pretending to have to think about it.

"How big is your bed?"

"I'll get a bigger bed," I promised. We both looked at Jax.

"I'm just trying to process everything right now." He laughed. "I went from just trying to say I'm sorry, to me saying I love you, to you asking us to move in together."

"Say yes, baby." Charlee nudged him.

"Yes, say yes, baby," I echoed. Heat flared in his eyes.

"If I say yes, what does that mean?" Jax asked.

"It means I'd marry you both right now if you'd let me," I confessed. I heard Charlee give a sharp intake. "But if all I get is living together, you being my boyfriend and girlfriend and letting me love you, I'll be happy with that." Jax wanted us to talk, he wanted honesty, he wanted to know what I really felt—well here it was. Beating around the bush hadn't gotten us anywhere so I wasn't going to do that anymore. Here it all was. The raw, honest truth. It may be fast. It may be bold. It may be a lot. But it also felt like just enough. Hopefully it wasn't too little, too late.

"Are you asking us out, Dr. Hennessy?" Jax asked, trying to lighten the heavy emotion with a little teasing.

"I believe I am, Jaxon Berman. Permanently, if you'll have me."

"What do you say, wife?" He turned to Charlee. She answered by pulling him down for a kiss, then turned and kissed me—all of our lips just breaths apart. I wondered what my parents' neighbors would have to say later about this drama happening on the front lawn.

"I say yes." She smiled sweetly. "Yes to moving in, job or no job. Yes to loving you, and loving *you*. Yes to us being together no matter what anyone has to say about it. Yes to forgiveness. Yes to all the kisses."

"And sex," I added, winking.

"And sex." Jaxon pulled me in for a hug, sandwiching Charlee between us. She giggled, wriggling a little and for a moment everything was absolutely, irrevocably perfect.

"I want you to come in—to the party. Eat, meet my family, let me introduce you properly," I said, not ready to let them go. I hadn't even let go of their hands.

Charlee looked hesitant. "Your mom probably hates us."

"She loves you. Because I love you." I'd never been more certain of anything in my life.

"We may as well pull the awkward Band-Aid off now or we'll just be prolonging the inevitable," Jax said, ever the sensible one. "We can't exactly avoid her until the wedding," he joked with a crooked grin.

"Don't say things like that." I shoved him playfully.

"Why not?"

"Because I want it." The words dropped from my mouth, heavier than I expected, shadowing my chest with quiet hope.

"Be my boyfriend first," Jax said, but he didn't say no—and

that was enough to light something inside me. Something that felt like trust. Faith. Patience for what was to come. No matter how long it may take to get there.

"Come on, let's eat." I tugged them toward the house, fingers still tangled with theirs.

Charlee wrinkled her nose. "My anxiety about seeing your mom is making me nauseous. I don't think I could eat."

"If anyone has anything negative to say about either of you they'll have to go through me first," I announced. "Besides, I'm about to come out to my entire family, so I think that'll keep everyone a little distracted."

Jax guffawed as I opened the door—and nearly ran right into my mother.

"Oh, I was wondering what was keeping you." Her tone was gentle, but wary. My mother was the most loving person I knew —gracious, forgiving—but she was also fiercely protective of me. I saw it in her eyes, the flash of a memory of me, hollowed and broken, curled in bed.

"Mom." I let go of their hands and stepped into her embrace. "We talked. It's all good—perfect even. They're moving in with me." I paused. "We're gonna get married—someday."

Jax cleared his throat. "I—uh..."

"Okay." I laughed, flushing. "No one's technically asked me yet, but I told them—I want that. I love them. I know this is a lot and... I know it's fast. But I'm so happy, Mom."

I was rambling now, overwhelmed with how to explain it all. Of how to do this. How to show her what this felt like. The peace. The certainty. The love. It was all rushing out of me in this messy, happy, open joy—and in that moment, I didn't care how I looked. I was ready to dive right out of the closet in front of everyone, if that's what it took.

*Yes,* my inner child applauded, *we're done hiding.*

My mother gave me a kiss on the cheek.

"I knew you'd find your way back to each other. True love has a funny way of doing that."

Relief broke through me like sunlight.

Then she turned to Jax and Charlee. "And you, my darlings." She hugged Charlee first, then Jax. Something inside me healed as I watched her arms wrap around them.

"All people make mistakes. But great people apologize and grow from their mistakes." She kissed Charlee on the cheek. "I'm just so glad you're both okay."

Then my mother slipped an arm through hers. "Now come—just in time. We're just about to start a slideshow of Liam's baby pictures, and I'm pretty sure there are a few naked ones in there."

Charlee giggled as I groaned, trailing behind them—two of the three most important women in my life. I didn't know what I'd done to deserve this but *healing* felt really, really good.

I pulled up extra chairs at my table so they could sit next to me during the slideshow. After it ended and my mother gave her speech, my brothers voiced how thrilled they were to see both Charlee and Jax, and they all fell into comfortable conversation, catching up. Remi and I had a silent exchange across the table, and he quickly understood that all had been forgiven. He brought Jax a beer and clapped him on the back with a welcoming hug. Charlee waved off his offer of a drink, saying she'd have to drive home. I wanted to make her a plate of food, but she said her stomach was still in knots over the interview and everything that had gone down today, so she couldn't handle a big meal. She agreed to let me make her a plate of freshly cut fruit, and I filled a bowl with strawberry sorbet.

Most of the guests were now dancing on the makeshift dance floor near the pool. Others had changed into bathing suits and were lounging in the hot tub, which left my immediate family and closest friends surrounding me where we sat around the fire pit on various chairs and outdoor couches.

"Charlee and Jax will be moving in with me," I announced

quickly. Everyone's eyes turned to me. I felt my dad's gaze boring holes into the side of my skull.

"Y'all taking turns living in each other's apartments?" Lia joked. Thankfully her husband wasn't around.

"No. More.like.we.are.dating." I said it so quickly I wasn't sure anyone would understand me, but the collective deep breath from the group told me they had.

"You're dating both of them?" Landon clarified. I nodded quickly. I felt Charlee stiffen when no one said anything.

"You're dating Jax?" my oldest brother, Leo, asked, sounding confused.

"I'm bi." It came out like a whisper, but it felt like a scream—to my ears and my heart. My heart that drummed against my rib cage. There, I'd said it.

"Oh." My sister-in-law seemed to verbalize it for the whole group.

"Y'all are married, right?" Levi confirmed. Jax nodded. My heart still hammered in my chest.

"So, like you're, like, polygamists?" my youngest brother, Landon, questioned.

"No," Shaen interjected. "That's one man who marries a bunch of wives. This is polyamory, which is an open relationship between the three of them. It's basically ethical non-monogamy."

"Huh." Lance, my other brother, mulled that over.

"Seems cool to me," my friend Carter crowed. I laughed—of course he'd be down for multiple partners. Nothing ever threw him for a loop. My laugh finally cracked the awkward tension.

"If anyone has an issue with it," Remi declared, "they'll have a meeting with my fist."

"No one has an issue with it," my father said, standing now, surprise still etched into his features. He came over to shake Jax's hand and give Charlee a hug.

"Welcome to the family," he told them warmly. "Let's talk later." He squeezed my shoulder. "I love you." I nodded.

"I love you too, Dad."

LATER THAT NIGHT, I watched Charlee and Jax pull out of the parking spot and head for the highway. They waved one more time, and I fervently hoped Charlee would get the job. I was almost there. I was just about to press play on the rest of my life. I'd graduated. I had a job. I had a new apartment. I'd come out to my family and friends. All I needed now was for them to be there when I woke up and went to sleep.

Then everything would be exactly how I needed it to be. I was so close. To peace. To love. To home.

I was bone-tired, and I hadn't even done anything too strenuous today other than direct the movers where to put our boxes. Maybe it was the back-to-back shifts I'd done during my last week of work, or the late FaceTime calls with Liam, or the intense round of sex with Jax last night to say goodbye to our apartment. Whatever it was, I could barely keep my eyes open.

I also needed to ask Liam to order me an antibiotic—I was peeing constantly, and although it didn't burn yet, I felt a UTI coming on. Perks of your boyfriend being an OBGYN. The word *boyfriend* still had the same thrill it did two weeks ago when we officially started dating. It almost didn't feel real, not after everything we'd almost lost.

I lay back on Liam's couch—*my* couch, I corrected. This was my apartment now too. This huge, spacious, freshly built condo was more like it. Three bedrooms, a large kitchen, two full bathrooms and a half bath, an actual laundry room, and the building had an elevator. No more hauling groceries up flights of stairs.

I closed my eyes, remembering the looks of shock on everyone's faces when Liam announced I was his girlfriend, and my

husband was his boyfriend. His family had barely skipped a beat. They hadn't stuttered with their questions. They hadn't judged or seemed upset—just confused. But even that had quickly cleared to acceptance. I knew my parents would probably get stuck in confusion and Jax's parents would stick staunchly to rejection. I hadn't known what such a loving family looked like until I'd seen Liam's firsthand.

As angry as Shaen had been before was just as loving as she was after. I ended up holding Billie for the rest of the party, and Liam had whispered that he wanted to practice putting a baby in me later. Shaen overheard and said, "Ew, Liam," before winking at me and laughing.

Just like Julia, Liam's father had also been amazing. So welcoming and accepting, Liam told me, on one of our FaceTime calls, that later on, when they were alone, his father had broken down crying, thinking about Liam not feeling safe enough to tell him he was bi.

"Everyone loves you, babe," he'd said excitedly, disappearing from the screen momentarily to pull on his scrubs for his first day at his new job. It had been two weeks now, and he just kept saying how happy he was. It almost made me feel like we were making up for how miserable he'd been not that long ago.

I smiled, snuggling deeper into the soft couch. I'd be starting my new job on Monday. It was a short drive from the condo, way less traffic than the city, and had much better hours. Jax's new position at the company meant he'd be working from home a few days a week—and a few of those days coincided with mine. It felt like a dream come true. A new boyfriend, a new condo, a happy husband, and a calmer work schedule. Maybe I'd even have time to work out—the pill weight was stubborn and my scrubs were getting tight.

Not a big deal body-wise but if it meant my hormones were still off, I wanted to address it. I made a mental note to ask Liam to order bloodwork too.

"I'm hooome," Liam called out, bounding into the apartment. He tossed his work bag and stethoscope onto the counter and ran over to me. We'd moved in while he was at work, so this was his first time seeing me officially living here.

I'd never seen him so happy—it was like he'd been walking on air for the last two weeks.

We hadn't seen each other in person since the party, because everyone's schedules had been so insane, so I was practically starving for his touch when he knelt beside me and kissed me.

"I love you, I love you, I love you." He kissed down my neck, under my shirt, and sucked on my nipple, through my bra.

"Ouch." I winced, suddenly sensitive.

"Oh fuck, babe, sorry—too much. I'm just so fucking psyched that you're here. You have no idea." He kissed the skin above my belly button, then pulled my shirt back down.

"Where's Jax?" he asked, kicking off his shoes and stripping off his scrub top.

"He went to get dinner." I watched him appreciatively, noting how his happy trail disappeared down past the waistband of his pants. "He asked what you want." I pointed to his phone.

"Ooh. Let me see." Liam opened our group chat. Jax had rejoined, and Liam had jokingly threatened to hurt him if he ever left it again. I'd changed the group name from *We at 3C* to *We at Unit 405* but it didn't have the same ring, so I just left it as *We*.

My phone buzzed as Liam typed.

LIAM:

Hey, baby. Thanks for going. I'll take wonton soup and sticky honey gochujang chicken

JAX:

Already got it. I know your favorites

LIAM:

God that's sexy

JAX:

What? Your boyfriend knowing your Chinese
food order?

LIAM:

Fuck. I think I just came a little

JAX:

Lmao. You're an idiot

LIAM:

Ur idiot

JAX:

Facts. See you soon. (Heart emoji)

LIAM:

We're starting without u, so hurry up (eggplant
emoji)


I snorted, then shrieked when Liam scooped me up and
shoved open the door to our room.

"I've been semi-hard all day thinking about christening this
room with both of you." He deposited me onto the bed and pulled
off his pants.

"That must've been awkward for your patients," I joked.

"Tell me about it. I had to keep running through the different
kinds of UTIs in my head to keep my boner from showing." He
pulled off his boxers and climbed onto the bed.

"Not to ruin the moment, but I think I have a UTI," I told him
awkwardly. I was fully comfortable with him, but telling your
new boyfriend you might have a bladder infection wasn't exactly
sexy.

"What are your symptoms?" He tugged off my sweatpants.
"Cloudy urine, low abdominal pain, urgency to pee, discharge,
fever…?"

"You're hot in doctor mode," I teased.

"I'm hot in any mode when I'm with you," he corrected. I lifted my arms willingly as he pulled off my shirt.

"Really just the frequent peeing."

He peered down at me, looking lost in thought.

"Hmm."

"Hmm what?"

He ran a hand down my ribs. I shivered. He kept going, hands resting on my pubic bone, fingers prodding and pressing around my pelvis.

"You're gonna make me have to pee again." I tried to wriggle away.

"Charlee…"

"Liam…"

"Your nipples are sensitive." He gestured to where they stood at attention beneath my bra, the wet spot from his mouth still visible.

"Yeah, so? I'm still waiting on my period. All the hormones…" My voice faded as he kissed my stomach.

"You're peeing a lot," he murmured. "You mentioned you were nauseous at the party. Did that stop?"

It hadn't. The smell of eggs yesterday morning nearly made me puke.

"The pill fucked me up, babe," I tried to protest, anxiety building. "I had some bleeding two weeks ago. Just not a full period."

I didn't tell him that it has been one wipe of red—not even close to "some bleeding."

"I can feel your fundus, Charlee."

His voice was quiet. Tone serious.

I sat up, grabbing my shirt, and covered myself. "No you can't." I looked down at my stomach in horror.

He left the room, returning with a Doppler and a pregnancy test.

"Stop it. I'm just bloated. I ate a lot of—"

"Lay back, baby. Let me take a listen."

He slipped his boxers back on. I guess searching for a baby's heartbeat in your brand-new girlfriend's uterus wasn't exactly a turn-on.

"No," I said, eyes stinging. I'd gained weight. I kept getting acne. I'd gone off the pill three weeks ago and still haven't gotten my period. I couldn't stop peeing. I was nauseous.

"No… No. No. No. No." I grabbed the pregnancy test from him and darted around unpacked boxes to the en-suite bathroom. I tried to shut the door but he followed me in.

"I'm not peeing in front of you, Liam! Get out." My hands were shaking. I fumbled with the packaging. My hormones just needed to even out. I ate two cinnamon buns at work two days ago, hence my bloat. I was getting a UTI. I kept crying because it had been an emotional few weeks. *Right?* I couldn't get the motherfucking package open. I threw it into the sink in frustration.

Liam came over, like he was approaching a feral cat. I could barely look at him and almost flinched when he rubbed my back with one hand while he held the package in the other and ripped it open with his teeth. *Why was that so hot?* He smirked and pressed a kiss to my temple.

"Sit, Charlee," he instructed gently. I wasn't wearing any underwear, so I just sat. He knelt and held the test between my legs. "Pee."

"Liam." I tried to stand. He pushed me back down.

"I am not fucking peeing on a stick that you're holding. Oh my god, Liam."

"Sweetheart. Your hands are shaking."

I looked. They were.

"Nothing could make me not be so fucking attracted to you. Not even you splashing pee on me. Honestly, it might even be hot. I don't know. We'll have to see."

I laughed and teared up at the same time. My bladder screamed in protest—I had to pee so bad. *I'm so scared. I'm so scared. I'm so scared.* My brain raced. *This was not part of the plan. At least not yet.*

I didn't know if I was ready to be a mother, to raise a new life. Not when I was still figuring out how to live this one myself.

"Look away," I told him.

"I'm looking at you, baby." He smiled and kept his eyes on mine, holding the stick between my legs until I finally gave in and let out a stream of urine. He leaned in and kissed me, then took the stick, capped it, and waited for me to finish. He handed me a bunch of toilet paper when I was done.

"You don't need to baby me," I grumbled.

"Yes I do." He watched the pregnancy test while I turned the water on to wash my hands.

"I'm not pregnant," I insisted. "I was on the pill."

We both said nothing as I finished washing my hands. I turned to dry them. "I'm not pregnant. I'd know if I was…"

"Yes you are," he interrupted.

My heart felt like it fell out through my feet.

"What?" I whispered. Shock reverberated through me.

He held up the test, grinning. Two dark lines. Very dark.

"Fuck me." My knees buckled, and his hand shot out to hold me up.

"I plan to," he said, lust strong in his tone, as he guided me back to the bed. I walked with him, robotically, all of my thoughts racing through my head at once. He lay me back against a pillow and took out his measuring tape. I just lay there, letting him do his thing. The two lines were burned into my vision.

"You're measuring around ten to twelve weeks. I won't know for sure until we do an ultrasound, but by palpation, that would be my guess. Must have happened when you first went on the pill."

"That was months ago." I was in shock. He nodded as he squeezed some ultrasound gel onto my pelvis and pulled out the fetal Doppler.

"Ready to hear our baby's heartbeat?" He sounded so excited that for a moment I forgot how terrified, how blindsided I was and smiled at him.

Just as we heard Jax open the door.

"Where y'all at?" he called. "I've got dinner and I'm starving."

*Fuck me.* I didn't know what to say or do. I didn't move.

He stepped into the bedroom moments later.

"What's that? Some sort of weird dildo?" He leaned against the doorframe, arm flexing from the effort. *He was so hot.* Yeah, my hormones were definitely out of control... *Lord help me, I was suddenly never hornier.*

"Jax."

He looked at me, concern instantly replacing his smirk.

"What's going on?"

"I have to tell you something..." I started.

"Charlee is..." Liam said at the same time.

I nodded at him, motioning for him to do the announcing part. I was suddenly swallowing back the nausea swelling in my throat.

"Charlee is pregnant, Jax," Liam finished.

"What?" Jax looked completely taken aback, then... excitement flared in his eyes. He crossed into the room in two big strides and sat down beside me, bouncing me slightly with his movements. "Are you lying?" He sounded apprehensive.

"Why would we lie about that?" I giggled nervously.

"She's around three months along." Liam still held the Doppler. Jax's brows furrowed as he paused to do the math.

"Wait. We always used condoms..." Jax's voice trailed off.

"Until I went on the pill," I reminded him. My fear morphed into guilt.

"We both came in you." He looked at me, stunned. I nodded. The horror of the unknown had been creeping along the edges of my mind since seeing those two lines but they crashed into me now, shaking my brave resolve as Jax verbalized it.

"I know."

"So we don't know…" His eyes flicked to Liam. Liam shook his head.

"Which one of us got her pregnant," Jax completed his sentence quietly.

"We both did." Liam turned the Doppler on and pressed it to my belly.

"I mean, scientifically…" Jax started, but the soft static sound from the Doppler cut him off.

"This baby was made by love. This baby will be raised with love. With two dads and a mom who adore it. So, in my mind, I don't give a fuck whose sperm got there first. I'll love all of my kids no matter who made them, because she will grow them—and that's what matters to me," Liam said emphatically.

Somehow, despite my racing thoughts, his words made everything inside of me calm and grow peaceful.

"Can we grow this one first before we talk about more?" I asked weakly.

Liam laughed—and then we all stilled. Suddenly, the fast rhythm of our baby's heartbeat filled the room.

I gripped Jax's hand as tears welled up in my eyes yet again.

"Is that…?" He looked between Liam and me, wonder spreading across his face.

"That's our baby." Liam's smile took over his whole face, and I got swept up in his happiness. The worry, the fear, the anxiety—all put aside for a moment.

"Our baby," Jax echoed. "Oh my god, Charlee. Are you okay? Did you lift anything heavy? We had no idea." Jax jumped into full-on overprotective dad mode.

"I thought it was the pill." I sniffled. "I've been having all the symptoms but I'm such an idiot…"

Liam moved the Doppler aside and leaned up to kiss me.

"You're not an idiot. Don't say that. A lot of the symptoms

overlap. You just didn't think of it." He gently wiped the gel off my stomach with a paper towel, then kissed me again.

"Oh my god." Jax was still reeling. Honestly? So was I. Liam seemed like the only one who was excited and chill at the same time. I needed a minute. My whole world felt like it had just been shaken up like a snow globe.

Jax leaned down, touching my stomach gently.

"Hi, baby," he whispered. "I love you. It's Dad." He looked at Liam. "You down to be Daddy and I'll be Dad?"

His question was so sincere I cracked up through my tears.

"I can be Daddy." Liam's eyes were suspiciously wet and he bent to press a kiss to Jax's cheek. Then he looked at me like he was saying, *he's such a sweet, sweet man, isn't he?*

Jax went back to stroking my stomach. I knew the movement was supposed to be heartwarming, gentle, and appreciating this gift—a shocking gift I hadn't expected but a gift all the same—that we'd been given. But his mouth was so close to… other areas of my body and we hadn't been near Liam in two whole weeks, and suddenly I was desperate for them. I couldn't take it anymore.

"I need to be fucked so bad," I blurted.

Liam paused from where he was putting the Doppler away. Jax lifted his hand off me, startled.

"I'm sorry, I'm just…"

"Why are you apologizing?" Liam stalked over, pulling his boxers back off. "You asking has me hard as a rock."

"Fuck." Jax seemed to still be trying to catch up—first baby news and now Liam's cock was in his face.

"Suck it," Liam ordered, acting like the bossy one now. And Jax did just that. Liam's fingers clenched in his hair as his mouth worked him over until he was straining not to come.

"Stop." Liam pulled out, squeezing the tip. "Fuuuck."

I watched greedily as Jax took off his clothes and joined him on the bed. Liam scooted behind me, flipping me so I was sitting in his lap, Jax came closer, behind me.

"This won't hurt the… baby… right?" he asked, hesitant. I was grateful Liam didn't laugh at his question. We both understood he just didn't know.

"Not at all," Liam confirmed. "Sex is very safe for normal, healthy pregnancies. I'll bring her into the office tomorrow to do blood work and an ultrasound to confirm, but as far as I can see and hear, everything looks perfect."

Jax nodded, reassured. I squirmed in Liam's lap, aching for him, feeling his hard cock beneath me but not close enough.

"Feeling feisty, huh?" Liam smacked my ass lightly. I moaned.

"Yeah you are, all the hormones and blood flow will do that to ya."

I could've laughed at how he was dirty-talking science, but he suddenly had his mouth on mine and his fingers in me.

"Oh fuck." I heard from behind me as Jax drew near. I felt him behind me, crowding me closer to Liam. Liam kissed me like his life depended on it. Jax lifted me slightly, and I felt him guide Liam's cock inside me.

"Oh my god," I gasped as he filled me, sliding in, thick and deep. Liam's eyes were fixated on the place he entered me, and I followed his gaze, watching it—slick, wet, and perfect. He kept moving, stretching me to a fullness that I desperately needed.

Jax kissed his way down my neck, then around to my breasts, weighing one in his palm.

"You're bigger," he said conversationally, as if I wasn't currently being wrecked.

"They are," Liam groaned, running a hand over the other. I sucked in a breath at the sensitivity.

"Is this what you needed?" Liam asked, bouncing me on his cock, gripping my waist. I nodded. "You needed Dad and Daddy to take care of you?" He winked, then threw back his head and laughed when I warned, "Don't ever fucking say that to me again."

"Okay, Mommy," he teased, cracking himself up once more. I shook my head.

"No!"

Jax ran a hand over the slight swell of my belly.

"Mommy is kinda hot," he admitted. Liam looked up at him, sweat beginning to form at his temples. His abs flexed with every movement, and I felt an orgasm begin its rumbling quakes in my pelvis.

"It is, isn't it," he gasped.

"I can't believe you guys are just chatting while we… while you… ah, fuck." I came, hard, clinging to Liam's shoulders, closing my eyes and giving myself over to the grip my pleasure had on me. When it passed, I rolled off Liam who lay there—spent, sweaty, and satiated. He didn't even open his eyes when he said, "I love you both so much, and I'm so happy we made a baby together. I can't wait."

"I'm scared," I admitted.

"Of which part?" Jax asked.

"Labor doesn't seem like the funnest thing a girl could do." I laughed, thinking of the many births I'd attended at work.

"We'll be there. I will not let anything happen to you." Liam's tone turned fierce. "I promise you, my love, I will make sure of it."

I believed him.

"And then… raising a kid. I want to be better than our parents were." I gestured to Jax and me. "I want to be like Julia."

Liam smiled softly at the mention of his mother.

"You won't find a better grandmother than my mom. If you want, she'll teach you everything she knows. She is going to freak out. Oh my god." He laughed, and I imagined he was picturing his mother's reaction to finding out about this baby.

*Grandmother.* I hadn't even thought of that. If we were going to go with the *they both made this baby route* then technically Julia would be our baby's grandmother, no matter what a paternity test ended up revealing. And what a gift I would be giving to my child. A family that offered unconditional love was better than anything I could ever think of.

"No one could be a better mom than you, Charlee," Jax said hoarsely.

"Thank you, Jax." I smiled at him—then moaned as he pushed his finger inside me, running it through the cum Liam had left behind.

He licked his finger clean, then sat beside Liam and pulled me into his lap. He cock slid in and I gasped at the sensitivity. Jax groaned.

"She's extra tight, huh," Liam said.

Jax nodded. "So tight."

Liam leaned over, capturing Jax's mouth with his. I watched as they kissed, appreciating how hot they were, and how much they enjoyed each other. Then something new happened—Jax tugged me forward and turned his face away, so Liam's next kiss landed on me.

"I love you," Jax said to both of us, as he handed Liam the gift of my lips. Liam groaned, "I love you both so much," against my mouth before he dove back in licking, biting, and kissing. I echoed the sentiment. Jax was pounding into me now, I leaned back, gasping, as his thumb swirled circles around my swollen clit.

"Shit. Shit," Jax muttered, slowing down, changing to deep, lazy strokes, taking his time as he slid in and out.

"Fuck that's hot." Liam leaned over and spit on me, leaving me glistening. Then he rubbed me while Jax picked up the pace again. Liam's scent and body surrounded me, and Jax came with a shout, I followed, moments later, with my second orgasm of the night.

One of them kissed me. Or maybe both. I didn't know. Didn't care.

"I love you," I whispered. "Thank you."

"Anytime, baby." They both chuckled.

I fell asleep in our big bed, their baby inside me, their love wrapped around me like a blanket. I didn't know what tomorrow would bring—but I was no longer afraid. My heart was full, my mind finally at rest.

We were going to get our happy ending. Finally.

To say I was in shock was an understatement. I hadn't prepared for this kind of curveball. When I told Charlee I wanted a baby, I'd imagined a baby that was half me and half her. Up until seven months ago, that was the only option our child could have been. Then things got interesting—to put it mildly—and here we were.

I didn't regret anything. I wasn't questioning anything. Liam enhanced everything about our marriage, our lives together, and even who I was as a human being. Waking up this morning, in our huge bed, in our new condo, to the sounds of Charlee snoring lightly to my left and Liam brushing his teeth in the bathroom had made me feel like I was finally, really home. So no, I wasn't regretting anything. And I wouldn't change the situation even if I could. But I was still in shock.

Liam came out of the bathroom and saw that I was awake. He told me he had coffee made for me in the kitchen, so I stumbled out of bed, just in my boxers, and went to drink the cup of coffee with him out on our deck.

We sat there silently, watching the sun cast beautiful colors across the sky. We had trees here—lots of them. And grass. Deer.

Flowers. Even squirrels instead of rats. I was enthralled with the whole picturesque scene of what living in suburbia had to offer. It was a welcome reprieve from the constant sound of horns, yelling, and traffic that I had grown used to.

"We're gonna be dads, bro. I'm so fucking excited." He brought it up first, startling me from my thoughts.

"How are you feeling about it? I know it's a surprise. And we all just moved in together," I deflected, asking him about his feelings instead of sharing mine.

"Dude, it's the best surprise. I've always wanted kids, and having one with you two? It's like a dream come true. Maybe the timing is a little wonky, but we're now a three-income household and we're three awesome people... What I'm trying to say is, I think we got this. Don't you?"

"I'm not worried about any of that," I assured him.

"Then what are you worried about?"

I shrugged. "I guess I just feel weird about not knowing who the biological father is," I admitted.

I felt bad saying it because if the baby Charlee was carrying was biologically Liam's, our baby would be smart, kind, tall, healthy, driven, funny, and good-looking. Literally a parent couldn't ask for better genes for their kid than Liam Hennessy's. But I still felt weird about it. It kind of felt like FOMO. I was fully ready to parent with both of them, and I didn't doubt for a second that I would love this baby and see it as my child no matter whose it was biologically. But I still had this innate desire to leave someone behind who was genetically mine. Call it the caveman in me, but I wanted a little part of me running around on this earth. Call it selfish, but I wanted to see myself in someone's eyes. I wanted proof that I existed long after I was gone.

Liam pondered what I said for a while before answering.

"I fully understand what you're saying. And not only that, but up until not that long ago, getting pregnant would have been something that happened just between the two of you. Her telling you she was pregnant would have looked different. You supporting her through the pregnancy would have been a bond just between you two. It would've been just the two of you becoming parents together. It was set to look a certain way, and now me being here has really changed the entire dynamic. And in a way I am sorry, because it's not how you imagined it going."

"No, I—" I rushed to tell him that I was okay with it looking different. I would never want to hurt his feelings. Our relationship with him was certainly not conventional, but I wouldn't have it any other way. He held up a hand to shush me.

"I know." He smiled. "I love you too, but the fact is, it's different. And that's okay. Everything about us is going to be different to society. The delivery room, date nights, PTA, our wedding..." He winked and made me laugh. "But in all seriousness, I have a plan. I didn't sleep much last night because I was thinking all of this through. Obviously only one of us is biologically this baby's father, and our relationship is still new—like you said you literally just moved in." We both chuckled at how right he was.

"But ideally, I see forever with both of you. And that hopefully means more kids, and legally protecting all of them. So my idea is —we do a DNA test, but for the first year only our lawyer knows who the bio father is, so legal proceedings can be put into place giving the non-biological parent power to make medical decisions, putting all of us on the birth certificate, etc. This will give us a year to fully bond and raise this baby together, not knowing whose it is biologically. Once the year is up and we all love this baby no matter what, we'll start proceedings for me to adopt the baby or for you to adopt the baby so all three of us will legally be the baby's parent. Once we know, I'm sure neither of us will love the baby any less—no matter whose sperm lost the race." Liam grinned at me, and I was yet again reminded of how smart and calculated he was.

"Lastly, once we know who fathered our first child, if Charlee agrees to have more, the other one of us will be the one to make sure she gets pregnant with his baby, so we each have a fully biological child. Just because it's nice to see how your genes play out. Ya know?"

"That's fucking genius." I looked at him, stunned. Of course he'd thought this through. Of course he'd found a way to make all of us whole.

"I know, but don't tell Charlee. She needs to get through growing this one first." Liam laughed and gathered up our coffee cups. "I need to run to work, but I love you." He smacked a kiss on my lips. "And I can't wait to see you at her sonogram later. Tell our baby mama I say bye—I don't want to disrupt her sleep."

"Have a good day." I watched him go, finally able to openly admire his ass in those scrubs and appreciating how much more relaxed I felt now that Liam had told me about his plan.

We were going to have a baby.

I wanted to yell it out to the whole neighborhood and send up a smoke signal in the sky. But I settled for leaning back in my chair, letting the sun beam down on my face, waiting for my baby mama to wake up so I could talk to her belly again and make her breakfast.

# CHAPTER THIRTY-ONE

## LIAM

E ver since finding out Charlee was having a baby, I eased right into impending fatherhood. I guess it came with the territory. Maybe it was my training—or maybe I just wanted her to feel protected in a world I couldn't always control. But truthfully, nothing alarmed me—pregnancy insomnia? No problem. I suggested magnesium baths, lavender sprayed on her pillow, some prenatal yoga before bed, and lemon balm tea. Low iron showed up on her blood work, so I instructed Jax to start cooking with a cast-iron pan and to make more iron-rich foods —which, of course, he did. Sharp, sudden pains in her pelvis? Not to worry, I told both Charlee and Jax it was called round ligament pain and suggested she start wearing a pregnancy binder for support. When her first stretch mark showed up, I brought over a homemade cream that Shaen made to prevent any more from forming. I don't know if it really worked, but her skin always felt soft and smelled incredible.

Over the next six months our chat was full of talks of constipation, vivid dreams, sciatic pain, reminders to eat potassium and magnesium-rich foods to avoid leg cramps, and strange pregnancy cravings.

Charlee once needed a very specific hot pretzel that she ate one time at a local fair. We couldn't find it anywhere. Shaen saved the day by baking some. Charlee said they weren't exactly the same but close enough that it healed her hot pretzel fixation. One night, she sent me on a goose chase for gummy candy—and not just any gummy candy. It had to be *very* specific Swedish candy. I ended up spending a small fortune trying to locate the right one. She ate a few, was happy, and the rest now sits in our pantry. One week, all she could stomach was Chipotle. The next week, Chipotle was an abomination and if any of us ate it, we had to brush our teeth and air our clothes out before coming near her. A few weeks after that she suddenly craved Coke—but it had to be *McDonald's* Coke. I tried to tell her that the soda machines were notoriously dirty, but she cried. So McDonald's E. coli-Coke it was.

Jax started listening to a pregnancy book on his phone. The chapter about actual birth made him anxious, but he didn't want to tell Charlee because he didn't want to make her anxious. Of course, neither of them thought that *I* might be anxious about this, because I delivered babies all the time. However, the closer we got to her due date the more my brain fixated on her going into labor and worrying about every little thing that could go wrong. I just kept redirecting my thoughts to all the successful deliveries I had done up until now. So many deliveries that Charlee even started keeping track of each one. She got a jar and began adding a pink stone for each girl and a blue one for every boy. Jax asked me what the few white stones were for, and I told him, "They represent the babies born sleeping." He had paled at that answer.

I wasn't a worrier by nature, but something about watching my girlfriend's body slowly expand—knowing my child was in there, her organs moving out of the way, her blood volume increasing by thirty to fifty percent—it affected me more than I'd anticipated.

I saw how much Jax already loved this baby, and I was happy to see that he had come around to the idea that it wasn't just DNA that made a baby yours. It was love. And your intention behind that love. My intention was to give this baby the best life possible. Not only would I show up as a dad, but my baby would also be loved by Charlee and Jax. My family. Shaen, Remi, and Billie. Jax's uncle. His sisters. Charlee's brother. Honestly, a kid couldn't ask for more.

I remembered when we told my mom that Charlee was pregnant. My poised, perfect mother dropped an entire casserole on the floor, made a huge mess, and clung to me, then Charlee, then Jax—mascara smudged tears running down her cheeks—telling us how excited and happy she was. It was a sheer contrast to Jax's parents. His mother said, "Oh, how nice." His father had hung up and blamed it on bad service.

At thirty weeks, Shaen threw Charlee a baby shower. All of her friends, Jax's sisters—even her mom—came. At the end, Charlee was so overwhelmed by the crowd and mountain of gifts they had brought that I found her doom scrolling on her phone and eating marshmallow fluff out of the container in a closet in Shaen's room.

"I already passed my glucose test," she told me when she saw me eying the fluff.

"I didn't say anything." I held up my hands in surrender. I had really just been staring at her, taking in how beautiful she was. She'd always been gorgeous, but now, watching her body change to grow our baby—it was something I'd never get tired of witnessing.

The twenty-week sonogram had revealed that we were having a little boy. Charlee had been ecstatic. Jax had cried. Now at thirty-eight weeks, we'd settled on a name that all three of us had brought pieces to. Being Jewish, Jax had chosen the Hebrew name Aziel for a first name. He wasn't religious at all, but he wanted to instill an appreciation in our kid for his heritage and the strength of the people who survived before him. I loved the name and the meaning behind it, and we all agreed that it was the perfect choice for our son. Charlee had chosen the name Wolf for his middle name, after her Native American grandfather, honoring her Tuscarora descent.

"Wolf means strength and courage," she told us. "And he'll need to be strong when the kids at school find out he has three parents, because I worry they're going to make fun of him."

"Then we better make sure he's good-looking, smart, great at sports, well-read, and hella funny so everyone realizes it doesn't fucking matter how many parents he has," I said. I would teach him how to be proud of his family—how to make 'different' look like strength.

"I just suggest we teach him how to throw a punch," Jax muttered.

I was happy to name our kid Aziel Wolf, I just told my partners that I wanted to hyphenate his last name to Hennessy-Berman.

"Kids gonna have a mouthful of a name I guess," Jax said in agreement.

"Guess so." I chomped happily on a steak sandwich he'd made me. Charlee was on chicken-only week, so she was eating a chicken burrito, reading arguments for and against giving vitamin K and the hepatitis B vaccine in the hospital or waiting till later.

"Are we gonna circumcise him?" she suddenly asked.

"For hygiene purposes, I vote yes," I piped up.

"It'll be another thing for him to get made fun of in the locker room if we don't," Jax told her.

"I know, but it seems so barbaric," Charlee complained. "And people online are saying it reduces sexual pleasure."

"I'm doing just fine in that area with my cut dick," I said, winking.

"Well, I leave it up to you guys. You're the ones with a penis."

Charlee struggled to get off the couch and had to resort to turning and grabbing the side to hoist herself up. She waddled toward the kitchen, putting her plate in the sink.

"Are you boys done Christmas shopping?" she asked, opening the fridge to get a drink.

"I haven't started," we said at the same time.

"Jinx," I said with a grin.

Jax was my boyfriend, my lover, my girlfriend's husband—but he was also my friend. A best friend. We laughed all the time. I loved hanging out with him. I enjoyed listening to him talk. We watched games together, cooked together, and hung out with the same friends. Apparently, we also annoyed Charlee together, because she rolled her eyes at us.

"The Christmas party at Julia's is next week. You have a Secret Santa gift to buy. It'll ruin the game if either of you forgets," she explained.

"We'll do it. Promise," I placated her.

She winced and put her hand on her stomach.

"Everything okay?" I was back to silently worrying.

"Yeah, there's just no room left in here. I'm gonna go finish organizing the nursery."

We had finished painting and putting up wallpaper last week. Jax and I put together all the furniture, and now Charlee was busy washing, folding and organizing all the baby clothes. It was hard to believe that in just two short weeks, our baby would be here and I'd be a Daddy.

With labor being imminent, it was something I was excitedly waiting for—and also anxiously dreading. I knew I'd have to be her partner, not her doctor. I'd have to be patient and not give my opinion too often, and just trust her provider to do their job. I knew it would be challenging for me not only because it was Charlee but because of my experience with Shaen's delivery and wanting to make sure everything was okay instead of sitting back and letting her doctor do his thing. But it was a challenge I was up for, I couldn't say I wasn't curious what it would feel like to be on the other side of things—with my own baby being the one she was giving birth to.

I was so excited, and I kept imagining a healthy, safe, easy birth for Charlee. Instead of letting my imagination go off to places where I knew she'd be in serious pain… those images didn't sit well in my soul.

"Let's go. Apparently, we have shopping to do," Jax told me.

"Tell me who you got." I grabbed my wallet.

"I'm not ruining Secret Santa because you can't wait patiently." Jax laughed.

"Asshole," I tossed back, chuckling with him.

"Your asshole," he corrected. I felt warmth sizzle through me.

"You know it."

The way he made my heart stutter, like I hadn't even realized how much I needed to hear it.

I went to say goodbye to Charlee and my baby, and then left the condo to do some Christmas shopping.

I t was crazy to me that just last year we had gone to Julia and Sam's for their Christmas party. One year ago, we all slept in the same bed for the first time and stepped into the unknown when we fooled around. Twelve months ago, I wore a really cute gauzy dress with a bow on the back, nice and fitted to my flat stomach—and this year, I was huge and couldn't find anything to wear.

My baby chose that moment to kick me, like he was telling me not to call myself huge. Just like his daddies kept telling me. Well, I felt huge. I couldn't see my toes or my vagina anymore. I couldn't even put my own socks on. I was due in ten days, and it felt like ten years. I couldn't sleep, my back hurt constantly, my pelvis ached, I peed every five seconds, and I had a baby kicking me in the ribs nonstop. I felt myself tear up because I couldn't find anything to wear to the Christmas party tonight and because I was desperate to get this baby out of me—but at the same time, I was petrified of giving birth. I knew how bad the pain could get, and while I assisted women in doing it every single shift, I *knew* I could do it, I still didn't relish the idea of actually doing it *myself*.

So, I just stood there, surveying my options in the closet,

299

feeling like a whale. My breasts strained against my bra. My feet felt so swollen, and my stomach got in the way as I tried to turn around.

"What's wrong?" Liam asked from behind me.

Crap. If he was already home from work, that meant I had even less time than I thought to get ready.

"Nothing fits." Even as I rolled my eyes at myself, I was crying. Over clothing.

"What about that dress that we bought specifically for this?" Liam sounded confused. As he should—just last week the three of us had gone shopping and picked out a gold, accordion-pleated dress with an empire waist and a twisted bow design across the chest. It fit well and didn't make it look like I had wrapped myself in a tablecloth.

But the dress put a sour taste in my mouth when I remembered the cashier.

Liam had patted his pocket, realizing he'd left his wallet in the car.

"I got it, babe," Jax said, taking out his phone to pay with Apple Pay.

The cashier had looked at me, and then at the two of them and said, "They both yours?"

I'd nodded.

No matter how many times something like this happened, it still stung. Not because I felt like we were doing something wrong—but because people in "normal" relationships didn't have to defend their love to strangers in checkout lines.

With Liam and Jax, I felt held. Safe in our unconventional arrangement. But the second we stepped out into the world, it was like all the tenderness got stripped away under someone else's scrutiny. Like we were a walking oddity, something to gawk at. I hated that we became a spectacle the second someone realized we weren't just a group of friends out shopping.

"Sheesh, girl." The cashier laughed, but I heard the venom in her tone. "Leave some for the rest of us."

I glared at her until she handed Jax the receipt. I *wished* I could have stalked away gracefully, but instead I'd waddled off on swollen ankles, looking more like an adorable penguin than an angry woman. In retrospect I wondered if I would feel better if I had defended myself.

"I haven't even unwrapped it," I admitted.

"Why not, it was perfect." Liam went to the closet and found the bag with the dress still inside. Tag intact.

"The cashier made me feel stupid." I knew how ridiculous I sounded. The dress had nothing to do with her, and her comment should have no impact on me wearing it tonight.

"She's the one who should be feeling stupid. She made it sound like we are an anomaly. There are like five hundred thousand openly polyamorous families in the United States. It may be a small percentage, but it's not unheard of. And it's becoming more and more accepted each year as people get their heads out of their asses. Anthropologists have found that lifelong monogamy wasn't even a historical human norm. Most ancient societies were more flexible, often practicing polygamy, communal parenting or open partnerships. The idea that we only get one partner for life is a cultural invention, not a biological truth."

Liam's usual speech full of stats made me laugh. He was so hot when he spoke nerdy to me. It also made me feel seen and validated. He looked up from where he was unpacking the dress from its bag.

"What?" He grinned.

"You're cute." I was distracted by a Braxton Hicks cramp squeezing my stomach, leaving me momentarily breathless.

"You okay?" He held the dress up in all its billowing, pleated, gold glory.

I nodded. "If these Braxton Hicks hurt this badly, I don't want to know what real contractions really feel like."

I turned as he unzipped the dress and readied it for me to step into.

"I know, baby. I'm sorry." He kissed my forehead as I turned back around so he could zip it up. I was already out of breath and I had barely done anything.

I knew I'd eventually forget and want another kid, but right now I couldn't imagine doing this again.

"You look amazing," he said softly.

I looked at my reflection in the full-length mirror.

I did.

Even with my face growing puffy from the water retention, there was a glow that came from growing life. I'd seen it many times before in my line of work but had never really understood it until now. Now, I could tell you that the glow represented the mama bear instinct hatching and growing inside of me alongside the baby.

I remembered once seeing a video circulating on social media where mothers were asked if they'd kill for their child. Some hesitated. A few said no. Most said yes. When I saw my son for the first time on the screen during my ultrasound, I knew the interviewer wouldn't have been able to finish his sentence before I gave a resounding yes. What do you mean, no? His first flicker of his heart on the screen, the first time his little feet tickled like butterfly wings inside of me—I *knew* I would tear someone apart if they fucked with him.

So yeah… that glow felt like a special halo that I and the rest of the mothers were given when the maternal instinct kicked in.

I looked at my reflection one last time. My hair had grown so long, and the soft makeup I'd applied earlier was still intact, even after my emotional spiral. I smiled. I looked even better with Liam standing behind me.

"Ten more days, baby. You got this." He ran a hand over my belly before helping me put on my shoes.

We each packed an overnight bag in case the storm they were predicting actually hit and the roads weren't drivable. I had him put my hospital bag in the car too, just in case. He placed it next to his work bag and wrapped gifts for his family.

Jax was already at the house—Sam had asked him and Remi to help build something. When Liam found out, he asked why his help wasn't needed.

Sam had laughed and said something about keeping his hands soft for the babies.

"I know how to use a hammer, Charlee," Liam had grumbled to me, fully insulted.

I'd talked him off a ledge, reminding him that his hands were insured and Jax literally ran construction sites while Remi worked on cars all day. Their hands didn't need to stay as delicate as his did. He'd stayed grumpy for at least ten more minutes.

DINNER WAS A FULL SPREAD, as to be expected. There was salmon in a pomegranate sauce and three different types of soup. Julia had even made a chicken soup with matza balls for Jax. The matza balls were such a hit, the whole pot was gone in minutes. She had platters of crostini smeared with feta and drizzled with honey, meat pies, potatoes made four different ways, brussels sprouts, ham and a roast—thinly sliced and served with a minty pesto sauce. I saw bowls of cranberry meatballs, salads, charcuterie boards, cheese platters, and I thought I heard someone mention lamb chops, but I could barely fit any food in me these days. Not with this baby taking up my entire torso and then some.

Julia found me in the living room, my feet propped up on a pouf, staying warm by the crackling fire.

"How are you, my darling?" She handed me a mug of tea, which I took gratefully.

"I am so done." I sipped the tea, tasting notes of cinnamon, cranberry, and orange. Knowing her, she probably made the tea from scratch. Never from a tea bag.

"You've officially reached the stage of get-this-baby-out-of-me," she noted. "I'm so proud of you for getting here."

I beamed under her praise. She always knew the right thing to say. Jax's mother had barely been a mother to him, let alone a half-decent mother-in-law to me. I'd never experienced this version of in-law love, and I had to admit I thrived under it. Julia took Shaen and me on weekly outings. Sometimes it was a massage, or a mani-pedi, sometimes it was to buy a piece of jewelry or get a facial. She was always checking in on me, always doing something kind—dropping off dinner or having a little something delivered for the baby. She made everyone in her life feel like they were the only one. The most cherished. The most loved. And I had been lucky enough to be added to her list of people. So would my son. I basked in that knowledge, knowing he would come into this world already so cherished by so many.

"Shit." I gritted my teeth when another Braxton Hicks overtook me. I'd had them for so much of my pregnancy that I was used to their off-and-on pressure, but these felt more painful than I was used to.

"Are you alright?" Julia noted the look of pain on my face. I nodded as the squeezing ache passed.

"Braxton Hicks," I told her. The ache in my pelvis still throbbed, and my back pinched, I shifted, trying to find a comfortable position, but my whole body just protested.

She nodded, then looked up as Jax and Liam came inside, followed by the rest of her sons and Remi. They were covered in snow.

"It's really coming down now," Jax told us. "It has snowed a few feet since everyone got here."

"A white Christmas. How fabulous." Julia clapped, looking excited. "Who's ready for dessert?"

She stood to go check on the kitchen as another wave of pressure squeezed my stomach. They were getting worse, more consistent. I focused on my breath, waiting for it to pass. My birth plan was simple: get an epidural. I knew all the breathing techniques, having practiced them with my patients thousands of times, but I wasn't planning on using them all the way through like Shaen had. But this wasn't labor, I was fine.

The pain passed, and I took another sip of tea as Shaen came to sit next to me. Billy was asleep on her shoulder. Her curly hair was getting so long, and Shaen had clipped it back in a little bow, which, rumor had it, made Remi emotional because his daughter was getting so big.

"What's happening?" Shaen asked.

"Nothing. I'm fine," I lied.

"You have a look," she pressed.

"Braxton Hicks," I said through clenched teeth as another contraction squeezed my whole body, every cognitive thought fleeing as all I could do was focus on getting the fuck through it. These were too consistent, too painful to be Braxton Hicks. *You're in labor* fear whispered from the recesses of my mind, but I stayed focused. Just breathing. Trying not to fight the pain.

People milled around, in the rooms nearby, voices and laughter filled the space, the sound of silverware clinking on china and children running in the hall. I let it all wash over me before finally turning to Shaen, who looked concerned, and whispered, "Please find Liam for me."

Liam showed up what felt like eons later, but was probably just ten minutes and two smaller contractions later.

"He was playing video games," Shaen said from behind him, sounding accusatory. "Sorry it took me so long to find him."

"All good." I tried to smile, but I knew my voice sounded more alarmed than calm. The grin slid from Liam's face.

"What's wrong?"

"I believe I am in labor." I finally said it, admitting it out loud to myself and those around me. Acknowledging that my baby had chosen Christmas Eve and a snowstorm as his day to join us. The words felt foreign coming out of my mouth, like I was finally giving in to this ancient rite of being a woman.

Liam handed Shaen the tumbler of whiskey he'd been holding and came closer.

"I can't drive…" he started.

"I know," I said weakly.

"Not 'cause of the alcohol. The snowstorm."

I nodded as a contraction hit. I gripped the arms of the chair. Fuck, they felt like an eternity. The squeezing, the never-ending ache, the awful sensation down below. All of it felt torturous. When it finally eased, I lay my head back, panting. Liam had his phone out, timer going, and I could see he was doing some math in his head.

"If those weren't Braxton Hicks earlier, that means labor has been going on for some time now. I need to check you."

"Can you get my mom and Jax?" he asked Shaen without looking up. He eased off my shoes and braided my hair back.

"I need to get the fuck out of this dress," I begged.

Remi stuck his head in. Clearly Shaen had clued him in on my unfortunate situation.

"I need my hospital bag from the car. It has an OB kit in it," Liam said, tossing Remi his key fob, which he caught gracefully and left the room without saying anything.

"I'm scared," I admitted, lips trembling, my eyes felt wet with unshed tears.

"I know, sweetheart." He smoothed a hand over my forehead. "But I'm here. I won't let anything happen to you."

I nodded as Jax came barreling into the room.

"Calm, Jaxon," Liam said. "We all need to remain calm. For Charlee."

Jax slowed his pace as he came to stand next to me.

"Well, this is shitty timing," I told him, grimacing as another contraction burned its way up my thighs, through my crotch, and around my stomach.

"Five minutes apart," I heard Liam note. "Lasting about forty-five seconds."

"Is that… good or bad?" Jax asked.

"It's neither, it just means she's likely in active labor." Liam was all business now that Remi had returned with his OB kit and Julia had joined us.

"We need to move her and I don't want everyone to see her when we do," Liam told his mother. I knew we needed to pass the dining room to get anywhere private.

"Remi," Julia instructed, "take everyone to the back porch and tell Sam we're doing the fireworks early." Remi nodded, giving me a sympathetic look before he left.

A few minutes later he was back, saying the coast was clear, for now.

"Can you walk?" Liam asked.

"I think so." Jax gently helped me to my feet and put an arm around me, holding me up as we went down the hall.

"Take the first guestroom suite," Julia said. "It has a sunken bathtub and a bench in the shower. Both will be helpful."

I heard her talking to Shaen and got bits about getting more towels and to change the linen to something a darker color. Julia had my overnight bag and helped me change out of my dress and into a pair of pajamas and a sports bra. Everyone left the bathroom so I could pee in peace. When I wiped, I saw that I was bleeding. I called for Liam who came rushing in. He assured me that the bleeding was normal.

"I still need to check you," he said again.

"Okay." I left my shorts off and waddled out of the bathroom.

Shaen had already changed the sheet on the big bed to a dark blue one instead of the cream brocade that had been there before, which eased my anxiety about making a huge mess in here— although I hoped I wasn't progressing much so that I could deliver in the hospital once the roads were clear. Jax helped me up onto the bed and everyone else turned away as Liam prepared to check me. He spread a blue chux pad under me and put on a pair of gloves.

"I'm sorry, baby," he told me as he slid his fingers inside. I grimaced against the discomfort but didn't make a sound. When he removed them, I saw blood again. He took off his gloves, wrapping them in the chux pad to discard.

"Can I make it till morning?" I asked hopefully.

"You're at a six, almost seven." He sounded sorry to tell me that he would likely be delivering our baby right here and tonight. I wasn't able to voice my disappointment because another contraction had me gripped in its claws.

ANOTHER HOUR PASSED as I battled contractions in the bed with Shaen guiding me in breathing through them. She asked Liam if I could go in the shower. Julia had lowered the lighting in the bedroom and bathroom, placing flickering candles everywhere. Soft instrumental music played gently in the background. Remi had gathered up all the pillows he could find to help support my back, Sam had been in briefly, checking my vitals and making sure I wasn't running a fever. Then he refilled my bowl of ice chips, before ducking back out of the room. Jax rubbed my back through every contraction while Liam timed them, writing things down on his makeshift chart and checking on our baby with his portable fetal Doppler, clearly perturbed that he didn't have all of his fancy hospital equipment available to him.

"People give birth at home all the time, Charlee," Shaen told me as she guided me into the shower. Jax had stripped down to his boxers and joined me, holding the handheld shower head against my back, applying pressure where I needed it. I leaned into him instinctively, needing his strength, needing to feel tethered to someone while my body unraveled. Even in this raw, stripped state, he touched me like I was everything. Like I was *precious*.

"In fact, I think I'm gonna try to do it at home next time."

"No you're not," Liam told her. Shaen stuck her tongue out at him and made me laugh. My sports bra was soaked, my braided hair stuck to my skin. I wore nothing else and any sense of modesty had departed when I realized that if Liam was doing the delivery and Jax would be holding one leg then it would likely be Shaen or Julia holding my other leg. But someone would have to be ready to take the baby so maybe Remi would hold a leg, Shaen would act as my doula and Julia, being a nurse, would be ready to take the baby. Either way everyone would be getting an up close introduction to my vagina at some point or another so I gave up on caring that only my breasts were covered—and just barely.

"I can't believe this is happening." I groaned out, humming with my next contraction.

"Rock back and forth," Shaen advised. I did, swaying my hips from side to side, Jax following with the shower head. The movement helped, just a bit. I let my body guide me. I moved when it told me to, I moaned, soft and low when it needed me to, I felt connected to myself in a way I never imagined I could. I felt powerful through the pain. My fear of doing this at home slowly waned to awe. *Like, watch me fucking go, I am so strong.* It helped that both Jax and Liam kept telling me I was.

Time lost meaning but after a while the rocking and the water pressure stopped helping and I began to feel half out of my mind with pain. I was shaking, teeth chattering, every part of me ached. The water shut off, a soft towel was placed around me, I was instructed to lift my arms, so I did, and a new bra was slipped on, replacing the cold wet one.

Jax guided me back to the bed.

"I need to check you again," Liam whispered in my ear, leaving a trail of kisses along my jaw. I nodded, miserably. I could hear the apology in his tone before he did it. My legs began to shake; my teeth still clattered against each other. Transition was an evil bitch and she had me in her grasp. I wasn't sure I could do this anymore. I wanted to crawl out of my body, escape the pain, the pressure, the fear.

"She's a nine," Liam said, sounding relieved. It will all be over soon. I'd be ready to push shortly. I'd have to push without any pain relief. I cried as I thought about it. The contractions were so close together now I found myself getting worked up into a frenzy. I felt helpless, laying on my back, my legs locked up as fire traveled up my crotch and pelvis every time a contraction hit.

"Breathe…" Shaen was back, placing a cool cloth on my forehead. How had she known I was burning up? I thanked her wordlessly, rolling from side to side, keening out my pain.

"Your baby is working so hard to get here," I heard her say. That caught my attention. *He was, wasn't he.*

"I need to get on all fours," I told her. My mouth was so dry, my lips cracked as I spoke. Jax helped me reposition and I felt immediate relief. In this position I was able to rock my hips and bare down as each wave of contractions hit. Shaen talked me through each one. Jax rubbed my back. Liam kept watch, talking to me, assuring me all looked perfect.

Then my water broke in a gush all over the chux pads and towels, and the need to push came on faster than anyone could grab more towels to clean up the mess I'd made. Everything began to feel raw and primal. I was at the mercy of my body's demands.

"I can't lay down," I gasped out, still on my hands and knees. I was not in charge—my body was. It was telling me to push, so I did. Long, mind-numbing pushes. I focused on nothing else but Jax's hand in mine and Liam's voice guiding me through each push, helping me help his son come earthside.

"Stop," Liam demanded. I eased off my push, although the urge to keep going burned through me, but I listened. I waited for him, giving him control because I trusted him implicitly and knew that he would never lead me astray.

"I see the head, honey," Julia announced after a moment of silent agony. Relief washed over me. I was powerful. I was made to do this. I *was* doing it. I was so fucking close. If I could just endure this part…

"Okay, one more push, love," I heard Liam say from behind me. To my right was Shaen, up on the bed next to me, encouraging me, speaking hope and strength into me—representing the literal epitome of womanhood. To my left was Jax, eyes full of unshed tears, his hair a mess from having dried from the shower in whatever disarray his worried hands had left it, love for me clear and obvious on his face.

"I love you," he said, confirming my thoughts. I bottled it all up. All of the emotion in the room. Jax's love, Shaen's encouragement, Remi's loyalty from where he hovered with Sam in the doorway, Julia's excitement, and Liam's fierce devotion and focus —and I funneled it all into my last push. I basked in my strength. I channeled all of the love I had for everyone in this room and for the one almost joining us and I pushed with everything I had and then some. I felt like I was tearing open—mind, body, soul—but it was worth it. Every part of me burned, but I wasn't afraid anymore. The famous ring of fire everyone had warned me about only lasted a moment as I felt my body expel the baby I had grown for the last nine months. I felt euphoric as it happened, like magic occurred as his life left my body and his face hit the air for the first time. I turned my head to see Liam catching our son and his voice shook with emotion as he asked Shaen to hand him the bulb syringe.

The flames from the candles flickered softly as shadows on the walls in my peripheral. The scent of essential oils and candle wax mixed with the sharp tang of blood clung to the air, grounding me in this surreal moment.

I saw him take the baby blanket from his mother as our son let out his first cry. Jax helped me turn and lay back to prepare me for Liam to put our baby on my chest. He let go of my hand to follow Liam's instruction on how to cut the cord and then my baby was on me, his skin against mine and a love I had never experienced before exploded inside of me.

"Oh my god, oh my god." I touched his little body, feeling slightly dissociated from the entire experience. Almost like I was floating above myself. "Hi, baby," I murmured to him. I had my baby. *I had my baby.* I was so happy and so tired all at the same time. He was slick, warm, and real. The tiny weight of him against my chest anchored me back into my body. A hush fell over the room, feeling sacred, as if the air understood the magnitude of what had happened here tonight.

"You did so good." Liam was checking our baby's vitals as he praised me, pressing a soft kiss to my lips.

"Is he o-okay?" I asked. I was shaking from the adrenaline now, so Liam wrapped the baby up and handed him off to Jax, who stared at our son in awe.

"He's perfect, my love. You made him absolutely perfect," Liam assured me. He was back between my legs now as Julia brought over a heated blanket, wrapping me in it, murmuring to me. I heard our baby cry and Jax soothed him in that deep voice of his.

"He recognizes your voice from all the time you spent talking to my belly," I told him weakly as Liam guided me in delivering the placenta and then Julia helped him by massaging my stomach to encourage my uterus to contract down and slow the bleeding.

"Did I rip?" I asked as I watched Liam prepare a needle of lidocaine.

"Not much," he told me. "Which is quite amazing for a first birth." I winced as I felt him injecting the needle. He kept apologizing even once I was numb and he sewed me up.

I felt Julia removing the dirty towels and chux pads and replacing them with fresh ones. Remi procured my hospital bag from Liam's car so Liam was able to prepare a pair of mesh underwear with pads, witch hazel, and numbing spray and pull it on me. He helped me change into a big T-shirt and re-braided my hair. His kisses were gentle and soft.

"Thank you," I whispered. "I could have never done this without you. It's because of you that this was such a calm and good experience."

"No my love, it's because of all of us—but mainly you. You were determined to get our son out. I am—I am so proud of you." His voice hitched and my heart skipped a beat as he wiped away happy tears.

"I just love you all so much."

Jax had come to stand next to us, our son curled up in his arms. Liam pressed a kiss to the side of our baby's head, which was covered in a tiny hat, and then pressed a matching kiss to Jax's temple. We stayed like that for a moment, basking in the magic of bringing new life into the world. Everything suspended in time, slowed by the snowstorm raging outside and the love evolving inside. We were now parents and our bond deepened into something even more tangible as the result of our affection and devotion to one another was now suckling at my breast, making funny little noises, his hand splayed across my skin, his tiny fingers holding onto me.

Liam went to figure out what to do with my placenta, Shaen and Remi had gone to sleep in the room next to ours. Julia had brought me a spread of food and a bottle of electrolyte water before going off to bed herself, and Jax lay on the bed next to me, eyes red-rimmed with exhaustion, but his face peaceful and loving.

I looked down at my baby, who had now fallen asleep. My body felt sore, a reminder of how hard I had worked to give him life, and I smiled.

"Hello Aziel Wolf Hennessy-Berman, welcome home."

I was coming down the stairs when I heard Aziel and his friend in the front hall.

"So, like, you have two dads?" he asked. I froze, even after all these years that question still hit me in the chest, making me weary.

"Hell ya I do. It's awesome," Aziel replied, his voice cracked and I winced. He hated when his almost deep voice did that, giving him away as still going through puberty. At fourteen he already stood at five-ten but when he opened his mouth you were reminded of how old he really was.

"My one dad is a doctor. He's also really into sports so we play all the time, and he made me a sick workout routine."

I grinned, imagining my son flexing his muscles.

"My other dad works in construction. You know that huge mall in Valley Cottage…"

"Ya."

"My dad built it."

He sounded so proud that a quiet pride bloomed in my chest. After all of Charlee's fears about how the world would treat our son, he spoke with such certainty—so sure of who he was, and

proud to be ours. Our love hadn't ruined him; it had given him roots to stand firm.

"What about your mom?" the kid inquired.

"My mom? My mom is the best. She's a nurse." Their voices faded as they left through the front door as his friend's mother had come to pick him up and in perfect timing too as all of our family was about to arrive for our daughter, Shaela's, twelfth birthday party.

For the most part Aziel was a spitting image of Jax, tall and broad with dark hair and a strong jaw. But he had Charlee's amber eyes and a year-round tan complexion due to the Native American blood from her grandfather Wolf. Yet his personality was all me. He was popular, funny, always up to something and a fan favorite amongst the girls in his class. We had already had a how birds and bees practiced safe sex talk and I had made it very clear this bird wouldn't be sticking anything into any bees any time soon.

"Sheesh, Dad. Stooop," Aziel had groaned, turning red, rubbing the back of his neck in discomfort, just like Jax did when he got nervous. He had taken to calling both Jax and me "Dad" which made it slightly confusing for everyone and Charlee had been renamed, "Mom" because Mommy was way too 'cringe' apparently. Raising teens was not for the weak, that was for sure.

Shaela, on the other hand, was all me physically. From the dirty blonde hair, to the bright blue eyes, full lips, and ever-present smattering of freckles she was practically my twin. She would probably end up somewhere around Charlee's height but she had all the mannerisms of Jax. She was sweet, quiet, and thoughtful. She preferred to bake with her godmother Shaen, or cook with my mom Julia than go to the mall with her friends. She also loved to build things with Jax. They had just finished putting together a bird feeder for hummingbirds and were outside installing it. She may be wearing her fancy birthday dress but she was out there wielding a hammer, not afraid to get a little dirty.

"Hey, bitch," Remi called to me as he came in through the front door, followed by Billie and their ten-year-old daughter, Nova.

"Dad, that's a bad word," Nova chided.

"It sure is, sweetheart," he agreed. "And what did we say the rule is?"

"You and Mommy can say bad words but we can't say them till we're sixteen," Nova repeated. I chuckled.

"Exactly. Now go find your cousins." Remi shooed her off as Shaen pushed the door open with her foot, carrying the birthday cake she had made for Shaela.

"Damn Shay Shay." I admired the white cake with realistic fondant flowers all over it. Charlee came over and guided her to the dessert table to safely deposit it there. My mom arrived with a bunch of my brothers' kids and they raced through the house and then out to the backyard, laughter floating in after them through the door that sat slightly ajar.

Jax's sisters arrived next, followed by Charlee's brother, his wife, and kids. Everyone carried gifts and much to Shaela's dismay she was soon the center of attention as the party began.

In honor of Jax's heritage and tradition today we celebrated Shaela's bat mitzva, a special milestone in the Jewish community. We had a fancy multi-course dinner, time spent for speeches, a fierce dance-off, a slideshow made by my mom which made us all cry because it started off with a photo of Charlee holding Shaela, having just given birth, this time in a hospital, and lots of time spent celebrating our daughter and all of her accomplishments.

Now all our guests milled around, some exploring the huge treehouse Jax had built for our kids, others signing the guest book and all the while the sound of kids' laughter sounded around us. Jax stood to Charlee's left, myself to her right, we each held one of her hands, the metal of my wedding ring felt cool against my warm palm. So many years, so many versions of us— and we were still choosing each other, again and again.

The scent of frosting and blown out birthday candles permeated the air. The rustle of the leaves on the trees sounded nearby, the breeze washing over my face was a welcome caress.

We watched as Aziel wiped some glitter off of Shaela's eyebrow and she giggled as he blew it off his finger, then fake punched her in a manner only teenage boys did and she pushed him away, rolling her eyes. I knew she was thinking what an idiot her brother was. My heart swelled in my chest as it always did when I watched my kids interact. I didn't know what to do with all of the love that grew inside of me when I saw the two amazing humans that we had made. Sometimes I caught myself watching Aziel and could still see the baby whose first cry I caught in my hands. They'd never know how much of us lived inside them, how every laugh of theirs rewrote any broken pieces from our past.

"I love those fuckers," I murmured. I looked over at Charlee. Time had been kind to me, my age only showing in the crinkles around my eyes from smiling so much but my hair was still thick and I kept my body muscular as always. Charlee didn't look a day over thirty-five. Her hair was glossy, her skin glowy, her lips full, and her eyes sparkling with happiness.

"Even when they complain that there is nothing to eat in a kitchen full of food." Jax chuckled. We both looked at him. Closing in on forty-seven, his temples had begun to gray, giving him a silver fox look that enthralled both myself and Charlee. I liked to call him daddy in bed sometimes to annoy him but despite his vehement protests we agreed that Jax secretly got a kick out of it.

"Even then," I agreed.

Jax closed the space between him and I, encircling Charlee as he placed his hand in mine, bending our heads together, our breath mingling as one.

"I love you," he said, kissing me gently, then Charlee. She molded into our bodies, still so reactive to us even after all these years. Her hands rested right over where her I love you, joined by Jax's, Aziel's and Shaela's handwriting, was inked on my chest.

"Ew Mom. Ew Dads," Aziel called as he raced by heading to the basketball hoop in the driveway.

"Yeah, ew Dads." Charlee grinned. I chuckled, holding their hands tighter, reveling in this moment. The breeze rustled my hair, the love surrounding us permeated my bones, and a feeling of peace overwhelmed me for a moment. We'd started out as three separate people, three separate hearts, and we'd been lucky enough to build one life. There was something nostalgic about tonight. It felt more emotional than I had anticipated. No one had ever told me that the most permanent thing in my life would arrive in the fashion it had but I was so grateful that all the pieces had fallen into place the way they did, our three puzzle pieces had become one. I had looked up one day and realized that the life I had yearned for was here. Complete. Whole.

I heard the inhale of Charlee's breath and the hushed laughter coming from Jax and I closed my eyes as I finally heard it—the sound of life actively being lived. It was beautiful in its silence and I just breathed, the love we felt for one another tethering us together. We were three hearts once; now we were one rhythm. The beat sounded like home.

The End

# ACKNOWLEDGMENTS

Wow. Here we are—book three is complete. You know what they say: *once is a chance, twice is a coincidence, three times is a pattern.* If writing books is now a pattern for me, then I'm absolutely here for it.

To be a little vulnerable for a moment—writing the books is always the easiest part. The hard part is putting them out into the world. Handing over something you've poured your heart into… to the boiling, writhing thing that is BookTok. Sometimes, posting stories, videos, and swipe-through posts feels like shouting into the abyss. Like, *please*, all you beautiful readers— read my book. Love my book.

But then, on some days, I get messages that shake up my entire world and remind me why I keep going. People telling me that my books changed their life. That they cried. That my writing is "exquisite" (yes, truly—someone said that! Lol). And wow, what moments those are. I save every one of your messages on my phone. They mean *that* much to me.

And from all of that comes Shaen and Remi, Jessa and Kian, and now Liam, Charlee, and Jax.

With each book, my hope is that you *feel* something—that a specific emotion lingers, or maybe you walk away with something new to ponder. And I know that each story will speak to each of you in a different way.

With *We,* I wanted to explore what the "taboo" could look like if we stripped it of its shame and made it feel *normal.* What happens when the rules life placed on you don't get to define your future? I wanted to show birth as the beautiful trauma it is. I wanted to highlight the strength of found family, unbreakable bonds, and heartbreak that ends in hope.

I believe I accomplished that—but ultimately, that's for you to decide. Just know this: I appreciate every single one of you more than you could ever imagine. Thank you for your support, your posts, your messages. This one's for *you*.

Thank you to my family—even though most of you haven't read a single one of my books (at least you say the covers are pretty, lol). To my cover designer, thank you for taking the jumble in my head and turning it into an experience that lives on the front of every story. To my editors, proofreaders, beta readers, and ARC readers—thank you for catching every little thing and helping me shape this into my best work.

And lastly, to all of you who are a *Liam*—I hope the world is kind to you. And I hope you are kind to yourself.

XOXO,

**Rae**

# ABOUT THE AUTHOR

Rae Lloyd is a romance author with a deep passion for the written word. Having been an avid reader since a very young age, she was inspired by the thousands of books she consumed since childhood. Rae's dream of having her writings published has finally come to fruition. She can be found writing in between living life with her three daughters and her husband, as well as hanging out with her many adorable pets, baking gluten-free desserts, or cultivating beauty in her wig salon. This is Rae's third book but she has many more stories brewing in her mind, stay tuned for more to come.

To stay in touch and receive all book updates, subscribe to get emails at https://www.raelloyd.com.

You can also find Rae on TikTok and Instagram @raelloydwrites.

You can join Rae's Facebook group called Rae's Readers.

# ALSO BY RAE LLOYD:


This Is What It feels Like (where we originally meet Liam)
https://amzn.to/4fD4bx5

Love's Crescendo
https://amzn.to/45Qg6Eo

www.ingramcontent.com/pod-product-compliance
Lightning Source LLC
Chambersburg PA
CBHW021022310726
48969CB00006B/1501